CORPSES IN ENDERBY

George Bellairs (1902–1982). He was, by day, a Manchester bank manager with close connections to the University of Manchester. He is often referred to as the English Simenon, as his detective stories combine wicked crimes and classic police procedurals, set in quaint villages.

He was born in Lancashire and married Gladys Mabel Roberts in 1930. He was a devoted Francophile and travelled there frequently, writing for English newspapers and magazines and weaving French towns into his fiction.

Bellairs' first mystery, *Littlejohn on Leave* (1941) introduced his series detective, Detective Inspector Thomas Littlejohn. Full of scandal and intrigue, the series peeks inside small towns in the mid twentieth century and Littlejohn is injected with humour, intelligence and compassion.

He died on the Isle of Man in April 1982 just before his eightieth birthday.

CORPSES IN ENDERBY

An Inspector Littlejohn Mystery

GEORGE BELLAIRS

ipso books

This edition published in 2016 by Ipso Books

First published in 1954 in Great Britain by John Gifford Ltd.

Ipso Books is a division of Peters Fraser + Dunlop Ltd

Drury House, 34–43 Russell Street, London WC2B 5HA

To
ANN and CECIL
and the happy memories
of GLENDOWN.

CONTENTS

Chapter One
The Night of the Storm

M onday, October 26th, was a pleasant autumn day, but there were gale warnings on the six o'clock news. At eight o'clock, the storm broke at Enderby, with high winds and driving rain. It kept it up all night and quickly cleared the streets.

Rising above the Market Square was the steeple of the church clock, its hands at fourteen minutes to ten. The last bus to Rutland was standing in one corner, its windows streaming with rain, which made it look like a large illuminated aquarium. Inside, the driver and conductor were smoking and talking to the solitary passenger. The conductor put his head out and looked at the clock, the driver appeared, climbed down and ran and mounted his cab. The bell rang and the bus swished away, casting a feather of spray on each side. Then, the place looked gloomier than ever.

The square was illuminated by naked electric bulbs on the tops of high standards, which threw down a dim diffused light on the wet pavements. One of the lamps stood before a large old-fashioned shop in the best position in the block. A sign in the shape of a large key swung to and fro in the wind and on a board over the door the words, *E. Bunn,*

Ironmonger, were just visible. Somewhere in the dark a loose shutter banged rhythmically.

The light on top of the police box under the church-yard wall began to flash and a policeman who had been sheltering in a doorway appeared, ponderously crossed the square, and took out the telephone. Someone had locked a dog in an empty house in Queen Street and it was howling the place down. The constable blew through his moustache, swore into the wind, and made off, his cape streaming with water.

Opposite the ironmonger's, lights were showing in a pub, with *Freemasons' Arms* etched on the ground-glass of the vestibule door. A car drew up, the door opened and was hastily slammed and a hurrying figure vanished inside the hotel. It was Dr. Halston, a local practitioner, arriving for his nightcap.

The bright lights indoors dazzled the doctor and he screwed up his eyes. There was a long passage with a bar at the end and behind the glass front the landlady, a huge blonde woman with her bust supported on the counter, was counting the money from the cash-register. The landlord, Blowitt, was leaning against the front of the bar in his shirt sleeves, a little tubby man with a black moustache.

"Evenin', doctor."

The landlord looked too depressed to move.

"Evening, Blowitt. Evening, Mrs. Blowitt. Shocking night."

"Bad for trade. Nobody in all night except your little lot."

"Bring mine in, will you?"

The doctor opened a door on the left and entered a small private room. Three men, sitting round a table, gazing reflectively into the fire, looked up and greeted him.

"Evening all. You look very cheerful."

"What's to be cheerful about, doc?"

Snipe, the man who spoke, was thin and sanctimonious-looking and he could take any amount of drink without the least visible effect. He kept a faded outfitter's shop in a side street, drank a lot, and nobody knew where he got his money from.

Another of the party was half-seas over, a town councillor called Dabchick and the next man for mayor. He was short and stocky with a fleshy mouth and a ragged moustache, and a club-foot gave him a bad limp. He merely greeted the doctor with a wave of the hand and then subsided to brood over his almost empty glass.

"This'll kill 'em off for you, Halston."

There was no mistaking from the loudness of the tones and the trace of insolence in them that the speaker was the bigwig of the party. This was Edwin Bunn who owned the business over the way. His great bulk filled the large arm-chair and he was tolerably sober. His suit was of good grey cloth of a conservative cut, his linen white, his face pink and properly shaved, his crisp hair neat, his moustache trimmed. He made the rest of them look shabby, even the doctor, whose long grey hair, hollow cheeks, old shoes, and general air of untidiness gave him the appearance of a bro-ken-down musician.

A buxom barmaid entered, holding a tray with a double whisky in one hand and patting her platinum hair with the other. It was only then that Bunn showed any signs of inter-est. He turned his head, gave the girl a mysterious twisted smile, looked her boldly in the eyes, and put her out of countenance.

"Your whisky, doctor," she said, and, as the doctor fumbled in his pocket for the money, she swayed self-consciously, aware of Bunn's scrutiny from head to foot and then back again. She backed out awkwardly and silence fell again as the men drank up. It was as though the weather had drowned every topic of conversation; the rain was pelting down and the shutter still banging.

Before anyone could try to start the ball of sociability rolling, voices rose outside. Blowitt, the landlord, was getting annoyed.

"You can't have any more. You've had enough as it is."

"Where's Bunn? Is he in? I wanna see Bunn...I know he's 'ere."

And before they could stop him the drunken man was in the room. He was soaked with rain. A little sandy fellow with pale blue eyes, wearing a dripping raincoat and a velour hat too large for him, with the brim turned down all round. He went straight for Bunn with Blowitt making up the rear.

"Don't you bother Mr. Bunn, else I'll have to chuck you out, Mr. Hetherow, and that would be just too bad."

But Mr. Hetherow wasn't listening. He was talking to Bunn in a whining voice.

"Bin tryin' all day to raise the money and can't. This weather's put the tin-lid on it, Mr. Bunn. I can't go anywhere else to-night. I'll 'ave it in a week."

Hetherow owned the shop next to Bunn's and Bunn held a heavy mortgage on it. He was going to foreclose and take over the premises for extensions.

"Don't bother me here, Hetherow. We've had all this out before. What's the use of keeping your bankrupt draper's going. I want the shop and I intend to have it."

The man in the large velour swayed unsteadily. He could only think of one thing; he didn't want to leave his shop.

"It's been in the family for nearly two hundred years, Mr. Bunn. What am I to do if it's sold up? At my age, with an ailing wife..."

4

"You're not old, Hetherow ... You'll find work. I'm taking over the premises, whatever you say, in a month's time, so you'd better arrange things. And now you'd best be off to bed. You'll get your death ..."

The sopping figure before them suddenly seemed to sober up.

"Is that your last word?"

"Yes."

Bunn looked pleased about it. He stretched out his legs to the fire, smiled to himself, thrust out his chest, and put his thumbs in the armholes of his waistcoat.

"I'll kill you before I'll give up the business that's been in the family for ..."

He was pointing threateningly and Blowitt seized the chance to take him by the arm and tow him to the door.

"Touch my premises and I'll kill you ..."

Hetherow managed to get it out and then the door closed. He argued loudly with Blowitt who steered him to the vestibule and gently pushed him in the direction of his darkened shop.

"I'm going, too. Bed's the best place on a night like this."

Bunn rose and stamped his feet to restore circulation. He was almost six feet tall and florid. He was a bit merry from his drinks. He slipped on his overcoat and set his black bowler carefully on his head.

"Good night!"

The others looked up as if they couldn't believe it. Dabchick's voice had a note of disappointment.

"Don't go yet, Ned."

"Good night."

Bunn halted in the vestibule for a minute to brace himself and then crossed the road to his shop. All the blinds were drawn and the only trace of light was a small halo in the middle of the door, caused by a peephole cut in the blind. Bunn put his eye to this and snorted. He took out his keys, selected one and slid it in the patent lock. Then he snorted again, this time more loudly. The door was already unlocked.

The ironmonger softly entered and crept through the shop to the door of the living quarters behind, beneath which a chink of light was showing. He hastily turned the knob and flung it open.

"So ... I thought so ..."

The room was small, cosy, and almost brimming over with heavy nondescript furniture. There was a large fire in the grate, and a table-lamp cast a circle of light on a couch on which Bunn's daughter, Bertha, and his shop assistant were still sitting in close embrace as though Bunn's sudden appearance had converted them into pillars of salt. There was in their eyes a momentary, questioning look, like that of actors who wait for the producer of a play to tell them their caresses are realistic enough. Then they both stood up to face the music.

Bertha Bunn was well on the way to forty and she and Wilfred Flounder, the shopman from whose arms she now disentangled herself, had been in love for over ten years. She was a big, fair girl with a good figure and regular features and since Flounder, who was a few years younger and two inches smaller, thin and pale, had arrived, she had taken complete possession of him, courted and mothered him, greatly to his joy and satisfaction, for Wilfred was short of initiative and was content to leave it all to Bertha.

"What did I tell you both ... ?"

Bunn had told them often enough. Not a penny for Bertha and the sack for Wilfred Flounder if he caught them at it again, to say nothing of letting them get married.

Mrs. Bunn, a pale shadow of a woman to whom her daughter was devoted, had been dead six months. Until then, Bertha had put up with her father's bullying for her mother's sake. Wilfred, of course, was a cipher in the whole affair. Now, he stood blinking through his glasses, making up his mind.

"Look here, Mr. Bunn..." he said at length. His chin was set and it looked as if they were going to have it out once and for all. Bertha had inherited five hundred pounds from her mother and they'd already planned to leave the old man if he wouldn't change his views.

But Bunn had had enough of talking. The veins on his forehead stood out like cords and a pulse started to throb in his temple. He pulled himself up and looked two inches taller and he towered over Wilfred Flounder for a minute and then seized him by the collar.

Bertha Bunn started to scream and then, impelled by a spasm of maternal solicitude, began to beat her father's back with her fists. Meanwhile Wilfred, his feet off the ground, wriggled and twisted in Bunn's grip. The old man shook off his daughter, kicked open the door of the living-room and, holding Flounder with one hand, turned the key with the other and locked Bertha in.

"Now, my lad... I'm throwing you out and you stay out. You're sacked. I'll send you a month's wages and your cards to-morrow and if I see you about here again, I'll horsewhip you. Get that?"

"Look here, Mr. Bunn..."

Bunn did not heed him. He flung open the outer door, took a few short running steps, and propelled Wilfred Flounder half-way across the pavement, leaving his momentum to do the rest. Flounder vanished into the dark and rain and before he could gather himself together, Bunn was back' on his own doorstep and entering the shop.

Then, it happened.

At first, it looked as if some invisible man were throwing out Edwin Bunn in exactly the way he had dealt with his daughter's lover. There was a crack, like that of a whip, a flash inside the shop, and Bunn made another run for the street, flew through the air, pitched into the gutter, and lay still.

Everything seemed to start at once after that.

Bertha Bunn managed to break out of the room behind and rushed screaming through the shop. Wilfred Flounder materialized from the dark and started to mill around in the rain calling plaintively for Bertha and Mr. Bunn. P.C. Burbot appeared on his way back from pacifying the dog and the door of *The Freemasons' Arms* opened and emitted a crowd of unsteady customers. The wind still blew and the rain was coming down in torrents.

"What's goin' h'on?" asked P.C. Burbot. He had to shout at the top of his voice and even then he didn't get an answer. So, he turned on his torch and revealed the white face of Wilfred and the red one of Bertha, whose eyes glowed with horror, like those of a rabbit caught by headlamps in the dark.

" 'Oly mackerel!"

P.C. Burbot couldn't think of anything else to say, but he acted promptly to the tune of rushing in the shop, turning on all the lights, and pulling up all the blinds. The blaze of illumination revealed Edwin Bunn lying in the gutter with a stream of water flowing over him.

In no time at all, a crowd had gathered. Stragglers from the local cinema, which had just turned out a thin audience, joined the clients from *The Freemasons' Arms* and, in spite of the drenching rain, they formed a ring, two-deep, round the body of the prostrate ironmonger.

"Now, now ... Make way ..."

P.C. Burbot started to shout almost as soon as he left the police-box by the church, whence he had been summoning help from the police-station behind the square. Nobody heard him, but they gave way to him when he arrived. He was followed by Dr. Halston, who happened to be police surgeon and, therefore, took charge at once.

"Get him in the shop."

They picked up the dripping body of Edwin Bunn. Now that there was somebody to give orders, there were more offers of help than were needed. Eight men started to carry Mr. Bunn and began to jostle one another for right of place.

"Four will do ... You've sent for the ambulance, Burbot?"

"Yes, doctor."

The quartet of picturegoers, chosen because they were sober and steady, shuffled indoors, bore the body through the shop, and into the living-room behind. Then they stood there, their raincoats dripping and making little pools on the carpet.

"That will be all. We won't need you any more."

The helpers filed out. Faces were pressed against the panes of the shop window; pale, wet faces, with questioning eyes and fearful stares; faces with lank hair, like some strange monsters from the deep.

"Move along there. You can't do any good gettin' soaked in the rain. Get 'ome!"

P.C. Burbot drove them all away and they vanished into the night like wraiths.

Inside, when the constable returned, he found Bertha Bunn sobbing hoarsely on the breast of Wilfred Flounder, which, on account of their different heights, was rather a difficult feat. Dr. Halston had told them that old Bunn was dead.

Bertha raised her streaming face.

"But how did it happen? I know he was quarrelling with Mr. Flounder and was annoyed because he found us together…"

In spite of the shock, Bertha's tones grew a bit bashful as she skated over the circumstances of the discovery.

"…He was annoyed to find us here at this hour and was showing Mr. Flounder to the door. He got in a temper… Did he…? Did he have a stroke, doctor?"

Dr. Halston rubbed his chin and tightened the muscles of his face. His long grey hair was wet and matted, for somewhere in the dark, he had lost his hat.

"No, Miss Bunn. It wasn't a stroke. I'm afraid he was murdered. You see, there's a bullet-wound in the head .. in the base of the brain. He wouldn't know it had hit him…"

"Eeek!"

Bertha made one shrill sound, looked hard at her lover, and then collapsed in a dead faint.

Dr. Halston looked round at the room crowded with furniture, the body on the sofa, with Wilfred Flounder's trilby hat beneath, just where he'd put it before he started to embrace Bertha in the old man's absence.

"Isn't there another room somewhere? Take her to it and get her in bed."

Wilfred Flounder and P.C. Burbot looked at each other fearfully. True, Wilfred was Bertha's lover, but he hadn't bargained for this! And P.C. Burbot had only just started courting!!

"Is there anythin' I can do?"

It was Mrs. Blowitt from over the way. Just in time, she took it in hand and after the two men had manoeuvred Bertha to her room above, she set about making the unconscious woman conscious again by slapping her face. Over the fireplace, a portrait of the late Bunn glared down on Bertha's bed, and Mrs. Blowitt turned it to the wall and then she descended to make some cups of tea.

P.C. Burbot was a young, fresh-complexioned bobby with a large handlebar moustache. The situation was a new one for him. He had never been in at a murder before and he didn't know what to do. He whistled softly through his teeth as he waited for his superiors to arrive. The doctor stood with his back to the dying fire, drying his hair with his handkerchief. Flounder was sitting in an armchair with an antimacassar on the back, stiff and solemn, like somebody awaiting his doom.

"It looks bad for me, doctor, but I didn't do it. I haven't got a revolver..."

"Nobody's accusing you."

"Yes... But... There was only me about. It looks as if I did it. Well, I want you to know I didn't."

"It's nothing to do with me. That's the business of the police."

The door of the shop blew open and the signal bell over it rang lugubriously. The wind rushed through the place, causing the buckets, saws, chains and other ironmongery hanging from the beams to clash together like the drummer's odds and ends in a jazz band. Then the ambulance drew up and a police car. The body was removed to the morgue and the Inspector-in-Charge took off his dripping cape and his wet hat, hung them over a chair in the shop, and returned to the fire in the room behind.

Inspector Myers was about forty-five and well thought of by his superiors. He was tall, well built and quick on his feet. His face was large and square, with a strong chin, broad forehead, and a determined projecting lower lip. His eyes relieved the stern set of his features; grey, straight, with an ironical twinkle, as though he knew all about it beforehand but just asked questions to confirm his own thoughts.

"What's been happening?"

The doctor told him, and Flounder then added his own tale of what went on before Bunn met his death.

"Did you hear anybody moving about in the shop whilst you were in the room behind? I take it you were courting, Mr. Flounder?"

The ironic grey eyes met Wilfred's steadily.

"Yes, we were. And we didn't hear anybody. In fact, the wind was so wild, we wouldn't have heard much above it unless there was a *big* noise."

"Where were you when this happened?"

"Mr. Bunn was mad at finding us together in the house alone. He ordered me to leave and he got a bit rough and pushed me through the shop and into the street. I stumbled when he pushed me and fell in the gutter."

Again the ironical, searching eyes.

"Tell me, Mr. Flounder, did the old man *chuck* you out?"

"Yes, he did, if you must know."

"Why didn't you say so, then? We must have the truth."

"Well, it's not very pleasant for a man like me."

The Inspector didn't seem to hear.

"And as you were picking yourself up, you...?"

"I heard Mr. Bunn go in the shop, and then he came out, as though somebody had thrown *him* out, too. There was no light except from the street lamp and that was swinging in the wind. He seemed to fall and I went in his direction. Then Bertha... I mean Miss Bunn, came out and things started to happen."

"Have you a revolver, Mr. Flounder?"

"No. What would I do with...?"

"Let me ask the questions, please."

The doctor was getting restive; his hair was still wet, he felt a cold coming on, and he wanted his own fireside and another stiff whisky.

"If you don't want me, I'll ..."

"Quite all right, sir. See you to-morrow. Miss Bunn is here, I think you said?"

"Yes. In bed. She took it badly and fainted. Nothing I can do. Mrs. Blowitt's with her ... Good night!"

"We were talking about revolvers, Mr. Flounder ... Do you sell them in the shop?"

"Yes. You have to have a permit, of course, but we did get them for people who were allowed ..."

"Have you any in stock?"

"Yes, I think there's one. It was ordered and the man who wants it hasn't called for it yet. There's ammunition, too."

"Where is it?"

"This way ..."

They passed into the shop again and Flounder, hidebound by custom, went behind the counter and faced the Inspector across it. He almost said, "What can I do for you ... ?"

But Inspector Myers wasn't interested in Flounder any more, for there on the counter, like an exhibit in a collection, lay a very efficient-looking little revolver, loaded in every chamber and with one shot fired.

CHAPTER TWO
SEND FOR SCOTLAND YARD!

In the afternoon following the murder of Edwin Bunn, Wilfred Flounder took a rope from the shop and prepared to hang himself. He was highly-strung and impulsive, and he thought he might as well get it done before the public hangman did it for him.

The storm had blown itself out in the night, the sun was shining, and the pale blue sky, flecked with high white clouds, looked as if somebody had given it a shampoo. Bunn's shop was closed, but the town was busy; it was market-day and stalls had been erected in a cobbled corner of the market-place. Regardless of the tragedy, the stallholders were shouting their wares: fruit, vegetables, clothes, carpets, cheese, eggs and pots. All eyes kept turning in the direction of the ironmonger's shop and when anything happened there, silence fell expectantly, leaving only the hucksters' voices still yelling. "Oranges...Every one's a Jaffa!" "Nylons, lady?" "Monkey Nuts!..."

Wilfred Flounder took no heed of it all. He had been with the police all morning and his stamina had ebbed away. Had Bertha supported him, he felt he could have borne it; but since the discovery of her father's dead body, she hadn't spoken a word to him, except "Go away!" Her eyes accused him of the crime and she kept him at arm's length when he tried to approach her and protest his innocence.

"You'd better not leave town; we shall want you again," the police had told him in far from friendly tones. In fact, Inspector Myers had looked ready to arrest him, but the Chief Constable of the County had stopped him. Colonel Cargrave was a cautious man, who had once been a party to a wrongful arrest with dire results. Now he never acted without being quite sure. A tall, austere official, who might have been mistaken for the Duke of Wellington during the Peninsular Wars, huge nose and all.

"I don't believe that fellah did it," he told Myers. "Too timid; too rabbity. Everything seems to point his way except the fellah himself. Better not arrest him yet. Keep a man to watch he doesn't bolt."

"But, sir..."

"Do as I say."

Inspector Myers shrugged his shoulders and after the Chief had left the room, he sat back and swore horribly. He ran over the case again in his mind and tried to find the flaws in it. Outside, policemen kept tramping in and out of the charge-room, booking parking offences of which there were a lot every market-day. At the end of the street an old man was playing a violin— "Scenes that are brightest..." —and pausing now and then to thank passers-by who put something in his hat. Whenever he halted, he started at the beginning again.

They had brought Wilfred Flounder in for questioning before nine that morning. The shop assistant had seemed determined to incriminate himself. In the middle of the interview, the vicar had arrived to testify to Flounder's good character and say how truthful and honest he had always been. It didn't do Wilfred much good.

They got him to tell his tale without interrupting him. Then, a policeman took it down in shorthand, typed it out, read it over, and Wilfred signed it.

"You didn't like Mr. Bunn, did you, Mr. Flounder?"

"No, I did not. He was mean, and he treated me more like a shop-boy than his assistant. I'm thirty-three and I've been with him more than ten years."

"Are you engaged to Miss Bunn?"

Flounder's Adam's apple moved up and down and he pulled the joints of his fingers and made them crack.

"Not exactly... Unofficially, I mean. Her father wouldn't consent to it."

"Why?"

"He said I was after her money. I assure you I wasn't. We'd arranged to leave him and go away and get married, even if he cut her off without anything. We couldn't stand it any more..."

"So you kept on at Bunn's shop and didn't try to get another job, simply to be near Miss Bunn?"

"Yes. She asked me to stay. Her father didn't want her to get married. She used to nurse her mother who was an invalid. Then when her mother died, her father said she'd to remain and look after him."

"And you didn't assert yourself and resist the old man?"

Flounder missed the slight note of contempt in Myers' voice, but the irony in the grey eyes was not lost. He flushed.

"Did you know Mr. Bunn? He was a snorter. If he didn't get his own way, there was a shocking flare-up. Sometimes, you just had to give way for fear he'd have a stroke."

"Yes, I knew him. Perhaps you're right."

So it went on and on until Wilfred Flounder grew limp and lost all his colour. They gave him a cup of tea and then it started again.

"...When Mr. Bunn saw me and Bertha sitting on our own in the room at the back of the shop, he seemed to see red and he just got hold of me, rushed me through the shop, and threw me in the street. I was helpless. He was big and heavy..."

"You're sure you didn't see or hear anybody else in the shop?"

"I told you before, I didn't. The shop was in darkness and the door to the room behind was closed, because Mr. Bunn had locked it to stop Bertha interfering with his throwing me out."

He told it all in a meek and mild way and in a monotone. Beads of sweat stood on his forehead and he had to keep taking off his spectacles and polishing them because the heat he was generating steamed-up the lenses.

The policeman at the side-table was taking it all down in shorthand, the tip of his tongue appearing now and then at the corner of his mouth as he made some tortuous outline or other.

"And now about the revolver again... It's funny there were no fingerprints on it except yours, if you say you hadn't used it."

Flounder looked nettled and cross.

"Look here... I told you already, my fingerprints would be bound to be on the pistol. It was kept in a drawer under the counter till Ericson, the man who'd ordered it, called for it. I'd handled it several times, cleaning it and moving it about..."

"Oh, yes. I remember. When did you last see the gun?"

"Yesterday morning. I went to the drawer to get out a new pair of scissors. I moved it then. Can't you see, my fingerprints would be bound to be on it?"

Myers rubbed his chin as though in doubt, but he knew the explanation was reasonable. He persisted.

"How came it to be loaded? Did *you* load it?"

"No. But the box of cartridges was with the pistol in the drawer. Anybody taking the pistol could have got them."

Flounder irritated Myers by calling the weapon a pistol. He turned to the shorthand-writer and shrugged his shoulders wearily.

"It's a revolver, Mr. Flounder. I thought you'd know that."

Flounder looked at the Inspector with glazed eyes.

"Yes..."

"Did anybody else know it was in the drawer?"

"Oh, yes. I can't say exactly who, but we always kept the pistols... revolvers there. Bertha knew, of course, and a lot of others... I'd say anybody familiar with the shop would know."

"H'm... And you found yourself in the street and were just picking yourself up when Mr. Bunn was shot and followed you in the gutter?"

"I said so before. Do I need to keep on...?"

"Not much longer. I just want to be quite sure. Mr. Bunn had turned round after leaving you. Had he got right in the shop?"

"I don't know. I was a bit confused and my glasses had got rain on them. He seemed to just get in the shop and then staggered out again and fell. I was nearly on my feet by then."

"And even though the lamp was on just in front of the shop, you didn't see..."

"My glasses were streaming with water, I tell you. Do you have to keep on and on...?"

Just then the Chief Constable arrived. He eyed Flounder and then Myers and sat down.

"Getting along all right?"

"Just taking a statement, sir."

The Chief's eyes lost their good humour as he eyed Wilfred Flounder over.

"You feeling all-in, Flounder?"

"A bit, sir. You see, I've been here three hours making a statement and now they're checking it."

"Read it over to me, Bradley."

Myers grew red and Bradley coughed and began to translate his notes in a loud, formal voice. Outside, they were bringing in a pair of drunks who had been fighting in the market. One was threatening to murder the other.

"I'll swing for you..."

Flounder started and turned a dull yellow at the sound of the threat. It was like a prognostication of his own fate.

"That'll do..."

Colonel Cargrave's face was grim.

"That what you told the Inspector, Flounder?"

"Yes, sir."

"Let him sign it and then send him home for a meal and a rest, Myers."

Myers looked put out.

"Could I have a word in private with you, sir?"

"Yes. Bradley, take Flounder and give him a spot of stimulant, brandy or something. He looks all-in."

Flounder was led off to the charge-room.

"Now, Myers. What is it?"

"In my view, sir, Flounder's likely to be our man. He's no alibi, nobody saw what he did at the time Bunn was shot, and we've only Flounder's tale to go on. Bunn had laid hands on him, after abusing him in front of his girl. The old man also seems to have led Flounder a dog's life, because he wanted to marry Bertha Bunn. He threatened to turn them both out if they persisted and cut Bertha off with a shilling, so to speak. The pair of them had planned to run away. The old man caught them ... ahem ... I suppose they were canoodling ... and he chucked Flounder out. What more likely than Flounder losing his temper, getting out the gun from the drawer under the counter, and taking a pot at Bunn in temper? Flounder's one of those chaps who stands a lot and then goes all beserk and does things ..."

"You think that?"

"Well, he's shown signs of temper here this morning. Looked ready to attack *me* at times."

The Chief smiled sadly.

"That's not proof. Don't get over-enthusiastic about theories, Myers. *Festina lente*, as we used to say. Slow but sure. What did Miss Bunn say about all this?"

"She was locked in the room at the back of the shop. The old man shut her in the better to deal with her boy-friend."

"And her father was dead when she got out?"

"Yes. She thinks Flounder did it, I'm sure. She won't have anything to do with him. They were here together and he kept pleading with her to believe him, but she said there was nobody else there, and he must have done it. She went off home in distress as soon as we'd taken her statement."

"She had no idea that somebody else might have been in the shop, hiding, say?"

"No. As I said, it all points to Flounder, who must have done it under extreme provocation ... One might almost say he was defending himself ..."

Myers' eyes had a questioning look, which the Chief shrewdly interpreted at once.

"Now, now, Myers. Gently. You're not going to persuade me into allowing an arrest yet. More work to do, more enquiring, more search for anybody who *might* have been there. Let Flounder go home now and tell him to stay around. He'll not bolt. He might be a timid customer, but

I've a feeling that there's a stubborn streak in him. Let him go for the time being...and watch him."

"Very well, sir."

Myers was disappointed. He felt sure that, given time and patience, he could break down Flounder's story. But he had to obey orders.

Once released, Flounder's main idea was not of flight, but to restore Bertha's confidence in him. He went back to the shop. The door was locked, so he hammered on the panels. Bertha's tear-swollen face appeared at the hole in the blind and her mouth moved in words of dismissal. A small crowd gathered and started to enjoy the scene. Flounder took no heed. Finally, he went to the extent of kneeling in the doorway, applying his lips to the letter-flap, and shouting through it.

"Let me in. I want to get my things."

The door opened and a voice from behind spoke huskily.

"Keep away from me. Murderer..."

The spectators round the shop-front recoiled and then looked at one another. Word started to spread around that Flounder had killed his boss and was going to be arrested. Nobody had liked Ned Bunn and normally his death wouldn't have stirred them at all. But now, they were like a wolf-pack out for blood.

"Come out and take your medicine, you little swine!"

Somebody started to kick at the door and then the police arrived and broke up the party.

Inside Wilfred was pleading. He was worn out after his police examination. All he wanted now was the comfort of Bertha's motherly arms and soft bosom, just as in the past when he despaired at her father's treatment of him.

"Get away...I never want to see you again. If you'd hit him and it had been a mistake I might have...But to shoot him from behind...After all, he was my dad and I thought a lot about him, even if he *did*..."

Bertha was now finding a lot of virtue in old Bunn.

"But I didn't..."

"Get out. I never want...I'm going to live at the Blowitts' till this is over and you can keep away. Get your things and go..."

And she ran upstairs and locked herself in her room.

Wilfred Flounder felt himself collapse inside. He stood there like one in a dream, recalling his happiness and comfort only twenty-four hours before; looking at the familiar objects of the room; remembering the terms of endearment between himself and Bertha; eyeing the couch on which they had embraced; thinking of their plans. He slowly walked to the shop, fumbled under the counter to where the clotheslines were kept, and took one out, a solid bale of rope with a ring on one end with which to hook it up on washing-day.

There was an old shed at the bottom of the yard behind the shop, which had originally been a place where they took down and cleaned lawn-mowers. The structure was held up by a large beam and there were hooks in it...

Flounder picked up the invoice pad and pencil from the counter and scribbled hastily:

Bertha,
    If you don't believe me, I don't want to go on living. Please forgive me taking this way out.

He thought a bit, drew himself up, and then wrote with a flourish:

As faithful in death as in life, your loving Wilfred.

Then he went to the shed.

Wilfred Flounder, having made up his mind, now started with his customary thoroughness to do a good job. He made a noose he'd learned when he was a boy scout.

He found the grass-box of an old mower, cleared a space beneath a large hook which held chains, threw the latter in a corner, and tested the strength of the hook. Then he fixed the ring on the end of the line to the hook, put the noose round his neck, stood on the box, closed his eyes, and jumped from his perch ...

Bertha Bunn, hearing noises beneath her window, pressed a tear-stained face to the pane and saw through the open door of the shed what was going on. She screamed and rushed downstairs. As she reached the back door there was a reverberating crash as though someone had dropped a bomb in the yard.

The shed had long been disused and the uprights which held the roof beam had rotted away in the ground. As the weight of Flounder strained the roof, the post on one side gave way, the whole crazy shanty rocked once and then collapsed like a pack of cards. The beam struck Flounder and laid him out beneath the wreckage.

Bertha started to claw and scrabble about among the splintered wood and corrugated iron and quickly cleared a space around the unconscious form of her rejected Wilfred, whose head and shoulders she commenced to hug, weeping over them, calling upon him to open his eyes, and begging his forgiveness. Wilfred Flounder, the slack rope round his neck, took no heed, but started to babble in concussed fashion, calling a woman's name. Fortunately, it was Bertha's he was calling for.

Bertha Bunn scrambled to her feet, rushed through the shop, and for the second time in so brief a period, roused the neighbourhood with her shrieks for help. At once, the shop doorway resembled the turnstiles at a football match;

people from the market, apparently eager to be of assistance, poured past the ironmongery into the room behind, on through the yard, to the wreckage of the shed, in which Flounder was now sitting in a daze.

"He's got a rope round his neck ..."

"He's tried to hang himself ..."

"Pulled the shed down on himself to try to kill himself ..."

" 'ere, 'ere ..."

The voice of the Law rose above it all and soon the procession was reversed back into the street.

So, Wilfred Flounder was returned, dishevelled, bruised, and gabbling from concussion, to the police-station, where they put him in a comfortable cell and sent for the doctor to deal with him.

The Chief Constable was still on the premises and he expressed himself in unprintable language about it all.

"The strain of the police interview must have driven him off his head ... I must say I think he was taxed beyond endurance by it."

Myers smiled grimly.

"It looks to me almost like a guilty conscience ... an admission of guilt, sir."

"Nothing of the kind. I grant you're an efficient officer, Myers, and I've no complaints, but murder of this kind is something new to us all ..."

Colonel Cargrave flung down his cap and stick and stopped a passing constable.

"Hi, you constable, get me Whitehall one-two-one-two."

Myers' eyes opened wide.

"You don't mean, sir ... ?"

"I do. We're getting help and, if it can be managed, I want the fellah who dealt with the case at Blow's Bank, at Nesbury ... Littlejohn, that's the man ..."

CHAPTER THREE
HAPPY FAMILIES

"And this is where it all happened..."

Inspector Myers led Littlejohn and Cromwell into the ironmonger's shop and through to the living-room.

All things considered, Myers had taken it very well. The hint that he might not be capable of handling the Bunn affair had come to him as a bitter pill. There was a vacancy for a Superintendent in a neighbouring town and Myers had been sure that the Chief Constable had him on the list. But just as he'd made up his mind that it was all off, the Chief had said quite casually, "Don't take it to heart my sending for Scotland Yard, Myers. They're more used to this kind of thing than we are. I've recommended you to the Committee for Superintendent at Selsby, by the way."

After that, Myers felt he didn't care a damn. On his way to the station he hurried home to tell his wife and then met the newcomers with a cheerful face.

"Seems all right about it," said Cromwell, who was always a bit anxious as to how the locals were going to take their intervention.

The same sort of town they'd been to so often before. The station a long way out from the centre; a long street leading to the heart of things; drab shops lining the route.

They passed a public library and a garden of remembrance, with a war memorial and a lot of seats scattered about on which old men and loafers were sitting gossiping. Then, round the church and to the police-station ... The file of the case and the story itself were short enough. There was so little to tell. A shot in the dark, nobody about as proper eye-witnesses, a serious suspicion of Wilfred Flounder, a difference of opinion between the Chief Constable and the Inspector about Flounder. That was all.

"Flounder tried to hang himself yesterday, but it seems to have been more because he'd lost his girl ... the victim's daughter ... than because we suspected him. They've made it up now and the Chief has sent him home under her care ... Perhaps we'd better go and have a look at the scene of the crime."

The market square was one of the most hideous Littlejohn had ever seen. There was a large forlorn-looking church at one end, with a tower and graveyard and, at the other, a huge Victorian nonconformist chapel built of crumbling sandstone, with a portico which looked ready to fall down. Between the two, a motley assortment of shops, the bulk of which seemed to be struggling for existence. Sedate nineteenth century drapers and tailors, a wool shop and a shoemaker's. In between, a lot of new tile and chromium grocers and dairies, milk-bars, tobacconists, butchers and multiple stores. Notices hit you from all directions. MILK SHAKES. REGISTER HERE FOR MEAT. HOT DOGS. SUITS, HALF-PRICE. FUNERAL PARLOUR, ARRANGEMENTS REVERENTLY MADE ...

And in the middle of it all, BUNN's shop, prosperous, well-stocked, conservative in structure, free from competitors, the best of the lot. The windows were choc-a-bloc with tools, small machines, fishing tackle, sporting guns, lamps, poultry appliances and garden implements. You almost had to fight your way in past the lawn-mowers and garden-rollers on the pavement and in the doorway and the rolls of roofing-felt and wire-netting which cluttered up the public side of the counter.

"Business as usual," Wilfred Flounder had said after being reconciled to Bertha Bunn and, single-handed, he had covered the pavement with the customary overflow of goods and set out the shop with the usual obstacles. He was now standing behind the counter in a grey overall, selling screws. As the sole remaining support of the Bunn emporium, Wilfred had been seized with a frenzy of efficiency and was trying to deal with three customers at once. The high-spot of the day's business had been when Mr. Ericson had called for the revolver he'd ordered, had been told that it had been used to assassinate Ned Bunn, had been impounded by the police, and was, therefore, not available. He had left the shop in anger, as though somehow this were just another piece of Ned Bunn's awkwardness.

The arrival of Scotland Yard in the room behind the shop caused a great commotion; there was hardly a square foot of space available. The Bunn family and its ramifications were widespread and mixed-up in every aspect of the life of Enderby. Ned Bunn's father had had four children, two sons and two daughters, and the other three had not confined themselves to a single child, like Ned. In all, Bertha had one uncle, two aunts, seven cousins and two second cousins in Enderby alone, to say nothing of her grandfather Bunn's relatives scattered in distant parts and now mustering for the funeral. The Enderby end of the family was a close clan, centred round Salem Chapel in the market square, which was their hobby, stronghold, matrimonial agency and source of spiritual power. Nothing went on at the chapel without the concurrence of the Bunn clan and if the parson fell out of their favour, he might just as well pack up and be off.

When Littlejohn and Cromwell appeared, the two aunts and Uncle Jasper were holding a family council with Bertha. Several of their offspring were sitting around silently taking it all in. They had been trying to persuade Bertha by weight of numbers that Wilfred Flounder wasn't good enough to be her husband. She had resisted, and was now enjoying a fit of hysterics. As the door between the house and the shop opened to admit the police, the cries of his girl-friend became plainly audible to Wilfred, who, brushing aside his customers, thereupon entered the family conclave and, taking the sobbing Bertha in his arms, challenged the clan to do their worst over his dead body.

"The police!"

A hush fell upon the gathering from which a small, unctuous man detached himself and started to act as spokesman.

"I am Jasper Bunn and I'm Miss Bunn's uncle. Since my brother's death, I'm head of the family. We have just called to comfort our dear niece who is sorely stricken."

"You seem to be succeeding very well..."

It was Cromwell who spoke and it was as though he couldn't help it. This was the kind of thing which appealed to his astringent sense of humour. Already he was starting to enjoy himself among this galaxy of queer characters. He eyed Mr. Bunn's bald head, pouched hazel eyes, bulbous nose and round pink face as though he were some kind of strange animal. It made Jasper quite nervous and he began to straighten his tie, polish his glasses, examine his clothing to see if all the buttons were fastened, and generally make moves which showed he was put out of countenance.

The family stood behind the newly-appointed head wondering what to do next. A tall woman, who strongly resembled Jasper, a small nondescript shabby sister, and a lot of cousins on the fringe and lost in the shadows of the room.

"We'd better go. We know when we're not wanted. But we'll be back..."

The tall woman took the initiative, pressed it home by thrusting an umbrella and a hat in her brother's hands, and led the party through the shop and into the street. The atmosphere cleared at once and Bertha even smiled.

"Good afternoon, Mr. Myers."

"These two gentlemen are from London to help in your trouble, Miss Bunn, and I'll be glad if you'll give them all the assistance you can."

"Pleased to meet you, I'm sure. This is Mr. Flounder, my husband-to-be..."

Then, Bertha and Wilfred told their stories for the tenth time, and they were just as unprofitable.

Littlejohn was smoking his pipe and looking through the window. A large yard, a lot of packing-cases, a workshop, and the tumbledown shed in which Flounder had tried to take his own life and had only succeeded in bringing it down about his ears. Beyond that, a lot of slum property built in narrow rows in shabby streets, with children playing on the cobblestones...

He turned his head.

"Had your father many enemies?"

Littlejohn had already seen the body of Ned Bunn in the town morgue. The square face, the massive and aggressive nose, the heavy chin, and the thrust-out swollen lips told, even in death, of a difficult man.

"He wasn't easy to get on with. He liked his own way and would quarrel if he didn't get it, but I don't think he had any enemies who hated him enough to kill him. Do you, Wilfred?"

Flounder awoke from his reverie with a jerk.

"Eh? No ... Not that. Not enough to do murder."

Myers was sitting at the round table in the middle of the room, his hat on his knees. He looked up.

"And yet, Mr. Flounder, you must admit that his survival put grave difficulties in the way of your own plans, didn't it?"

Flounder grew red.

"I don't see why you should keep picking on me, Mr. Myers. I didn't kill him. There must have been someone in the shop, hiding, someone who planned to do it. How else would they have loaded the revolver?"

"Did your father make a will, Miss Bunn, and do you know what was in it?" asked Littlejohn suddenly. Greed, lust, revenge, fear ... It might have been caused by any of them and it was as well to get the easiest out of the way first.

"He did make a will, but I don't know what's in it. Dad was like that. He liked to keep you on tenterhooks about your future."

That was obvious. In her younger days, Bertha Bunn had certainly been a good-looking girl. She was quite pass-able still, with her fair hair unblemished by grey, her clear complexion, and her Junoesque figure. But there was now about her the uncertainty, the nervousness, the eagerness of the maternal type who sees the chances of marriage passing her by. She was not *femme sole* of her own wishing; old Ned Bunn had been responsible and had driven away every man likely to deprive him of her presence and constant atten-tion. Bertha had always been on perpetual tenterhooks about her father's reactions to her various suitors. In youth, they had been many and they had all gone off and married somebody else after Ned Bunn had finished with them.

"Did he ever mention how he was going to leave his money?"

"Often. Sometimes he said he'd rather leave it to the Dogs' Home than to me. But that was when he was cross about something. He often talked about altering his will. Last time he threatened to alter it because of Mr. Flounder..."

"Is it with his lawyer then...?"

"Yes. Mr. Edgell across the way was his solicitor. He'll have it. Mr. Edgell's father looked after grandfather Bunn's estate, too. There's still a trust there that father got income from. I never knew about it; father wouldn't talk of it. He once said, I remember, that he ought to have had the money outright instead of tied up, but I wouldn't know what he meant."

Littlejohn took up his hat.

"Perhaps we'd better get to the bottom of this right away, Miss Bunn. I'll go and see the lawyer, but you mustn't expect me to tell you anything about the interview till after the funeral and the will is properly read."

"I quite see that, and thank you for being so kind. We both appreciate it, I'm sure. Don't we, Wilfred?"

Mr. Flounder vigorously concurred and with that the police left them, Littlejohn to visit the lawyer, Cromwell to look into the matter of their lodgings, and Myers to return to get rid of his day's routine.

There was a plate on a door adjoining a multiple tailor's shop: Edgell, Green, Bastable and Edgell, Solicitors. It was a strain to read it, as metal polish had worn it nearly all away. A shabby staircase and then a door with a ground-glass panel on which the rigmarole of names was repeated, with the injunction, "Come In." There was a sort of anteroom plastered with posters about property sales and a portion of it was shut off by partitions from behind one of which came a young lady chewing gum and patting her hair.

"Yep?"

"Mr. Edgell, please. Here's my card."

"O.K."

She looked nonchalantly at the card and then her attitude changed.

"Coo...er," she said, round the chewing-gum, eyed Littlejohn with profound admiration, rolled her eyes at him, and rushed off to announce him.

Mr. Edgell was free and eager to co-operate. He was a slim little elderly man with grey hair, a grey suit and a grey complexion. He looked to live among the masses of papers and files with which the room and every receptacle and available bit of space in it were filled. The best thing which could happen here, thought Littlejohn, would be a fire to rid Edgell of this incubus and, strangely enough, the thought must have been prophetic, for three weeks later the whole block went up in flames, papers and all, and a grey suit which Mr. Edgell was having made at the tailor's also dissolved in smoke with the shop.

"Well, Inspector, is it the Bunn murder you're here about? How can I help you?"

"That's right, sir, and just to be quite sure about the money motive, I wonder if you could tell me if the late Mr. Bunn made a will."

Mr. Edgell thrust the spectacles he was wearing up to his forehead and then put on another pair. This process seemed to help him to think, his face cleared, and he said he would do what he could.

"This is advance information, Inspector, and must be strictly confidential. The will won't be read till after the interment, you know...Let me see..."

Mr. Edgell thereupon turned and started aggressively to rummage in a pile of papers on his desk. He worked hard, like a rabbit digging a burrow, and in the heat of the job seemed to forget altogether that Littlejohn was waiting. At last, he came up for air.

"Dear me! Where did I put that copy-will...?"

He rang a bell on the desk and the girl with the chewing-gum entered again. She rolled her eyes at the Inspector as she approached the desk. She seemed able to read her boss's mind, for, without a word, she thrust her hand among the mass of paper before him, drew out a foolscap envelope, and held it out.

"This what you want, Mr. Edgell?"

The lawyer needn't have bothered hunting for the will. It was very simple. After all Bunn's shouting and threatening, he'd left every penny of his money to his daughter, Bertha, and she was to be his sole executrix.

"Well, well... Not so much there, sir, is there? Were the family... I mean the brother and sisters... acquainted with the will?"

"I'm sure I've no idea, but if you're seeking motive for killing Ned Bunn, I think you might bear in mind that it is always as well to know if you're included in a will before killing whoever has made it. As for Bunn's relatives, have you met them? Can you imagine any of them firing a revolver? They wouldn't know one end of the thing from the other."

"I'm not so sure about that, sir. You'd be surprised at some of the things a murder enquiry brings to light."

Mr. Edgell started to hunt for his first pair of glasses and Littlejohn pointed out that they were across his forehead. The lawyer seemed very grateful.

"Well, sir. Thanks for the help. I think that's all. It clears up one motive, at least. Now, we must seek for others."

Edgell smiled knowingly.

"That's not all, Inspector, by any means. There's another will. Not that of Ned Bunn, but that of his father, Jeremiah Bunn. The trust created by it is still alive. It will enter into the formalities when Ned Bunn's will is read, because the trust made by Jerry Bunn ended with Ned's death."

Littlejohn sat down again.

"And this second will is of interest in our case, sir?"

"It certainly is."

There then began another lot of frantic rummaging among papers until the clerk with the chewing-gum arrived again, put her hand in exactly the right place, and produced, this time, a folder as large as a pillowslip.

"This what you want, Mr. Edgell?"

"I'm very much obliged to you, Miss Whatnot."

"The name's Watson, sir."

"Ah, yes... So sorry..."

The folder was full of papers and it took Mr. Edgell quite a time to find the ones he required. Even then, he didn't open and read them; he held them in his hand as he spoke as though they gave him confidence.

"This is also strictly confidential until I read the will after the funeral."

"Of course, sir."

Mr. Edgell got to his feet, stood with his back to the fire, and read Littlejohn a lecture, which he punctuated with his forefinger.

"Jeremiah Bunn had four children; two boys and two girls. He married Mary Wood, but only three of the children were his... I heard all this from my late father and it is borne out by the nature of the trust. Before Jerry Bunn... he owned the same shop over the way and made a large fortune in it... before Jerry Bunn married her, Mary Wood had been seduced by a friend of her brother's, who ran away and left her in the lurch. A child was born and he was baptized Edmund .. Edmund Wood. Jerry Bunn came of a strait-laced family and his own moral views were a bit rigid, but he was mad about Mary Wood and determined to have her. He took her and her child, gave Ned Wood the name of Bunn, and brought him up as his own. But...But...when he made his will he wasn't going to treat Ned just like his own flesh and blood and give him an equal share of the family fortune. The other three inherited twenty thousand pounds apiece...A tidy sum, but remember, Jerry Bunn not only sold screws and nails, but every type of agricultural machinery and also was sole agent for certain firms of textile engineers at a time when industry was booming...He cashed-in properly...Ned Bunn took over the business on a mortgage to the family and has since repaid it. To cut a long story short, Ned Bunn received the income on twenty thousand pounds for life and, on his death, the trust ends and the money is divided among his surviving half-brother and sisters. The beneficiaries all know it..."

Mr. Edgell tittered and hunted for his spectacles again.

"There's a bone for you to worry, Inspector."

As Littlejohn made his way down the drab staircase, he smiled grimly to himself. So, Ned Bunn was really Ned Wood! He wondered what those of the townsfolk who had trembled all their lives at the very name of Bunn would do when they heard it should have been Wood. It seemed like being held up with a revolver and finding that it was a water-pistol after all, or being terrified by a masked intruder and discovering it was a practical joke played by Uncle Joe!

All the same, Bunn or Wood, Ned had been murdered, and that was no joke.

CHAPTER FOUR
THE MAN WHO SAID
HE'D SWING

"Hetherow said he'd swing for Ned Bunn..."

Mr. Blowitt, the landlord of *The Freemasons'
Arms,* leaned over the brass rail at the foot of the bed and
searched Cromwell's face to see if he'd startled him. The
sergeant didn't move a muscle.

"Oh ... and who's Hetherow?"

Cromwell wasn't in too good a temper. He'd been arguing about accommodation with Mr. Blowitt.

"We've only one room with a double bed in it and I doubt
if you'll find anywhere else to suit you in Enderby. We don't
get many class visitors." He thereupon showed the sergeant
the room, which was satisfactory in every way, except that
the bed wasn't big enough. Besides, he and Littlejohn had
never slept two in a bed on any of their previous excursions,
and a little whippersnapper like Blowitt wasn't going to start
them doing it now.

"That thing'll collapse if my chief and me get in it.
Nearly thirty stone together. We'll end up in the room
below. Better put another bed up."

"We haven't got one."

"Well, buy or borrow one, then."

Mr. Blowitt thereupon had a bright idea. Ned Bunn was dead and wouldn't need his bed any more. He'd borrow *that*.

"O.K. I'll borrow one."

The landlord of *The Freemasons'* having settled that point, then leaned over the bed-end and started to pump information into Cromwell. He slung his short arms over the brass rail between the two brass knobs. He had a habit of opening his eyes and his mouth together spasmodically as he spoke, like some strange fat fish.

"Hetherow said he'd swing for Ned Bunn."

"Who's Hetherow?"

"Owns the draper's shop next door to Bunn's. Ned Bunn lent him money on mortgage knowing all the time he'd never get it back and meanin' thereby to foreclose and turn 'Etherow out. Bunn wanted to extend his own shop..."

"And Hetherow objected...?"

Cromwell opened his suit-case and started to stuff its contents in the drawers of a rickety chest. Volumes of criminal and forensic works, handcuffs, a box containing equipment for everything from fingerprinting to setting a broken limb, a book on Yoga, some chest-expanders, and two tins of patent food. Mr. Blowitt watched it all, his eyes and mouth making gasping movements... Finally, a revolver over which Cromwell pondered a second before throwing it up in the air, catching it, and slipping it in his pocket...

"Like 'ell he objected. Wouldn't you? If you was losin' the shop you got your bread and butter by. And Hetherow with a sick wife on whom he dotes, an' two kids still at school. He's never done any other job in his life, 'asn't Hetherow... His shop's been 'anded down from father to son. Not that it pays 'im now. Times are bad, what with multiple stores and such."

"You'd think he'd be glad to get out if he was losing money."

"It's not that. It's the way Bunn did things. He went to church regular, but was never above a bit o' money-lending on the side. He must have known when he lent 'Etherow money, what he was goin' to do. What Hetherow thought was just a temp'ry setback became a permanent one, and Bunn put on the screw."

"All the same, if the shop didn't pay ..."

"Yes, but 'Etherow lives there, you see. And his wife's bedridden ... dyin' of cancer, between you an' me ... and how in the world is a man to get another house to let under present conditions? If Bunn had put him out, even if he *had* a place to go to, Mrs. 'Etherow would have folded up an' died. You see what I mean?"

Cromwell nodded and snapped the catches of his suitcase.

"So, rather than put up with it, Hetherow said he'd swing for Ned Bunn. That it?"

"Yes."

"When and where was this said?"

Mr. Blowitt caressed his unshaven chin with his fingers.

"More'n once, but he said it in front of a number of us the night Bunn was killed. In fact, he'd come seekin'-out Ned Bunn to tell 'im so. He was a bit drunk and I 'ad to chuck him out."

"I'll look into it. By the way, if the Chief agrees and if you put another bed in here, the room will suit us. You'll see the food's good and I'll have to have a word or two with you or the cook about my diet. I don't eat white bread, tinned stuff, or anything cooked in aluminium pans ... and just one or two other little odds and ends ... I'll tell you later."

Mr. Blowitt's eyes and mouth opened spasmodically.

"It'll be a pleasure," he said in tones which belied the words, and he hurried downstairs to make arrangements.

"I've never met anybody from Scotland Yard before," he told his wife, "an' I hope this is the last. He's mad. Chuckin' revolvers up in the air, won't eat off aluminium, an' he's got what looks like a strait-jacket in 'is bag. I 'ope we've got the right chap and not somebody who's escaped from a mad'ouse and thinks he's Sherlock Holmes."

His wife's tight lips did not relax.

"He's no worse than some I could name."

She was a heavy, temperamental woman with a tired, made-up face and hair hennaed to a deep purple. She had once been a small-part actress and still spoke as though every word were out of some lines she'd learned.

"Oh, come off it...! Nag, nag, nag... Will it never end?"

He was leaning on the bar, tearing at the tufts of hair on the sides of his bald head when Cromwell descended the stairs. His wife was striking an attitude; her bosom drawn up, her hands over her heart, her face twitching.

Hetherow's wasn't hard to find. A shabby, old-fashioned shop across the way, with braces, overalls, corduroy trousers and cheap blazers hanging outside. *Bargain Lines. Cut Prices.* The woodwork had lost all its paint and the goods in the windows were higgledy-piggledy and shoddy-looking. Cromwell cast his eyes around the square. There were three similar shops and a multiple store within a stone's throw. No wonder Bunn had made sure of getting the premises before he lent the money.

The shop was dark inside and somewhere in the depths as he entered, Cromwell could hear footsteps and fumbling. Hetherow appeared from behind a barricade of soiled men's vests and pants piled up on the counter and marked, *For the Cold Weather—Half-Price While They Last.* They looked like lasting for ever! There was nobody else in the shop, and Hetherow grew convulsive to oblige. He rubbed his hands. "Well, sir...?"

He only seemed pleased with his mouth and teeth; the rest of his face was haggard and sad. His head was bullet-shaped, with a tuft of wiry grey hair on the top. He wore strong cataract glasses and you couldn't see properly what his eyes were like, for they seemed, through the lenses, to be deep in his head like stones in a pool. He was sallow and tired and kept looking from side to side, as though, among the rows of raincoats, frocks, carpets and shirts, relief were hidden and ready to emerge and save him. The nails of his stumpy hands were bitten to the quicks and his clothes hung on his thin frame like shapeless garments on a coat-hanger.

And this was the man who had said he'd swing for Ned Bunn!

Hetherow showed no sign of emotion when Cromwell said who he was. Only the corners of his lips turned down and the teeth vanished. He had reached the bottom of his endurance and anything else didn't matter much.

"You knew the late Mr. Bunn, sir?"

Mr. Hetherow started to giggle. A hard, dry, sobbing noise. He took off his spectacles and wiped his eyes. His appearance changed completely without the glasses. The eyes were small, twitching and expressionless.

"Did I know Ned Bunn! You're joking, sir. He lived next door, and, had he continued to do so, would have put me and my family in the street next month. I don't suppose for a moment he's left me anything in his will, but his daughter will be better to deal with. She's a friend of my poor wife's... unknown to her father, of course... and, on that account, I'm glad somebody killed Bunn."

"You didn't do it yourself, sir?"

There was a hush. It was as if death were in this place, as well as next-door. The overalls swayed about like men on the gallows; the white shirts hanging at the back of the shop looked like a cohort of wraiths; and, to crown all, somebody had broken the head from a fully-dressed male dummy and he stood in a gloomy corner like one who had risen from the executioner's block to finish off one or two jobs before yielding up the ghost.

Upstairs, where life and laughter and the voices of children had sounded in better days, there was dead silence.

"Me?"

"Yes, sir. You threatened to kill Bunn, didn't you?"

Cromwell found it difficult to put it in the way Blowitt had done. He'd swing for Bunn. Hetherow didn't seem the type who would use the expression. He was obviously a well-educated man, one who had been to a good school paid for by the profits of this now decayed business. He'd known better times, which made it all the more difficult for him to face the present hopelessness. Cromwell looked at the close-bitten fingers, the wild topknot of hair, the deep unfathomable eyes, which, when the spectacles were removed, had a blank, mad expression.

"I said I'd kill Bunn? Yes, I did. I was drunk, but I remember it. I recollect Blowitt putting me out of his hotel. I'd been pleading with Bunn. He wouldn't see me, so I went where I knew I'd find him; with his cronies having a drink. I took one or two bracers of whisky to give me Dutch courage. Bunn laughed at me in front of his friends. As I went I tried to dramatize the event. I turned and said I'd kill him. And he *was* killed. I can see the folly of it now. But I didn't do it, I assure you. I might fire a revolver, but I could never hit anything with it..."

"Where were you when it happened, sir?"

"I came straight in from *The Freemasons'*. I must have been making myself a cup of black coffee. I daren't appear before my wife half-intoxicated. Fortunately she was asleep when I got in. She's an invalid ..."

A spasm of anguish crossed his face, as though sometimes he could forget it, and then when the truth returned to his mind, it was too bitter to bear.

"Did you hear any noise next door, sir? A shot, or anything?"

"No. It was blowing a gale, you'll recollect ... Or perhaps it wasn't at Scotland Yard ..."

His voice trailed away. He began to fold up some shirts on the counter with fussy, concentrated movements, as though the world depended on their being straight and properly put away.

He suddenly lifted his head and looked at Cromwell; the concentric rings in his pebbled glasses were like spirals boring into his head.

"Who sent you here? Was it Blowitt?"

He didn't wait for an answer. His mild, tired voice gathered strength and venom.

"Did Blowitt happen to tell you, as well, that he himself hated Bunn? Did he tell you that they had a good-looking barmaid at *The Freemasons' Arms* and that Blowitt became infatuated with her and nearly ruined the business by spending so much money on her; and that Mrs. Blowitt used to make scenes and throw hysterics about it in front of customers; and that Blowitt was ready to run away with the girl ...?"

Cromwell was amazed at the vehemence of the little humble man. His face had grown flushed and he was throwing his arms about wildly. A customer looked in at the shop door, saw what was going on, and hastily retreated.

"Yes... He was ready to run away with the girl, but she ran away first. One morning Blowitt got up and found she'd gone. He was like one demented. Then it leaked out. It had been known that Ned Bunn, a nasty one where women were concerned, had taken a fancy to her and she wouldn't have anything to do with him. She preferred the little half-bankrupt publican to Bunn. So Bunn took his revenge. He made enquiries about her from her previous places. She'd been in prison for helping herself to a till, and she was already married but had left her husband. Bunn bullied her out of town in a rush. Then, he boasted about it... How do you think Blowitt feels about Bunn? It wasn't as if the girl had proved flighty and unfaithful... She was just chased out."

Hetherow folded the last of the garments, gave it a slap with the flat of his hand, and smiled a crooked smile at Cromwell.

"Now! Think about that when you start suspecting people. Blowitt was once a sergeant-major in the Army. He can handle a revolver, believe me. I never thought of shooting Bunn. That's not my strong point. I might have tunnelled into the shop next door and blown it sky-high and Bunn with it... A sort of Guy Fawkes... I hadn't got down to details though..."

He started to laugh hysterically. Another customer, a woman this time, thrust her head round the doorway and was about to withdraw. Hetherow cut off his laughter suddenly, like switching off the radio, and ran to bring her back.

"Come in, Mrs. Keith... Come in... Don't go..."

Every penny counted in the takings of this bankrupt shop, and Hetherow even had to beg customers to come in. Cromwell bade him good-morning and went away. He came upon Blowitt quarrelling with his wife again.

"I tell you I never touched Annie. Every barmaid we get you're jealous of. We've got to have a barmaid; we can't afford a man. Nag, nag, nag..."

They saw Cromwell and stopped. Mrs. Blowitt had one hand on her bosom again, as though her breathing troubled her; the other she passed across her brow in the conventional fashion of melodrama years ago. Then she bit into her handkerchief and stumbled from the room, like someone making an exit amid sympathetic applause.

Blowitt shrugged his shoulders at Cromwell.

"Women!" he said. "Are you married?"

"Yes."

The way Cromwell said it shut Blowitt up.

"You weren't fond of Mr. Bunn yourself, were you, Mr. Blowitt?"

The landlord suddenly sprang into life. The hopelessness of his married state was forgotten.

" 'Ere. Who's been tellin' you things? Is it that little perisher, Hetherow, gettin' his own back because I chucked him out?"

"I don't know about that, but I did hear about Bunn being a bit vindictive about a barmaid you once had."

Blowitt's jaw dropped and his mouth slackened. He seemed to grow smaller somehow, sagging at the shoulders, like somebody stabbed in the back.

"Effie!" he muttered, turned on his heel, filled a tumbler full of whisky at the bar, and drank it off in two quick gulps.

Then he dashed the glass to the floor, where it smashed to pieces. He staggered away to a room behind, slammed the door, and Mrs. Blowitt emerged and swept up the broken glass silently.

"Have you fixed us up?"

Littlejohn had entered unseen during the commotion, and stood watching the landlord's wife working with the brush and dust-pan. For all her bulk, she somehow contrived to get down to it gracefully and enact a touching scene, mingling her tears with the debris. Two men arrived carrying an enormous bed with brass knobs. They shuffled upstairs and then another followed struggling with a spring-mattress. He must have been the town comedian, for as he got half-way upstairs he saw Mrs. Blowitt and pretended to play the harp for her on the mattress.

"That's your bed going up, sir," said Cromwell. "I wonder where he's got it from."

"I saw them trundling it across as I came here," replied Littlejohn. "And it's *your* bed, not mine. It was presumably the connubial, and later the widowed bed, of the late Ned Bunn and it's all yours ..."

The man was still playing the harp on the mattress and Mrs. Blowitt, thawed by his attentions, stood with a shovelful of broken glass in one hand and threw him a theatrical kiss with the other.

In a room behind, somebody started to play the piano. Schumann's *Papillons*, beautifully played.

The man with the mattress cocked a thumb in the direction of the music and spoke to Littlejohn.

"That's Blowitt. Must be in the dumps. Always plays the pianner when he's *low*. Played in an Army orchestra once't... No good in a pub, though, that sort o' stuff. Over the patrons' 'eads, you might say."

The difficult, swirling music continued.

CHAPTER FIVE
THE TRIBE OF JERRY BUNN

Had Ned Bunn known what would happen at his inquest, he would have been very annoyed. In life, he loved being made a fuss of; in death, it looked as if they were trying to settle it all and get him buried with as little publicity as possible. Nobody except the family, the necessary officials, and a sleepy local reporter knew when and where the inquest was to be held and they did not noise it abroad because of its unsavoury nature. In fact, all the Bunns feared that more horrible things would come to light and disgrace them. ...

The Coroner was a man called Surtees Green and he looked it. As he sat on his rostrum, he seemed to be in the throes of a rough Channel crossing and his complexion matched his name. A thin faggot of a fellow, whose wife had bullied all the spirit out of him; so much so, that he kept glancing over his shoulder and peering myopically into the distance to make sure she wasn't there. Littlejohn, sitting with the rest of the officials in the well of the court, looked from the Coroner to the public places and back again; it reminded him of a gathering of a strange religious sect. The Bunn family were all there, except the second cousins, two small boys named Enoch and Caleb, who were away from home at a denominational boarding-school.

Jasper Bunn gave evidence of identification. He wore a frock coat and carried a top hat, which he took with him into the box and balanced on the ledge whilst he took the oath. He then coughed in his hat, testified, and looked angry when told to step down. Jasper had been rehearsing the part he would play as head of the clan in the proceedings. He was going to deliver a kind of funeral oration on his late brother, but Mr. Green, after a furtive squint over his shoulder, slipped a bismuth lozenge in his mouth and said that would be all.

"If I may be permitted..."

"Later, later..."

Jasper returned to the pew where his family awaited with sympathetic looks. They were all dressed in black; Mrs. Jasper Bunn, née Louisa Freer, a fat fair woman who had once been very good looking and the belle of Salem Protestant Chapel, but who now resembled a feather-bed, took up two seats. She ate a lot of chocolates and read romantic novels. In days past, the affair of Jasper and Louisa had been the romance of Salem and, in spite of the sanctimonious nature of the courtship, had ended in a rush for the altar, for little Paul was already on the way. Paul, now grown-up, was sitting beside his mother, lanky, very swarthy, pug-faced, heavy jowled, and with a stiff growth of beard which needed removing twice a day, but never was, hence giving him the look of a pious burglar. His brother, Silas, sat beside him and resembled him, although in a feebler mould, for he had been a backward boy and a great trial to his parents. Their wives were insignificant echoes of their husbands and had been told to stay away. Paul's wife, Leah, the mother of Enoch and Caleb, now and then rebelled against authority and took to gin, a phenomenon which was explained away at church as migraine.

Jasper Bunn sat down next to his wife, mopped his brow, put his hat on the floor and examined all his buttons to see if they were right. Then he pushed away his wife's comforting hand, which was a sign that there was trouble brewing. He and his two sons had public-spiritedly absented themselves from their successful business of making eyelet-holes for shoelaces, and this was what they got!

Wilfred Flounder had been sworn and was now telling his tale for the fourteenth time.

"Speak up," said Mr. Green. The result made the Coroner hold his hands over his ears. "I said *speak*... not yell your head off."

Bertha and Wilfred sat apart from the rest of the family, who were only half on speaking-terms with them. Bertha wore a ready-made tweed costume and a green hat with a pheasant's feather waving above it; Wilfred was in a multiple-tailored brown suit and a green tie. This show of disrespect for the dead had further angered Mr. Jasper, who had sworn to have a "few words" with them afterwards, a masterpiece of understatement, for once started, Jasper never knew when to stop.

"It was dark in the street and I couldn't make out what was going on. My glasses were running with rain, too."

"Wait a minute... I've got to take all this down."

Mr. Surtees Green, using a quill pen, scratched and scrawled and looked over his shoulder and at the distant door.

"Go on."

At this point, a dog entered the court and proceedings were suspended.

"What have we come for? I do think we ought to have been called before *him*".

Sarah Agnes Fearns, née Bunn, and briefly called Sr'Agnes, thought she was whispering to her husband but her voice rose like a dull chant.

"Silence in Court!"

Sr'Agnes was the tall, scraggy elder sister, around whom centred all the resistance to Wilfred Flounder. She had a pale, heavy face, the pugnacious pug-nose and heavy jaw of the Bunns, and she wore a shapeless black costume, black stockings and black gloves. On her head was a small hat of lacquered straw. It looked as if good taste, having been stifled whilst the rest of her clothing was being chosen, had suddenly recovered and insisted on being represented by the hat, which made all the rest look shoddy. Her husband, John Fearns, sat with her, a small slip of a man, with dark eyes, a sensitive face and a ready smile. Side by side with his wife, he looked like the mate of a predatory female spider, ready to be devoured when his functions had been fulfilled. If you'd asked him why he ever married Sarah Agnes Bunn, Fearns would have been at a loss to explain, but, in her younger days, she had been good-looking in a ferocious amazonian kind of way; Fearns, who attended Salem Chapel, had been chosen, enmeshed, and married before he quite knew what he was doing. She had borne him three children. Barnabas, who was never mentioned, for he had at the age of nineteen gone abroad with a doctor's wife, aged twenty-nine, and had never been seen again. Henry, their second son, was with them; smaller than his father, light on his feet, and locally known as Little Titch. Their daughter, Helen, had been told to stay at home. By some freak of nature, she was phenomenally beautiful and upset the men wherever she went. This was a constant thorn in her mother's flesh, for, instead of being proud of it, she somehow had the idea that in bringing such a lovely snare into the world, she had assisted the devil in his work.

"We carried him indoors..."

Flounder, adjusting his speed to Mr. Surtees Green's quill pen, dawdled on and on under the malevolent eyes of the Bunns and the encouraging nods of Bertha, who had been weeping and whose face resembled a boiled pudding therefrom.

Here again the proceedings were interrupted. A noise like the hooves of a lot of cattle was heard on the marble floor of the ante-room and a cheerful chirping voice was raised, explaining something to the usher.

"We thought it started at half past eleven...Was it eleven?"

"Silence!"

There was a pause and then the hooves resumed their tapping. Down the passage, across the well of the court, and to the vacant seats on the other side.

"Late again! Always late!"

A stage whisper from Sr'Agnes echoed round the rafters. The recipients of the criticism were not in the least put-out. They bobbed and bowed to the rest of those present, made an awful noise getting in their pews, selected seats, changed them, and giggled at their own discomfiture. Mr. Green flung his quill pen into the well of the court in a rage. His seasick-looking cheeks turned a dull mauve.

"And what, might I ask, is the meaning of this gross disrespect to my court?"

Somebody retrieved the pen and handed it back. Mr. Green, who was prone to little fits of temper, flung it from him again.

"We thought it started at half past, instead of on the hour. We're all sorry."

There was a murmur of concurrence from the newcomers which sounded like 'hear' 'hear'.

"So you ought to be! What are you all doing here, anyhow?"

"We're close relatives of the deceased."

"That is no excuse for arriving at this hour. We're nearly finished. Sit down. Where's my pen? Has anybody seen my pen?"

Mr. Jubal Medlicott sat down. He was the husband of Ned Bunn's younger sister, a little, nondescript woman, who in her early days had been pretty and clever, but who had deteriorated under the struggle of making ends meet. Her husband kept the only first-class tailor's and outfitter's in the town, and it had declined in the teeth of competition. Mr. Jubal Medlicott had not declined with it. In appearance, at least, he kept his head above water. Every morning this little, dark-eyed, brisk, elderly man, with a close-clipped beard and gold-framed spectacles, started from home in a natty grey suit, a foulard bow-tie, a flower in his coat (placed there by one or the other of his ugly twin daughters), white spats over his shoes and a grey soft hat on his head, escorted by his two girls to the shop, where they all worked. He couldn't afford to employ the girls, really, but he loved them too much to turn them out to work elsewhere. The Bunn family gazed with astonishment as Jubal entered in his pearly grey business suit with a large chrysanthemum in the buttonhole.

Mrs. Jubal Medlicott was born Anne Bunn and theirs had been a love match. From the day Medlicott, the new assistant-cutter in the tailor's business he eventually bought with his wife's money, entered Bunn's shop with a rose in his buttonhole to buy a pair of scissors, she had loved him to the exclusion of all else. She was in her early twenties then and managed the shop during her father's frequent absences in search of business. Although in his dandified fashion, Medlicott had run through her little fortune, been frequently unfaithful, and left her to worry about his mania for squandering money and aversion to hard work, she still thought there was nobody like him. He always came back to her with his troubles and she still felt pride in his immaculate appearance, his energy, and his unending optimism. Their twin daughters resembled their father; round-eyes, globular foreheads, sharp pink-tinted noses, giggling optimism... Only what in the sprightly Jubal Medlicott was attractive, in the two girls was plain, almost repulsive. There was a joke in the town that Mr. Medlicott had offered a complete wedding rig-out from his shop to whoever would take his daughters from his hands. Dorothy and Mary—Dolly and Polly—were their father's darlings, the foils for his wit, the Mrs. 'Arrises of his anecdotes, and he treated them with a mock courtesy of bowing scraping and blowing kisses to which they responded in kind. Among her exuberant family, Mrs. Medlicott looked worn and faded, her pale invalid's eyes followed them around full of fondness, her tired hands served them, and she went shabby herself to balance their budget.

"... the bullet entered the skull from behind, travelled through the cerebellum and the corpus callosum, and made its exit through the frontal bone over the right eye. ..."

Dr. Halston was saying his piece and Mr. Green was slowly taking it down. A dull thud, and Bertha Bunn slid to the floor in a dead faint. She hadn't understood the medical report, but it sounded terrible. There was a scrimmage as Wilfred Flounder, two ushers and a constable carried her out. The leaders of the Bunn family were unmoved. They were used to it. In fact, they resented the interruption. Mrs. Medlicott alone detached herself from the group and, with slow tired steps, followed Bertha's retinue into the ante-room.

The inquest was adjourned. The family looked a bit surprised, as though they'd expected a verdict similar to that of a murder trial. They hesitated momentarily in their seats, whispered among themselves, and then rose and made for the door in procession. Presumably, Jasper Bunn should have headed it, but he stayed behind to consult the Coroner's officer; so his sister, Sr'Agnes, with her diminutive husband and even smaller son, led the way. She kept turning to see what was going on and muttering. There was an order of precedence in the Bunn family, strictly adhered to, like those rituals of jackdaws in which the higher one pecks the one immediately below it to keep it in place.

Mrs. Jasper Bunn and her two sons hesitated, formed a minor procession of their own, and went out without their leader. Mrs. Jasper fished deeply in her large handbag, took out a slab of chocolate, bit it, like a tobacco-chewer taking a quid, and began to munch contentedly.

Littlejohn gently tapped Jasper Bunn on the shoulder.

"Could we have a word together, sir?"

Jasper jumped, dropped his silk hat, rescued it, and started to restore the nap by rubbing it along his sleeve.

"You gave me a shock, Inspector. Shouldn't startle me like that. My heart's none too good."

He ran his fingers down the buttons of his waistcoat to see they were all decent and in place.

"We can't talk here; they're shutting up shop."

He was right. Mr. Surtees Green had vanished from his pulpit, the police and other officers had made an exit through a private door, and only Cromwell remained with Littlejohn, holding two hats and looking expectant.

"I must confess the inquest was a bit of a farce. I'd quite a lot to tell Green, I can assure you."

"Suppose you tell me ..."

Jasper Bunn looked a bit nonplussed. He'd only been wanting to talk a lot of hot-air and now it all seemed irrelevant.

"It hadn't exactly to do with the murder. I wanted to give Green our alibis, but he wouldn't let me speak. He's only half-baked, you know. A brilliant lawyer gone completely to seed, Inspector. That's what comes of getting married to a half-wit of a woman. Green knew there was a streak of insanity in the family. Now, she leads him a dog's life. Up half the night nagging him and chasing round the house after burglars and such like."

Mr. Jasper was just having his 'few words'!

"Let's go and have a drink, sir, and I can talk better with you then."

Mr. Bunn raised this thick black eyebrows and his pug's face grew set.

"I'm teetotal. Very much opposed to strong drink. I don't mind, however, a glass of port wine. I take it as a tonic."

Cromwell was attacked by a fit of coughing behind his hand and seemed busily occupied with the two hats he was carrying.

They found Mr. Blowitt of *The Freemasons'* in a livelier mood. He had, over breakfast, apologized to Cromwell for his behaviour of the previous day.

"I get a bit out o' sorts, sometimes. Temperamental, you know. In this place all day and every day gets on me nerves now an' then. I used to be a musician in the Army and when things like this Bunn business crops up, it gets me down and makes me wish I never left...'ope you'll think no more of it."

He thereupon shook hands with Cromwell, gave him an alibi for himself for the night Bunn had been killed, and ended up playing "Smoke gets in my eyes" on the piano, just to show his spirits had been restored.

Mr. Blowitt seemed surprised to see Mr. Jasper Bunn. He even got a bit sarcastic.

"Not offen you grace our 'umble pub, Mr. Bunn."

Mr. Bunn hung up his silk hat carefully on the hat-stand, dilated his pug's nostrils at the smell of beer and spirits, and snorted.

"You know my views, Blowitt."

Mr. Blowitt smiled as he served two beers and a dock glass of port. He winked at Cromwell. Mr. Bunn drank half his port, coughed, ran his tongue round his mouth and then finished the glass.

"Same again, Mr. Blowitt."

Cromwell couldn't resist it.

"I'm thirsty after that inquest," said Bunn, mopping his reddening face with a silk handkerchief. "What did you wish to know, Inspector?"

"Just where you and the family were at the time your brother died, sir."

Mr. Bunn sipped his next glass like a hen drinking.

"At 'ome, of course. We're great 'omebirds."

"Your sons, too?"

"Yes. We were having a meeting about some repairs for the church. I am a deacon, sir, and my two sons are on the council. So, we said we might as well meet the parson. You won't know him yet, Inspector. A Mister 'Ornblower... A very good preacher, I must say, but a bit *weak* doctrinally... Yes, a rather h'empty vessel on doctrine... Hic... Pardon me."

"Wasn't your brother interested in such a meeting, sir?"

"Who? Ned? Oh, yes. But this was an informal meetin', if you understand what I mean. Confidentially... confidentially... my brother liked to run the whole place. Liked wot he said to be law. Tried to dominate the meetin'. So we had to arrange beforehand what we wanted and form a strong h'opposition to him at the formal meetin's. See what I mean?"

Littlejohn nodded.

"Cut and dried beforehand?"

Mr. Jasper Bunn beamed. Here was a man after his own heart! He drank his second glass of port.

"Exactly. That's the only way of dealin' with dictators. A bit of secret democracy. Wot?"

He chuckled.

"For a teetotal drink, port wine's the best of the lot."

He hiccupped again and begged pardon.

"Anythin' more, Inspector?"

"Had your brother many enemies, sir?"

Mr. Jasper brooded alcoholically.

"No, sir. Not as might want to kill 'im. That is, not as far as I know. Unless it might be that Flounder fellow. A bounder, sir, he is. Flounder, the bounder... Not so bad, that? No... He's only after my niece for her money and as Ned wouldn't 'ave it, perhaps he did the murder to get his own way. Crime of passion, so to speak. Not that I would condemn a pore erring brother unheard. See what I mean? Fair's fair."

His face assumed a sanctimonious expression.

"There's none of us should judge another,
For fear our judgment's wrong,
Perhaps our own eye has a beam...

I forget the rest. Once saw it in an autograph album; thought it good. Eh?"

Mr. Jasper Bunn wasn't too drunk to stall. Littlejohn could see it in his fishy, protruding eyes. There was something he wasn't going to talk about. Perhaps it was old Jerry Bunn's will. At any rate, it would all come out after the funeral. Jasper was on his feet putting on his hat a little rakishly.

"I don't feel very well.... My heart.... Must be the emotion of the death and inquest."

He tottered unsteadily.

"Better go 'ome in a cab."

And that ended the inquest and the first formal rally of the Bunn clan; the players in the drama Littlejohn was to watch for some days to come and which, according to some, was to terminate in his worst failure.

CHAPTER SIX
THE SUPERANNUATED PARSON

M r. Blowitt, the landlord of *The Freemasons'*, stood in his shirt-sleeves at the door of his public-house, watching the passers-by. The eternal cigarette hung from the corner of his mouth and he seemed in a melancholy way to be enjoying it more than usual. He had just had another dramatic quarrel with his wife, who, this time, had accused him of making overtures to the girl who brought the milk. He sighed and went indoors to join Littlejohn and Cromwell, who were awaiting lunch.

"They say smoking shortens your life," he said, removing his cigarette and coughing loudly, after making sure that his wife was within earshot at the bar. "All I says is, the sooner the better with me." He lit another cigarette from the stub of the last. His wife thereupon made a gulping noise, bit her handkerchief, and made her famous *East Lynne* exit.

Mr. Blowitt immediately became more cheerful.

"Everybody seems to be gatherin' for the funeral. Bunns arrivin' from all over the shop." He took the policemen to the window and showed them the latest newcomers from the bus. A fat woman with a florid complexion and dressed in black from top to toe was ponderously entering Bunn's shop, followed by a thin, tottering, blue-nosed old man, also fully clad in mourning and wearing a billycock hat with a broad black band.

"That's old Gilbert Slinger and his missus. She was a sister of Jeremiah Bunn and they're both over eighty if a day. Rollin' in money, though you wouldn't think so to look at 'em. They used to run the eyelet-'ole works as Jasper Bunn and his sons now has."

It had been going on all day. Numerous as the tribes of Israel, the Bunns had been foregathering for the funeral on the morrow and were sorting themselves out and inflicting themselves for the night on various local relatives. It had been a busy morning, too, for tailors, dressmakers, hosiers, hatters and outfitters as their stocks of black were raided, and the undertakers and the parson had been commissioned exactly concerning the parts they were to play.

"I thought of goin' to the funeral myself," said Mr. Blowitt cheerfully. "But if I did, the wife would suspect me of kissin' the gravedigger's daughter, so I'd better stop away."

After lunch, Littlejohn made his way to the Manse of the Salem Chapel to confirm the alibis of Jasper Bunn and his family. The house, like the church, was the worse for wear. A stone wall which had shed all its mortar, surrounded the dirty brick building. An iron gate with a smashed catch, and held in place by a piece of rusty wire, hung at the end of a mossy stone path, which led through a neglected garden. Old trees and lank bushes made an avenue to the front door which badly needed a coat of paint. Littlejohn had to hammer on the panels because the bell was broken. As he mounted the steps, the middle one tilted dangerously.

A little, grey-haired smiling woman opened the door. She looked tired and determined to be cheerful whatever happened. She read the Inspector's card, shook hands, and asked him to enter. The hand she gave him was hard from work. Her clothes were shabby but carefully brushed and mended.

The Manse was large and frugally furnished. The hall was covered in linoleum, without carpets, and their footsteps sounded hollow as they crossed it. A wide staircase rose from the left and there was a big window glazed in ruby glass on the landing. The place seemed empty and barren and the air smelled of vast, neglected, dusty rooms. All the doors downstairs were closed. Mrs. Hornblower tapped at the first on the left and ushered Littlejohn in. It was the minister's study, stuffy and overcrowded, overlooking the wild garden. There was a collapsible dining-table in one corner with two dining-chairs. It looked as though the parson and his wife made this their sole living-room when she was not working in the kitchen.

Mr. Jasper had said, in his tipsy confidences, that Mr. Hornblower was doctrinally weak. The man who greeted him did not look a weakling. He had a pale, craggy, clean-shaven face, thick white hair swept back from a broad forehead, a large nose, firm chin and a wide, loose, sarcastic mouth. He was tall and heavily built, spotlessly clean in his shabby clerical clothes and linen, and the hand he offered Littlejohn was well-kept. He must have been between sixty and seventy.

"I hardly expected a call from you, Inspector..."

Mrs. Hornblower closed them in and you could hear her steps echoing down the hall. The two men sat before the fire in the old-fashioned grate in two saddlebacked chairs upholstered in horsehair. There was an old skin rug before the hearth and the paint and wallpaper of the room were shabby and needed renewal. Over the fireplace, a portrait of the Rev. Hornblower as a young man, clad in cap and gown and holding a diploma prominently in his clenched fist.

The alibis of Jasper Bunn and his brood were in order. Mr. and Mrs. Hornblower had attended the informal meeting at their home on the night Ned Bunn was killed and they had stayed to supper and left about eleven.

"I suppose you know a lot about the Bunn family, sir."

Mr. Hornblower passed his hand over his hair, looked in the fire, and regarded Littlejohn with grey eyes which seemed to grow paler whenever he grew excited.

"More than I could put down in several books, Inspector. I've known them for almost forty years... intimately..."

"Forty years! You haven't been at Salem Church all that time!"

"No. Twenty years altogether, in two separate spells. I was there as a young man for fifteen years. Then I left to take a living elsewhere. I worked in various fields until I was superannuated. Then, five years ago, I received another invitation to Salem. They couldn't afford to pay a full-time pastor, and asked if I would do part-time there, with my pension to make up the rest. I agreed... though it doesn't seem part-time to me. I seem to work as hard... harder, in fact, than I did as a young man. Perhaps it's age makes the work seem heavier."

"Could you tell me something about the Bunn family? I don't want any breaches of confidence, sir, but you could help, you know."

Mr. Hornblower started to fill an old briar pipe and Littlejohn followed suit.

"They are obsessed by money... All of them, without exception. Even Anne, who married Medlicott. She, of course, has to be miserly to keep the wolf from the door. Medlicott has made away with all the money they ever had. Yet, she is devoted to him."

"Is the family a large one?"

"Very...and very close-knit. Jeremiah Bunn, the father of the Enderby line, had four brothers who, in turn, had branches of their own. There will be a huge gathering at Edwin Bunn's funeral, although, as you perhaps know, Edwin wasn't really a Bunn at all. He was adopted by arrangement between his mother and his foster-father. That caused resentment among the rest of Jerry Bunn's family, a feeling which has grown with the years."

The Manse must, at one time, have stood in fields on the verge of the town, but opposite had been built rows of terraced houses. Men in their shirt-sleeves stood talking at the doors, children played in the street, and in the dilapidated gardens of the cottages, women were hanging out washing to dry. An angry mother was beating a child, her hair tumbling about her livid face, her arms rising and falling as the boy yelled and squirmed.

"I believe his brother and sisters will come into quite a tidy fortune apiece now that Edwin Bunn has died. His share of his foster-father's fortune was in trust for them, with Ned taking the income till his death. Now they'll inherit over ten thousand apiece..."

"And Bertha will get what her father leaves in his own right?"

"Exactly. How do you know?"

"Between you and me, Mr. Edgell, the lawyer, told me."

"Edgell...Ha! A great friend of the family. He was engaged to Anne Bunn until Medlicott came along and carried her off. Quite a local scandal. Edgell never married. Some people say it turned his brain a bit. You see, they'd bought the house, and all that. I'm not so sure that Medlicott was the better choice. He's run through all Anne's money, begotten two daughters as silly and irresponsible as himself, and generally made Anne's life a catastrophe. Yet, she loves him. Beautiful, tragic irony of life!"

Littlejohn looked at the fine face, the sarcastic lips of the man sitting beside him. Perhaps Jasper Bunn was right, after all. He glanced at the titles of the books nearest to him and which covered three walls of the room. Dusty volumes of sermons by dead-and-gone divines, theology, psychology, essays and memoirs; but bright and to hand, shabby and well-thumbed, Anatole France, Marcel Proust, Aldous Huxley, Sartre, Donne, Berdyaev and Kierkegaard... All from a world far beyond Enderby and the Bunns. Very doctrinally different from Jasper and his vast flock of relatives! There were galley-proofs of a manuscript on the desk under the window. Littlejohn wondered what Hornblower was working on and what the pillars of Salem would think of it. Actually, the book was, twelve months later, to lose Salem for Mr. Hornblower and earn him a scholastic reputation.

"I haven't learned much about the elder sister; Agnes, is she called?"

"Sarah Agnes, yes. The most formidable of the lot. Married to a very decent fellow, too, of distinct promise as an architect in his young days, but gradually since his marriage, all the sap of life and art has been squeezed from him."

He looked in the fire and twisted his fingers, puffing away at the pipe which hung on his chest.

"Her son, Barnabas... Barny, as his friends called him, rebelled and made a mess of his life. His mother manacled and secluded him so much by her domineering ways, that he fell frantically in love with the first good-looking woman he met... a married woman wedded to a brute of a husband. The situation was almost theatrical, but they ran off together..."

"And haven't been heard of since...?"

Littlejohn gave the minister a searching look. Here was a man to whom people would come in, or after, trouble.

"They went abroad..."

"That doesn't answer my question, sir. Have *you* seen or heard of them since?"

Mr. Hornblower removed his pipe.

"What are you getting at, Inspector?"

"Were you a friend, a confidant, of Barny Bunn? Do you know exactly where he and his woman went?"

"They went abroad. He wrote to me, once. He was fond of his father and wanted news about him from time to time... The woman he ran away with died of fever."

"Where is he now, sir?"

"In London. The family don't know, and I promised they shouldn't. So you must swear to keep..."

"I can't swear anything, sir, but I'll use the utmost discretion. Have you his address in London?"

"No. He will write if he wants anything. I reply care of the Post Office he gives."

"If you hear from him, you must let me know."

"I will, if you will promise to take no steps without talking it over with me."

"Very well. That's agreed, sir. What of the other members of Sarah Agnes's family?"

"A son, Henry... In his father's business, but a bit of a wastrel. And Helen, a daughter... most beautiful... a bright bird among a lot of sparrows, and her mother will make a sparrow of her as well if she has her way."

"Why?"

"Possessiveness. That woman dominates all she comes in contact with. She has interfered in two of the girl's love-affairs already. There was an American doctor at the camp here during the war. Helen was in her 'teens. They were a suitable, happy couple. But America was too far away for Sarah Agnes... Her long arm couldn't stretch so far. When it was all over, John Fearns told me of intercepted letters, fierce quarrels, constant nagging... The young doctor went away and was killed on 'D' day."

"And the other cases?"

"A penniless reporter who came for a spell on our local paper. He attended Salem for a time. A very decent lad. He and Helen got very friendly... Then he packed up and left after an interview with Sarah Agnes. One day, Helen is going to follow Barny's example, take matters in her own hands, and perhaps wreck her life, too."

"What a crew!"

Littlejohn said it half under his breath, but the parson heard it.

"You're right, Inspector. The family held all its members in its grip... except, funnily enough, Jasper. They didn't approve of his wedding to the flighty Louisa Freer, but the loving couple forced the issue... Louisa was going to have a child, so the family had to stand aside. That's how it always happens in the Bunn family. They corner their members and impose their wills on them. Then, every so often, the victim strikes back. Jasper and Louisa... Anne and Medlicott... Barnabas and Mrs. Lemont... It even went as far back as old Jerry Bunn when he married Mary Wood. Mary had an illegitimate child and the family said 'No'. Jerry eloped and adopted Mary's child."

"And now... Now with Ned Bunn, sir?"

The parson looked up keenly and then fearfully.

"Now...? You mean, Inspector...?"

"Someone has killed Ned Bunn. Which one had he cornered, tried to impose his will on, thwarted...?"

"I don't know."

The room was very still. Somewhere in the house, they could hear Mrs. Hornblower rattling tea-things. In the street, a knife-grinder was busy at his wheel with a crowd of children watching and taking it all in.

"Yes, sir. History repeats itself. Sarah Agnes Bunn, or Fearns, drives her son frantic with repression..."

"She kept him in knee-breeches till he was seventeen and gave him threepence a week to spend. He took her jewellery and three hundred pounds of her money with him when he ran away. He returned the jewellery when he got a job."

"Ned Bunn drove his daughter the same way. That is so, isn't it?"

"I suppose so. As a youngster, she was quite attractive. Like her mother, then. Ned Bunn, like the dominant animal in a herd, chased off all the young men who came after his girl. Then, finally..."

"Yes?"

"Her mother died. She was very fond of her mother and she was afraid to incur her father's displeasure which he'd vent on his wife if Bertha left home. After her mother died, it didn't matter."

"And Flounder came along and Bunn started his old tricks..."

The parson sat up with a jerk.

"My dear Inspector, you're not trying to deduce that Bertha Bunn killed her own father because of his objection to Wilfred Flounder! She could very well have eloped as her grandfather did."

"But without her father's fortune, she and Wilfred were penniless?"

"Not quite. Her mother left her a little..."

"But not a fortune ..."

Mrs. Hornblower entered with tea. She had brought out her silver service and best cups. The cloth on the tray was of fine linen with a little darn in the centre, so neatly done as to be almost invisible.

"We're just going through the tribe of Bunn and their many shortcomings, Alice."

Mrs. Hornblower laid down the tray carefully and began to pour out the tea.

"We ... I mean ... the Bunns have made our life here rather difficult ... But my husband always says we can't have life made to our own specifications. We must take it as it is and have courage."

She bent her grey head over the cream jug in a kind of pathetic resignation which spoke of tragedy and filled Littlejohn with pity for something he couldn't define.

"You needn't have bothered about tea for me, Mrs. Hornblower. It's very kind of you."

"Pour him out a cup, mother. He'll be ready for it after all this talking."

The parson put down his pipe and rose to help his wife, touching her gently as he passed with a sort of comforting gesture.

Hornblower had called her "mother", and Littlejohn took it up almost instinctively.

"Your children are grown-up and gone from home, then?"

There was an eloquent pause and Littlejohn wished he hadn't spoken.

Mrs. Hornblower laid down a cup and took from the table on which the tray was laid, a photograph in a frame. It was of a young man in his early twenties, dressed in uniform, with the delicate well-moulded features of his mother and his father's eyes and brow.

"That was our only child ... our boy. He was a war correspondent and was killed in Korea."

As Littlejohn held the picture, Mrs. Hornblower went on with her tale, like a little lament.

"I didn't want him to go. But he was so restless and ... there was some trouble with a girl. He used to be a reporter on the local paper and they said he had a great career in store. He was to have gone to London ... Fleet Street. But he got unsettled ... I must get some cake ..."

She fled hurriedly from the room.

Littlejohn's eyes met those of the minister and took in the tired, lined features and the ironic twist of the generous mouth.

"Helen Fearns?"

Hornblower hung his head. Littlejohn could scarcely hear the reply.

"Yes."

What was it Hornblower had said earlier?

Beautiful, tragic irony of life!

CHAPTER SEVEN
THE ARRIVAL OF AUNT SARAH

Cromwell ruled a line under the report he had written in his black notebook, closed it with a snap, and slid it into his large inside pocket. His long face wore a look of distaste and he kept sniffing disgustedly. He had just washed his hands with the pink soap provided for the purpose by the Blowitts. It was scented.

"Smells like a…"

He sought in his mind for a suitable simile, found one which wasn't quite decent, and let it go.

"More of 'em…"

Mr. Blowitt was still standing at the window watching the procession of Bunns coming and going at the shop opposite. The coffin with the corpse had just been taken in and figures in black kept entering eagerly and coming out with either tearful or resigned expressions. A large taxi, like a hearse itself, drew up bearing a black burden of such weight that the vehicle heeled over dangerously.

"Hullo. Aunt Sarah's come."

Several of the family emerged, fawned on the contents of the taxi, and then hoisted out an enormous woman, larger than any two of the reception committee. A fat face under a black bonnet, a lot of double chins, and a look of perpetual annoyance.

"She's the next to die on the list, chronologically, as you might say. Worth a lot of money. The family all keep well in with 'er."

Mr. Blowitt's roving eyes suddenly fell on his wife and opened wider. His mouth followed suit.

The man who had on the previous day brought in the mattress and pretended to play the harp on it was holding a whispered conversation with Mrs. Blowitt.

"Go on with you!" she said, and gave him a playful push.

The bed-man, small, slim, frisky, with a face like a robin, eyed the hennaed hair with admiration.

"I mean it," he said, and buried his little beak of a nose in his pint pot.

He was a widower and the mock kiss blown to him by Mrs. Blowitt the day before had shaken him.

"Hey!" said Mr. Blowitt loudly. He could flirt to his heart's content, but his missus must be beyond reproach.

The little man slowly removed his face from his mug of beer, which he carefully placed on the counter.

"Hey, wot?" he said, rocking on his heels in challenge. He violently thrust out his arms before him to jerk back his cuffs, ready for a set-to if needs be.

Mr. Blowitt climbed down.

"No wastin' time," he said, and left the room.

The little man tittered, shook down his sleeves again, and tipped his pot-hat over his left eye. Then he chucked Mrs. Blowitt under the chin.

"Still say it. This is no place for a fine woman like you. You oughter..."

"Go on with you..."

"Excuse me..."

Cromwell was fed-up with the amours and jealousies of the Blowitt ménage. He wanted Sarah Agnes Fearns' address and said so. Mrs. Blowitt gave it in a dramatic voice.

"Thank you..."

"Very pleased, I'm sure."

Outside, the square was almost deserted. A multiple tailor's was giving jigsaw puzzles as advertisements and a queue of boys was forming. A newsboy stood near the church with a sheaf of papers and a placard: *'Daily Trumpet'. Brompton Murder. Dooley to Hang.* Nobody took any notice. They had a murder of their own in Enderby.

The Fearns family lived just outside the town in a large, square, brick house surrounded by a high wall and a trim garden. All the family did the gardening and Mrs. Fearns saw to it that they mustered frequently for the purpose. There wasn't much left in the way of flowers. A few chrysanthemums and a clump or two of Michaelmas daisies. Dead leaves all over the lawns and paths. Mrs. Fearns was too busy at the time to bother with the garden. All the curtains and blinds of the house were drawn.

Before Cromwell could ring the bell the door opened and Mrs. Fearns appeared letting out the cat violently. At the sight of Cromwell she halted. She was wearing an apron which she hastily removed. Cromwell couldn't quite gather whether he or the cat was the cause of Sarah Agnes's sour looks. In her black ready-made frock she looked like a tall, scuttering cockroach. Her pug's face was set in grim lines and, above it, her hair had just been waved ready for the funeral.

"Well?"

She seemed to mistake Cromwell for some underling connected with the forthcoming ceremonies. He is frequently taken for an evangelist, theological student, or undertaker.

He handed Mrs. Fearns his card.

"Come in." She didn't sound pleased. "This way..."

Through a porch and a vestibule shut off from the hall by a door with a stained-glass panel. The hall was wide and full of odds and ends. A heavy barometer on the wall and three large pictures, badly painted. The brass lamp hanging from the ceiling was corroded and looked ready to fall down. There was a large, wilting palm in a pot at the foot of the stairs. Sarah Agnes almost pushed Cromwell into a room on the right. There was no fire, the place smelled of damp and stale cigar smoke and was heavy with Victorian furniture. Over the fireplace was a framed photograph of a formidable, middle-aged woman, in a freakish Edwardian get-up. The glass was broken slightly in one corner. It was of Aunt Sarah, Mrs. Wilkins, née Bunn. The usual Bunn face, even more puggy than usual. Until to-day it had been in the junk room, but Aunt Sarah had just arrived to stay at the Fearns' house over the funeral. Cromwell could hear her in the adjacent room.

"Who was it?"

The reply was inaudible.

"Speak up!"

"A man on business."

Mrs. Fearns closed the door and stood with her back to it.

"What did you want?"

She seemed anxious to get it over and didn't even offer Cromwell a chair.

Cromwell gave her his best smile.

"Sorry to trouble you at a time like this, madam, but I'm sure you're as anxious as we are to get your late brother's death cleared up."

"Yes?"

"We're just checking where the various members of the family were on the night Mr. Edwin Bunn died."

Sarah Agnes folded her scraggy arms over her tightly-laced bosom and advanced a step.

"Do I understand that you think some of *us* might have done it? Because if you do, you're mistaken."

She sucked in the saliva from her lips and shook her head aggressively. The permanent waves of her grey hair trembled like a lot of springs.

"Oh dear, no, madam. Just a formality. We have to do it, you know. It's part of the regulations."

He smiled again. Sarah Agnes' face softened to the extent of two lines disappearing from the root of her short nose, and her tight nether lip slackened and became fleshy.

"We were all at home ... every one of us."

Cromwell sighed. 'Ome-lovers, Mr. Jasper had said. Proper 'ome-lovers. He wondered if every member of the Bunn clan was tightly hedged behind a home-lover's alibi for the night of Ned's death.

"Your son and daughter, too?"

"Of course. Did you think they'd be walking the streets?"

Her voice rose in a crescendo.

Cromwell didn't know what he thought.

"No ... I just want to be sure. Were you entertaining, madam?"

"Yes. We had visitors ... The Mayor, his wife and their son."

From the way she said it, Cromwell judged that Sarah Agnes was very well satisfied about the Mayor and his family.

The *tête-à-tête* was interrupted by the arrival of Aunt Sarah, who thrust open the door of the room without knocking and entered slowly, panting, her eyes all over the shop. They fell upon her portrait in its place of honour and she malevolently noticed the cracked glass.

"What does *he* want?"

She panted and hissed as she spoke and her many chins shivered like jellies. She was enormous and walked with the help of a stick which she now pointed at Cromwell.

Her eyes were everywhere, curious and contemptuous. She raised her free hand and revealed an ear-trumpet which she elevated to her head to get the answer.

The huge bulk of the old woman had completely hidden the girl behind her who now advanced to pacify her. Cromwell had heard of Helen Fearns' good looks, but he hadn't imagined anything like this. It quite took him aback. Like a lovely sunset, or sweet music, or a fine picture... beauty that made you a bit melancholy, he told himself later by way of excuse for his susceptibility.

She was medium built, slim, and of the dark fine beauty of old Spain. Her hair was almost black, the eyes large, brown and clear, the eyebrows gracefully curved, and the brow broad and serene. The bone formation of her face was exquisite and tapered from the high cheek-bones to a short firm chin. The delicate arched nose, the fastidiously chiselled nostrils, the generous mouth and full red lips, the tender lines of the neck and shoulders... These were what caused Helen's mother so much apprehension.

Cromwell had seen both the father and mother of the girl, who seemed in her middle twenties. He found himself soundlessly whistling *Sally in our Alley...*

How such a couple could beget,
One half so fair as Sally...

"Eh?"

"Just a gentleman on business about uncle's funeral."

Helen spoke right in the ear-trumpet. Her voice was quiet, with a faint deep huskiness, but Aunt Sarah saw no charm in it.

"No need to yell ..."

Helen looked at Cromwell, the corner of whose lip curled, and she shrugged her shoulders slightly.

"Come on, Auntie. You'll get cold in here."

"Yes. Go on, Aunt Sarah. I'll soon be back."

Sarah Agnes, half-named after the old woman, added her assistance in persuasion.

"I'm not goin' to be told what to do by anyone ... Do you hear, *anyone* ... Not even YOU."

She pointed her stick at Cromwell as though he were a vigorous party in the campaign to get her out of the way.

"And you needn't think I don't know about you trying to hook up your Helen with the Mayor's son, because I do. Jasper told me and I don't approve of it. I don't like Jabez Stubbs, Mayor or no Mayor, and as for his son, Hubert, I like him less. Him with his little moustache and his pimples ... I don't like him, even if he does go to Salem Chapel twice every Sunday. They'll get no money of mine if they get wed ... Remember that ... If they get wed, no money."

Crimson to the roots of her hair, Helen did her best to tow the old woman to the door. Panting and snorting, Aunt Sarah delivered herself of a verbal broadside at Sarah Agnes with every step until finally she left the room, Helen manoeuvring round her like a graceful tug round a battleship.

"And don't you let 'em, Helen. If they try to make you, you tell me ... Not a penny of mine if ..."

The door closed and they could hear the muffled roaring going on in the next room.

Sarah Agnes, white with shame and embarrassment, breathed heavily, wiped her lips on her handkerchief and looked hard at Cromwell to see how he had taken it.

"She's old and queer in her mind ... She doesn't know what she's saying half the time."

It all seemed very intelligible and sensible indeed to Cromwell, especially when, afterwards, he compared notes with Littlejohn and heard about the history of Helen's forlorn love affairs. He also had a word with Hubert Stubbs, the current runner in the matrimonial field, later, and his admiration for Aunt Sarah grew considerably after that.

Jabez Stubbs and Son (Enderby) Ltd., Silk and Nylon Manufacturers. Cromwell had found their mills just behind the police station and now stood in the office waiting for father, or son, or both. They arrived together. The mills seemed old but very busy. The sound of machinery filled the air like the rush of many waters. The offices were of new brick and up-to-date in a flashy kind of way. Light woodwork, green decorations, a lot of chromium chairs and fittings. Like a modern picture palace. When you saw Stubbs and Son, in person, you understood why.

Mr. Jabez Stubbs, Mayor of Enderby, was a little, fat, prancing man, full of his own importance. His face and neck were fat, too, and he had blue, watery, roving eyes, which reminded you of poached eggs. He wore a heavy, light-grey tweed suit and light brown boots. He had made a lot of money out of his nylons and was spreading himself in all directions. A large car stood at the door.

"Well, officer...Come in, come in...Come into the office...into my private room...Drink? Cigar? No? Take a few then...I know you can't smoke on duty...Take a few for after. They're good ones....Here, put these in your pocket...Don't be shy."

Cromwell shook Mr. Stubbs off with great difficulty. He clung like a leech with his embarrassing ministrations and patronage. He screwed your nerves up so much that you felt like hitting him.

"This is my son, Yewbert."

Hubert wasn't quite as bad as his father, but he was bad enough. He stood around like an apprentice or understudy, domineered by his parent. He wore a check sports jacket of the hacking variety, a yellow pullover, and corduroy trousers. He was on the small side, too, and had sandy hair and eyebrows. A small sandy moustache sprouted from his upper lip and his chin receded. At his father's age, Yewbert would also have poached blue eyes; now they were bleary with beer and late nights. There was a livid pimple in the middle of his forehead. Cromwell ranged himself on Aunt Sarah's formidable side at once.

"Cigarette?"

Hubert flashed a gold case in Cromwell's face; a kind of attenuated version of his father's act with the cigars.

"And now ... What can we do for you?"

Mr. Stubbs was overflowing with unction and oily good will.

"Well, sir. We're just checking alibis, purely formal, for the night Mr. Edwin Bunn was killed."

Mr. Stubbs flung up his hands and threw back his head, revealing two even sets of dentures and hairs sprouting from his nostrils.

"Dear me! Terrible, terrible ... I say, 'orrible ... Ned Bunn and I were good friends ... almost like brothers."

Hubert thought he ought to speak.

"Just like that." He laid his index finger on top of the second and thrust them in Cromwell's direction. His father eyed him curiously. Was "junior", as he fondly called him, was "junior" mocking him ... trying to be a bit funny?

"Sure you won't have a drink ... Whisky, sherry?"

Cromwell shook himself free again.

"What can we do to help the police, then, in this shockin' affair? As Mayor of this town, I feel it my duty to do all in my power to end once and for all the dreadful state of suspense and anxiety which prevail."

Mr. Stubbs reeled it off like a speech on a political platform or at the weekly meeting of the Town Council. He was carried away by his own eloquence.

"Excuse me, sir ... I just wanted to know if you could confirm your visit to the Fearns's home on the night Mr. Bunn was killed and how long might you have been there?"

Mr. Stubbs applied the brakes and smiled benignly at Cromwell and then conspiratorially at his son.

Hubert cleared his throat, stood with one foot—clad in a suede shoe with a sole of rubber an inch thick—on a chair, and massaged his little moustache.

"Of course. Very glad to assist. We was at the Fearns's home on that night. In fact, we got there at about nine and we were just having a bite of food when the phone rang to announce the 'orrible news. Yes, we was there."

"Thank you, sir. And were all the family—Mr. and Mrs. Fearns, Mr. Henry and Miss Helen—present, too?"

Mr. Stubbs thrust out his chest like a pouter pigeon and smiled across at his son, who glanced back nonchalantly.

"Oh, yes. All there. As a matter of fact, officer, it was somewhat of an 'appy occasion, spoiled, I regret to say, by the 'orrible news which broke on us. My son, Yewbert, and Helen Fearns, have long been friends ... Been brought up at Salem Chapel and Sunday School since they was that high."

With a podgy hand, Mr. Stubbs denoted the exact height from the ground of the happy couple when they first met. He did not say, or perhaps he did not remember, that for his violence to a doll which Helen had carried everywhere in those days, Yewbert had arrived home with a broken nose.

"Since they was that high ..."

Mr. Stubbs's eyes grew more poached from sentimental wallowing.

"They've always been very fond of one another and now... well... it's changed to something else, officer. This was a special family gathering... an 'appy little affair to celebrate what we hope will soon be a betrothal."

Yewbert, his back to the fire, was looking like a man of the world, fiddling with his moustache, trying to appear as if he was a bit bored by it all.

"So, you see, we've good reason to remember every detail and can easily confirm the times. Oh, yes, you can put me down for confirmation of the alibis when the time comes, officer, and very glad to be of assistance."

Cromwell's eye fell on the glowing pimple in the middle of Hubert's forehead. His mind went back to Aunt Sarah.

"Thank you very much, sir. I'm very grateful for your help."

"Not at all. And, by the way, when he can spare the time, please tell Inspector Littlejoy I'll be very glad to see him at the Mayor's Parlour. We don't often get famous detectives down here, thank God, and I'm anxious to do 'im the honours."

That put Cromwell definitely on the side of Aunt Sarah! In fact, he almost felt like going to Fearns' home and telling her so.

"The name's Inspector Little*john*, sir, and I'm afraid he's very busy."

The Mayor looked at Yewbert and then at Cromwell. He scented an affront but couldn't be quite sure.

As he left the flashy offices of Stubbs & Son, Cromwell was whistling under his breath:

And when my seven long years are out,

Oh, then I'll marry Sally...

But not in our alley! It was in Aunt Sarah's alley, however, for Cromwell read in *The Times* almost a year later that Helen had been married from the home of her aunt, Mrs. Wilkins, Throstles Nest, Melton Mowbray, to a barrister called Shakespeare.

Chapter Eight
"Whispers"

When Jerry Bunn married Mary Wood he bought for their home a large, old house surrounded by matured trees on the edge of Enderby. Mary was romantic in those early days and called the place *Whispers* because of the gentle noises made by the trees. She never told anyone what they whispered to her later when her husband's fancy began to roam.

Jerry Bunn left *Whispers* to his daughter, Anne, to repay her for her past labours in the shop. When the Medlicott family moved in, they had enough money to keep-up the place, but after Jubal had dissipated his wife's fortune, the great house became a millstone. Finally, it ended as a block of flats, six in all, with the Medlicotts occupying the top rooms because they commanded a good view and fresher air.

Littlejohn thrust back the heavy, rusty wrought-iron gate and made his way along the forlorn gravel drive between overgrown bushes and shabby trees. The house itself was of dirty brick, square in shape, with rotting stone ornaments and decaying woodwork. The front door was scarred from the kicks and blows of tenants and was reached by three worn steps, flanked by tall, unused gas-lamp standards, survivals of the days when the Bunns entertained local bigwigs to dinner and processions of carriages came and went along the drive. Neglected lawns and sour flower-beds fronted the house and on a patch of weeds and unkempt rose-bushes stood a plaster statue of a nymph without a head. On her outstretched hands were hanging a bowler hat and a cloth cap.

The owners of the headgear, a small man in a green baize apron and a fat one like a superannuated boxer, in his shirt sleeves, were busy moving furniture from the bottom front flat and stowing it in a van. *Kosy Homes. Furnishers of Taste. Credit terms arranged.*

The bottom flat had missed paying two instalments and Cap and Bowler had arrived to take away the Kosy sideboard, armchairs, bedroom suite and dining table.

"Next week it'll be the other bedroom."

The deprived owner, a little pasty-faced man in crooked specs and old plus-fours, alternately pleaded, threatened, argued and sized-up the two Kosy men, wondering whether or not to try force or irrevocably give in. At the window, his wife and three small children watched his futile tactics with open mouths. The smallest child kept raising bewildered eyes to her mother's face and then pointing to the furniture which the pugilist handled with ease and stowed in the van with mechanical skill.

Browning, Mander, Cuffright, Pouter, Medlicott... The names of the tenants were plastered on bits of sticky paper spread on the panel of the door. Littlejohn entered and started to climb the wide stairs with a strip of thin oilcloth down the middle.

Layer on layer of homes with the tenants all back for the day, for it was past six. Sounds of quarrelling, housework, asthmatic coughing, bumping and banging, and the hammering of the man in the third flat, Pouter, who made galleons for a hobby and sold them to make ends meet. Wireless blaring from three or four stations at once. Smells of cooking, stale food, washing, drains, and sweating humanity. The railway ran behind, entered a short tunnel, and the engines whistled as they neared the town station. A train roared past, seemed to hit the house and crawl up it, over the top, and down the other side ... From the flat where the Kosy men had now finished their foreclosing, came strange cries and noises of strife.

The staircase was dingy and the walls soiled. Outside one flat, somebody had written a message on the wall in pencil. *Leave milk at flat opposite.* A man in his shirt and trousers and with a cigarette dangling from the corner of his mouth, emerged from the communal bathroom leaving behind the loud noise of gurgling water. He eyed Littlejohn insolently and disappeared into one of the flats. At once, the door opposite opened and a woman in a loose wrapper scuttered to take his place.

The Medlicotts' flat had been the attics. Littlejohn knocked at the door, which bore the name of the owner on a card in a brass frame. Inside, there had been noises of twittering and giggling as Jubal Medlicott and his two girls did the washing-up. When Littlejohn tapped, all grew silent. He could imagine the occupants waiting anxiously to see who was there. Dolly and Polly opened the door between them and stood goggling at the Inspector, round-eyed, shining globular foreheads, pink noses, figures like little bolsters tied up in the middle. They both wore small lace aprons and in the background could be seen Mr. Jubal Medlicott taking off an apron and rolling down his shirt sleeves. He put on his coat, a wilting chrysanthemum still hanging dismally from the buttonhole.

"Come in, Inspector. Come in."

Mr. Medlicott was hearty. It might have been a social call. Dolly and Polly stood aside, grinning, exchanging glances.

This was the living-room and it looked full of the furniture Jerry Bunn had left behind long ago. Heavy plush curtains at the windows, faded holland covers on the chairs, a large table covered with a plush tablecloth, an aspidistra in a pot, old armchairs in front of an ancient gas-fire, a moth-eaten turkey-red carpet, a lot of little bits of china on the mantelpiece and large ugly sideboard. In one corner an ancient piano with a faded silk front and a cover over the top, which made Littlejohn think of a horse draped in a blanket. The inside of the piano must have been loose, for with every step of the occupants, every reverberation from the trains outside or the tenants indoors, the wires clanged, jingled and gave a blurred aeolian melody.

Mrs. Medlicott was sitting in one of the fireside chairs, a workbox on the floor, fixing the strap on one of her husband's white spats. He was still wearing the other. She looked frail and tired in her old shapeless dress, with wisps of grey hair hanging across her face. She stroked back her hair and looked apprehensively at the Inspector. Medlicott and his two girls bared their teeth in smiles. They didn't seem capable of taking anything seriously.

"Well, Inspector... And to what do we owe this honour? Not going to arrest us, I hope."

The girls giggled and whooped at the joke.

Jubal Medlicott rubbed his hands together, looked down at the flower in his coat, tore it out, and threw it in the fireplace.

"Sit down... Take the armchair... A drink?"

He produced a half-empty bottle of pale sherry, eyed it apprehensively, and seemed relieved when Littlejohn refused.

"I'm sorry to intrude, sir, but I'm just checking the movements of all those concerned on the night Mr. Edwin Bunn died."

There was a hush and Mrs. Medlicott's hands fell limp in her lap. Her husband spoke. He seemed to be the first to pull himself together. The two girls stood motionless, like a couple of ventriloquist's dummies.

"Sit down, Dolly and Polly... Don't stand gawking there."

The twins seemed thunderstruck. Jubal Medlicott didn't as a rule address them so; he must have been rattled. They looked ready to rush from the room for a good cry, but they sat down instead on the rickety dining chairs.

"We were all at home, Inspector."

Littlejohn had expected it! Every one of the Enderby Bunns had told the same tale! 'Ome-lovers, that's what we are, Jasper Bunn had said.

Littlejohn glanced from one to the other of the group. The two goggling girls, Medlicott, the tired mother busy repairing her husband's finery. They all nodded, the two girls very vigorously with arch looks, half-afraid, half-cocksure. As though they'd already been through it all before.

"Are you sure?"

"Certainly, Inspector. Why should I say so... if..?"

Mr. Medlicott looked a bit hurt. The girls merely nodded their heads vigorously up and down.

"When did you last see Mr. Edwin Bunn?"

They all looked at one another and then left it to the spokesman.

"To speak to? Last Sunday at church."

"Last Sunday at church... oh, yes, last Sunday"

Polly and Dolly were eager to support Jubal.

"But we saw him on the morning of his death. He was putting something in the shop window as we passed. He just nodded."

"Nodded," came the echo.

They were all seated except Medlicott, who kept walking about the room, rubbing his beard, jingling keys and money in his pocket, parading around in his one spat, tapping his false teeth with a black propelling pencil.

"Sit down, Jubal."

Mrs. Medlicott sounded nervous, troubled by her husband's restlessness. He obeyed with an astonished look, as though he weren't used to being ordered around.

"Do you know anyone who might have wanted to kill Mr. Bunn?"

Another silence. Everybody seemed turned to stone. Polly and Dolly, more than ever like two dummies; Medlicott, a monument of whiskery amazement, and Mrs. Medlicott immobile and ashen-looking, like one on whom death had come in the middle of her task.

"No!"

Jubal bellowed it in a tenor voice and then:

"Certainly not!"

All his family thereupon woke up and corroborated his statement like mad.

An obstinate look crossed the face of Mr. Medlicott and the atmosphere grew strained. Littlejohn felt more than ever like an interloper who had spoiled a scene of domestic bliss. Like a broker's man or a rate collector.

Jubal crossed the room accompanied by the ghostly strumming of the ancient piano wires, took out the sherry bottle again and raised it aloft.

"Sure you won't, Inspector?"

"No, thanks, sir."

"Mind if I do?"

And, to the horror of his whole family, he filled a tumbler with the thin fluid and drank it off. His face was expressionless as the sherry spread itself inside him, then contorted as it entered his stomach.

"Good heavens!" he said, and sat down without another word.

No use prolonging the talk.

"Very kind of you to receive me so courteously."

Littlejohn said it to them all, and they all smiled as though an ordeal were passed.

"A pleasure ... A great pleasure indeed ... Hic, pardon me."

Mr. Medlicott hiccupped from the cooking sherry.

In the room below, someone turned on the wireless.

Because I love you,
I've tried so hard but can't forget,
Because I love you ...

On the stairs voices were raised:

"Keep that cat out of my flat, or I'll ..."

A door slammed. The Medlicotts exchanged shame-faced looks. Mrs. Medlicott took it all with bowed head, still sewing away at the white spat.

And this was the way things had ended for Anne Bunn! The clever girl of the family who might have married Edgell, the lawyer, and become somebody in the town. Instead she fell in love with the natty little, bearded tailor, who'd run through her comfortable fortune and fathered two giggling, half-witted girls on her. She looked ill, too, as if some fatal disease were gnawing at her. Her grey complexion, her thin, almost transparent hands, the wasted frame, the wilting look...

"We were all brought-up here."

Suddenly Mrs. Medlicott spoke, apropos of nothing particular, but as though trying, somehow, to excuse their present condition.

"...Yes, we were all born here...Except Ned, of course, who was born before...before my parents came to live here. It was very large then and so trim and tidy and we had such a lot of visitors. Dinners...And horse-carriages would come up the drive and the lamps outside the door would be lit. We children were supposed to be in bed, but we used to creep up to this very room and look through the windows and watch them all arriving...the men in their top hats and tail coats and the women...jewels and such lovely gowns...Things were all so different then."

She started and looked around, like some Cinderella who finds, on the stroke of twelve, the splendour suddenly changed to squalor.

"You really can't keep up these huge houses nowadays, can you, Mr. Littlejohn? Gardeners and servants are so hard to get and they want so much payment for so little work...It was better to retreat to our little attics and make a home there and let the rest of the house to other people who would do the work we couldn't afford to have done."

She looked pleadingly at Littlejohn, waiting for him to agree and perhaps ease her mind.

Littlejohn was sorry for her.

"Of course you can't, Mrs. Medlicott. Times have changed since houses like this were built. If one can't get help to run them, it's best to divide them up and share the work."

The tired woman looked grateful.

"We had happy times here as children...Unhappy ones, too. Things I could never mention...Horrible things."

Mrs. Medlicott was talking to herself. Her husband and the two girls stared at her in astonishment.

"...I like it best up here in the attics. Down below I could not bear to live...It reminds me of some poetry by Robert Bridges:

On such a night, when Air has loosed
  Its guardian grasp on blood and brain,
Old terrors then of god or ghost
  Creep from their caves to life again ..."

"Mother!!" Polly and Dolly screeched it out together.
"This house isn't haunted, is it?"

From down below, the answer came from the radio:

And though you left a tear
  As a souvenir,
It doesn't matter, dear,
  Because ... I ... love ... you ...

Mrs. Medlicott looked round.

"I'm so sorry. I expect it's remembering about this place again. You must forgive me, Inspector."

The twins were looking at the clock.

"I hope I'm not keeping you," said Littlejohn.

"Well ... There's a family gathering at Aunt Fearns' tonight. You see, Aunt Sarah ... that is great-aunt Sarah ... is staying there and we are all going to see her ... All the family ..."

Polly and Dolly got it out between them. Another family gathering of the Bunns! Littlejohn wished he could be among them. Old terrors creeping from their caves, as Mrs. Medlicott had said.

They all saw him to the door and the piano strummed a ghostly accompaniment as their joint weight made the floor tremble.

The stairs were illuminated by small electric lights; just a glimmer to prevent accidents. Littlejohn could make out the peeling wallpaper and the ornamental mouldings of the dusty ceilings. He passed along the corridors and down the stairs. The door of the Medlicotts' flat slammed. He could imagine them all scuttering round, putting on their best clothes to visit Aunt Sarah.

Littlejohn's footsteps echoed on the hollow stairs. All the noises were still going on; the radios, the coughing, the man hammering, tap-tap-tap-tiddity-tap...And as he neared the ground floor, the smell of stone, of large underground spaces, of cellars, rose among the odours of humanity like that of a crypt.

Outside the entrance to his flat, just behind the front door, the little man whose furniture had earlier been confiscated, was standing. He was still in his shirt-sleeves and plus-fours and there was a fag-end in the corner of his mouth. His sandy hair was plastered on his skull and he squinted in the gloom through his crooked spectacles, trying to make out who was descending the stairs.

"Evenin', Inspector."

Littlejohn was just turning the door-knob.

"Good evening."

"Don't look so surprised, sir. I saw yer picture in this mornin's local paper...Saw you comin' in, too, to see the Medlicotts, but I was a bit too occupied to speak to yer then...Had a bit of bother with the furniture people. But I'll make 'em sit up for it. I've money owin' to me and when I pay outright for the things they took away, I'll see somebody gets the sack for what they've done."

He peered into Littlejohn's face to see how the Inspector was taking it. Then he took out a full packet of cigarettes, offered one to Littlejohn and, when the Inspector refused, took one himself. Behind the door at the little man's back, the sounds of children crying and their mother trying to pacify them...

"It's not good enough to take the kids' beds. Proper upset they are. And wouldn't you be, sir, if somebody took your bed? I've just come out here for a breather. Can't stand to 'ear their 'owlin'. Breaks yer heart..."

His hands were long and bony with long dirty nails and he kept playing with his cheeks and mouth as he spoke. Littlejohn's hand went to the door-knob again.

"When my money comes along, we shan't stay here... Can't stand them Medlicotts. *She's* all right, but the old chap... Screwball Medlicott, I call 'im, and them two pin-up daughters of 'is... think they're too good for a family like mine. And wot for? They've no money. Can't even pay for repairs to this tumbledown place and always on the doorstep prompt for the rent. They'll 'ave to wait for mine till the money comes along."

So that was it! The little man—Mr. Browning, according to the ticket on the door—had been having trouble about his rent and had taken it amiss.

On the landing above, a door partly opened, letting out a streak of bright light and the woman in the wrapper Littlejohn had previously seen entering the bathroom, looked out. A man behind her saw Littlejohn and Browning and hastily bobbed back and closed the door. Browning sniggered.

"See wot I mean? This ain't the place to bring up respectable kids... As soon as my money comes... Just a minute..."

Littlejohn turned again. The crooked specs. were focussed on him; the eyes behind them pale, pouched, malevolent.

"You been after alibis for the night Ned Bunn died? You been asking Medlicott where 'e was?"

"What of it? Does it concern you, sir?"

Littlejohn was getting fed up with it.

"I was only trying to help. If Medlicott said he was in here at the time, he's not tellin' the truth. 'E was out. I saw 'im go about nine-thirty... I was just out for a breather, this time on the front lawn... if you can call that dump sich... and out comes Screwball, quiet like, thinkin' nobody saw 'im. It was dark and he didn't see me... I think if he's said 'e was indoors, you oughter ask 'im again."

Browning nodded his head vigorously, contentedly, like one who has done his duty.

Littlejohn looked hard at the shifty eyes, the cockeyed spectacles with a twist of wool over the nose where they bit into the skin.

"This is no place to discuss such matters, Mr. Browning. I'd like you to come along to the police station and make a statement. If what you say is true, it's very serious."

"Of course it's true... But I don't see why I should come with you. I've told you, 'aven't I? No need to believe me if you don't want..."

"All the same, we can talk better there. Get your coat on and come along. I'll wait for you at the front gate."

Littlejohn wanted a breath of air after the mixed smells of the Medlicott tenements. Browning, grumbling, went into his flat.

At the end of the drive, Littlejohn paused, filled his pipe, lit it, and waited. The road past the house was busy. A train roared through the tunnel and shook the place. Littlejohn imagined the piano in the top flat playing a ghostly tune. In the direction of Enderby there was a glow in the sky from the lighted town.

Browning was taking an unconscionable time. Quarter of an hour to get on his jacket! Littlejohn strolled back along the drive, the soft, mossy earth making little noise. The lights from the screened windows shone down on the

sour lawn and flower beds. The headless nymph held out
her grimy arms in the direction of the door. At the foot of
the statue lay a crumpled mass. Littlejohn ran the remaining distance. He shone his torch on the figure. It was
Browning and he was dead. Throttled, well and truly. His
swollen tongue protruded from between his teeth and his
features were contorted in a ghastly grin.

Littlejohn made up his mind at once. He ran indoors,
up the stairs two at a time until he reached the Medlicotts'
door, and he flung it open without knocking. Before the
fire, in his heavily-darned woollen underpants, struggling
to get into a pair of black trousers, was Jubal Medlicott. His
shoes were still on his feet; one spat off and one spat on. Mr.
Medlicott turned astonished eyes on Littlejohn.

"Really, Inspector!" He danced on one leg, almost fell
from the effort, made a wild plunge, and drew his trousers
on. From a room behind emerged Polly and Dolly, clothed
in pink underskirts. Both of them screamed, put their knees
together, and tottered back, like hampered runners in a
sack-race. Mrs. Medlicott's amazed face appeared round the
door-frame and vanished.

That settled the Medlicotts at any rate! There hadn't
been time for Jubal to put on the act of changing his pants
after strangling Browning. Besides, the soles of his shoes
were dry.

"May I use your telephone, sir? I'll explain later."

Mr. Medlicott was indignant. His whiskers bristled and
he puffed out his cheeks. He'd evidently just been washing
himself, too. His hair was ruffled and he was without a collar.

"You'll have a lot of explaining to do, sir. An Englishman's
home is ..."

"*Please!* There's been another murder. Where's the
phone?"

There were more squeals from the unseen listeners behind the bedroom door. Mr. Medlicott's humour changed. He pranced and danced around, wondering what to do next.

"We haven't got a phone. We use the one on the floor below in emergencies... Miss Mander's..."

Presumably the woman in the wrapper! This was going to be good! Littlejohn ran from the room and down the stairs without waiting for directions from Medlicott. He knocked on the door of Miss Mander's flat. There was a lot of scuffling inside. He had to knock again.

"Open, please. Police. I want to use your telephone."

More scuffling and then the key turned and the woman in the wrapper stood there.

"May I use your phone, please? I won't take a minute. Where is it, please?"

A small sitting-room, exotically furnished. Almost like a theatrical dressing-room. Two deep armchairs, a divan, a cocktail cabinet, a small gateleg table and two chairs. Framed photographs of theatrical nonentities, autographed, on the walls. Two dolls dressed in silk on the mantelpiece beneath which a gas fire burned. The place was stuffy and smelled of heavy scent. In one corner, a large wardrobe. Littlejohn thought of the man who had tried to get away and had bobbed back when he saw him and Browning. No doubt, he was doubled-up and almost choked inside the cupboard, anxiously awaiting discovery.

The telephone was under one of the dolls. Miss Mander was too put-out by the intrusion of police and the need to conceal her boy-friend—if he *was* a boy and not an ageing bigwig of Enderby—even to ask questions. She merely indicated the doll, leaned over, and extracted the instrument. She had next to nothing on under the wrapper and had to pull it together at the neck with one hand to maintain her decency before the police.

First, the Inspector rang up *The Freemasons'.* Cromwell was there, waiting for him. He told his colleague what had happened.

"...There's being a family gathering at the Fearns' house to-night. Presumably all the Bunns will be there. Go at once, as fast as you can, old chap, and see who's there. The Medlicotts are coming, but presumably they're late, as usual. Check particularly if all Jasper's family and all the Fearnses are present... I expect the home-birds will all have alibis for one another, but we'd better be sure."

Then the police-station to tell them to come and collect Browning and bring the technical staff. Miss Mander lit a cigarette and drew hard at it, taking in every word. At the mention of Browning's name, she let fall the cigarette. ... She was a tall blonde, with unctuous curves and golden hair. A real pin-up girl, with a face totally devoid of intelligence. She picked up her cigarette, put it in her mouth, and eyed Littlejohn from head to foot with admiring china-blue eyes. From the cupboard in the corner came shuffling sounds.

"Mice ..." said Miss Mander.

"Thanks," said Littlejohn and left her.

The occupants of the flats had scented something unusual and heads appeared round door frames.

"Excuse me," said the galleon-maker, a tall thin man with a face like a buzzard. His eternal hammer hung in his fingers. Littlejohn hurried past to meet the police.

They were able to attend to Browning at last, as he lay there in the light from his own window and with his unsuspecting family peeping round the blind to see what was going on. His wife at length made out the figure on the rank grass and ran out.

"Ronnie! Oh, Ronnie!"

She flung herself upon it. The police helped her indoors. There had been a bit of a scuffle on the wide flower-bed surrounding the nymph as Browning's assailant came upon him from behind. The soil was moist and told a plain tale. The pair, Browning and his killer, had met on the lawn; their separate footprints converged and then receded. They must have met as Browning took a short cut across the soil, spoken, and then parted. Then the murderer had run on his toes with shorter steps, taken Browning from behind, and killed him. There were no marks of fingers on the throat. It might have been done swiftly and silently with a scarf... One of the technical men pointed to one of the murderer's footprints. It was deep and couldn't have been better for the purpose. They were making a cast of it by the glare of the searchlights from the police-cars.

"But what's the use?" he said to the Inspector. "It'll be like playing Cinderella... Twenty thousand inhabitants in Enderby..."

"All the same, it might be useful. Carry on..."

Cromwell later reported that all the Bunn family were at the Fearnses, except the Medlicotts. They were always late. Aunt Sarah had played merry hell at Cromwell's intrusion and then co-operated valiantly to help him check the alibis.

"If you want anything, in future, young man, just come to me. I'll help you," she said as Cromwell left. "I *like* you, young man, and anybody I like I'll do anything for." And she gave him the smile of a benevolent bulldog.

Yes, the Bunns gave one another alibis again. A proper home-loving lot, quarrelling like Kilkenny cats among themselves in private, but a close, compact mass in trouble.

CHAPTER NINE
FUNEREAL INTERLUDE

It poured with rain for most of the day of Ned Bunn's funeral. Mr. Blowitt personally supervised the breakfasts, carefully giving attention to the preparation of *Strengtho*, the patent food on which Cromwell staked his reputation. Littlejohn preferred bacon and eggs.

"I can't make out wot's come over my missus," bleated Mr. Blowitt, addressing nobody in particular and rubbing his unshaven chin. "She's actually cheerful ... no tears, no complaints, no nuthin' ... It isn't 'ealthy, somethin's up ..."

Across the way the coffin was being moved to the home of Sarah Agnes Fearns. So many relatives had arrived for the funeral and so many carriages were likely to participate in it, that the police had intervened. There must be no congestion in the town square and no interference with through traffic. The starting-ground had, therefore, been transferred to the Fearns' home, which was more commodious into the bargain.

The blinds of the shop were drawn. All the flags were at half-mast on the public buildings, public servants kept passing *The Freemasons'* on their ways to work, dressed in black with toppers or bowlers, all got up for the day's events. The town was in complete mourning; even the rain looked black. The boys from the florists' shops kept scuttering backwards and forwards to the Fearns' home, carrying boxes of wreaths, bunches of funeral flowers and crosses of evergreens. A succession of carriages, cabs and vehicles of all shapes and sizes ran ceaselessly to and from Salem Chapel, where the service was to be held at ten o'clock, before the departure to the cemetery. After the committal, there was to be a funeral meal in the Sunday School, where at least one hundred guests were expected. They were going to do Ned Bunn proud and bury him with ham, tongue, veal and roast pork...

"Why the flower-bed? Why did the killer choose soft soil on which to impress his footmarks? Why didn't he stick to the gravel?"

Littlejohn said it suddenly, apropos of nothing much, but it showed that he was more concerned with his problems than his breakfast. Cromwell eyed him reproachfully.

"It's not good to think of work when you're eating, sir. It was one of Florence Nightingale's maxims that..."

"All right, old chap. I'll let it drop... Pass the marmalade."

Outside, Mr. Blowitt was arguing with someone.

" 'Ave you been up all night? The two gents is at breakfast. Can't it wait? Oh, very well..."

And Mr. Blowitt thereupon ushered in Hubert Stubbs.

"Mr. Stubbs wants a word with Mr. Cromwell, gents."

Yewbert was clad in black from head to foot and carried a bowler hat, the use of which had inflamed the pimple on his forehead until it resembled a navigation light. Black did not suit Yewbert. It made his sallow face even more dissipated and went badly with his sandy hair and moustache. He looked like a hangman, or, as Cromwell said later, airing a new word he had discovered, a patibulary assistant.

"Aunt Sarah wants a word with you, Mr. Cromwell. It's urgent."

Hubert Stubbs got straight to business. Cromwell noticed that he already spoke of his family opponent as though she were also a relative of his. In fact, he was one of the Bunn clan already.

When Cromwell arrived at the scene of the funeral and had sorted out Aunt Sarah from the ever-increasing mass of celebrants, he found the whole thing was a false alarm arising from a caustic remark made by the formidable old lady and, in his zeal to ingratiate himself with her, interpreted seriously by Yewbert.

It turned out that among the wreaths which were arriving in endless streams, two mysterious boxes had been delivered. And they had so perturbed Hubert that Mrs. Wilkins had impatiently told him there were famous detectives in the town and he had better consult them for a solution.

One box was filled with red roses and bore a card which the eager relatives had seized and whereon they had read with great consternation:

> Helen, thy beauty is to me
> Like those Nicean barks of yore,
> That gently, o'er a perfumed sea,
> The weary, wayworn wanderer bore
> To his own native shore.

There were loud and outraged cries from all sides, among which the reedy voice of Yewbert was loudest in lamentations, which increased when the other box was opened. This contained white roses and a further message of a non-mortuary flavour:

On desperate seas long wont to roam,
Thy hyacinth hair, thy classic face,
Thy Naiad airs have brought me home
To the glory that was Greece,
To the grandeur that was Rome.

Above the turmoil, Aunt Sarah was heard defending Helen and denouncing anybody who said a word against her.

"Whoever sent 'em had the right idea of wooing a girl... Sent 'em slap among all the funeral flowers. He's not only a poet but an original lover... And as for you, young man ..."

Whereat she pointed her stick at Yewbert,

"If you don't know who it is, better see a detective; there are some in town ..."

When Cromwell explained what had brought him, Aunt Sarah burst into loud Rabelaisian laughter, said it was a joke, and that Hubert would have to be his own detective and pretty smart about it if he wanted to win Helen. This sally was greeted by horrified looks from the rest of the expanding funeral party, although nobody dared utter a word against the old lady on account of the money she was due to leave and her obvious imminent decease.

"Nobody could weigh as much as Aunt Sarah and last long," one hopeful had said.

"Whilst you're here, you might as well stay," Aunt Sarah said to Cromwell. "There's lots of local colour, likely suspects, and a good meal in the offing. Besides, I like you, young man, and you can share my carriage with me. Just ring up your boss and tell him I say you've to see Ned Bunn under the sod. By the way, give me your card; I want your address."

Somewhat puzzled, Cromwell complied. The rest of the family held their breaths and then exhaled a loud collective sigh of disappointment and rage. They were used to Aunt Sarah's card trick. It meant she was going to include yet another beneficiary in her will ... "I knew it," said Miss Maria Bunn, who had a reputation for being clairvoyant.

Bunns of all ages, shapes and sizes had now assembled and it seemed that before long they would overflow from the house into the garage, the greenhouses and the potting-sheds. Among others was Mr. Jethro Bunn, next after Aunt Sarah in age and wealth. He had made a fortune as The Happy Dry Cleaners Ltd., whose title belied his miserable countenance. He wore a black tail-coat and a bowler, both gone green with age, and the wire showed round the brim of his hat. He was bearded like a patriarch and when indoors, after removing his headgear, covered his pate again with a smoking cap. Uncle Jethro was heard to say in a querulous voice that but for Ned Bunn, Helen, of whom Jethro was very fond in a possessive, senile way, would have married parson Hornblower's son. Ned Bunn had bullied Sr' Agnes into breaking up the romance. Cromwell made a note of this.

The assembly reminded Cromwell of a dog show. With one or two rare exceptions, all of the Bunn blood had faces like pug-dogs and their partners in marriage looked like their owners exhibiting them. There was some displeasure expressed at the sole pair of artistic oddities in the family. Augustus Bunn, an organist and teacher of music, whose main topics of conversation were César-Franck and Brahms and Johann Sebastian (as though Bach were a personal pal), arrived in a blue suit and tangerine-coloured shoes. He was therefore ordered by Uncle Jethro Bunn to borrow a suit more appropriate and some decent boots, and reappeared clad in garments of the late Ned, which were two sizes too large for him, as were also a pair of the deceased's boots. The other freak, Sylvester Bunn, was a literary man who wrote detective stories for popular magazines. He appeared in light tweeds and brown suede shoes, but nobody bothered; he was regarded as being quite mad and past curing.

There were thirty carriages in the cortège and Cromwell had a place of honour in the second one with Aunt Sarah, whose huge bulk made the cab ride askew, like a vessel the cargo of which had shifted in a storm.

The service in Salem went without a hitch. It was cold and damp and the place was not heated. A building like a huge barn with hard wooden seats for mortification of the flesh, each pew boxed in by a door, and the name of the proprietor written on a card on the door, like those of the flats at *Whispers*. Several people started to cough and sneeze and two poor relatives contracted colds which later proved fatal, but that did not affect the aggregate of the Bunn family fund, because the victims were penniless and lived on the old-age pension.

The Medlicotts were late as usual and entered the church after the obsequies had started. Jubal had a daughter on each arm and a white chrysanthemum in his buttonhole. He was told at once to remove it and rebuked for behaving as though the service were for a wedding. He had left his spats at home.

At the cemetery the first signs of something unusual occurred. The procession from the mortuary chapel, headed by the cemetery superintendent, turned left to the Bunn section of the burial ground, but the superintendent turned right. There was a hurried conference, Mr. Edgell was sorted out from the mass of Bunns and confirmed that the corporation official was correct. Ned Bunn had bought a plot on the right side and was, in death, going to rest as far away from the other Bunns as possible.

"That will be explained when the will is read," was all the lawyer would say and it seemed for a time that the outraged clan would refuse to agree to the committal of this rebellious member. They finally conformed with bad grace. Ashes to ashes, dust to dust, and that was the end of Ned Bunn.

The mass of Bunns then turned in procession and returned via the traditional family burial-place, which held a dozen or so plots, marked by broken pillars, weeping angels, miniature Albert memorials, Maltese and Celtic crosses, and several box-like structures made of stone.

"Where's Timothy?" Uncle Jethro was heard to ask. "He ain't here..." He indicated the black mass of Bunns. "And he ain't here..."; his arm swept over the plots holding the dead-and-gone Bunns, their numbers counted and their names enrolled.

There was a hush. Since the last gathering of the clan, Tim Bunn, a member of the Melton Mowbray branch, had, at the age of sixty, turned to drink, been sent as a remittance-man to the Isle of Man, and his name was never spoken. Somebody whispered brief details to Uncle Jethro, who protested at not being kept informed and made a note on an old envelope to cut somebody out of his will as punishment.

Thereafter, the clan adjourned to Salem Sunday School, where food was laid out for their refreshment. They steadily ate their way through it to the last crumb, for it had been paid for and one of the family mottoes was "Waste not, want not." After a substantial over-helping of pork, Mr. Jethro Bunn was taken ill and had to be sent to the Fearns' home to recover, which he did, greatly to the chagrin of many others.

Then, they all returned to Sr' Agnes's home for the reading of the will. As Mr. Edgell intoned the simple document, he looked like John Wesley preaching to a lot of unbelievers. The occasion was a very solemn family one, for it dealt with the apportionment of a section of the Bunn Consolidation which, however much it was laded and teemed within the clan, never leaked outside it.

Edwin Bunn left all his worldly wealth to his daughter, Bertha Bunn, *but*...

Here there was a concerted gasp. Hope still lived in many breasts, although they had to admit Bertha's rights as sole surviving issue.

But, to inherit, Bertha Bunn, pending any marriage subsequently contracted, was to change her name to Wood before entering into the fortune. Furthermore, on her marriage, her husband was to take the name Wood, which might be hyphenated with his own name coming first. To assure this, the money would be in trust till Bertha's marriage. "I have no doubt this will speedily come about as soon as the news of her inheritance spreads," Ned Bunn added, speaking from the grave.

"Bertha Flounder-Wood...Wilfred Flounder-Wood," said Wilfred Flounder loudly and hoarsely, and fell unconscious to the ground.

There was one other clause. Ned Bunn was to be buried in a plot he had chosen and the headstone was to describe him as Edwin Wood. "I never asked to be a Bunn, I was always a Wood. I despise the Bunns and would have changed my name back to my mother's had it not been expensive to do so and a lot of trouble."

The gathering broke up in confusion; many denounced the deceased and regretted the floral tributes which had cost good Bunn money. Some suggested the payment of their travelling expenses from the Bunn-né-Wood estate. They went one by one, with never a good word for the deceased. All except Aunt Sarah, who expressed her intention of staying with the Fearns family for some time.

"I want to see that Helen isn't bullied into wedding that Hubert Stubbs," she said. "She's the only one of our name who hasn't been afflicted with the ugly Bunn mug and I'm hanged if her chances of producing really good-looking children for a change are going to be ruined by a union with a little self-opinionated fellow with pimples and sandy hair, who, in any case isn't going to get a penny of mine for himself or his offspring ... And, as for you ..."

She poked her ebony stick at Cromwell and smacked her lips.

"As for you ... I like you, young man, and I'm going to help you solve this mystery and bring credit on yourself. I think you'll agree with me that Ned has had the last word and a good joke. Ned Wood, eh? That's a good one! I never saw the family so quick to depart ... Good riddance ..."

And with that, she switched off the hearing device she had acquired through the National Health Insurance, refused to hear another word, and relapsed into chuckling silence.

CHAPTER TEN
JUBAL'S ALIBI

From the point of view of real work, the day of Ned Bunn's funeral was, in legal terms, a *dies non*. You couldn't get at anybody except the police; the rest were either at the house, at the church, at the cemetery, or at the ritual feast. It was four o'clock in the afternoon before the will was read, the petard fired, and the Bunn clan sent scuttering home in disgust. Meanwhile, Littlejohn did some work at the police-station.

The footprint expert was excited about the plaster casts he had taken the previous night in the garden of *Whispers*.

"What do you think of those, sir?" he said proudly, as he placed his models on the table. "Notice anything peculiar about them?"

He stood back and looked admiringly at his handiwork, like a man who had suddenly found himself the father of a phenomenal child.

Under the instep of each of the casts ran a miniature trench about an eighth of an inch deep and just less than half an inch wide.

"The man wore spats?"

The expert looked disappointed but later told his colleagues, "You have to hand it to Littlejohn. He looks quiet enough, but there aren't any flies on him."

Inspector Myers jumped to conclusions right away.

"It's Medlicott! I thought so."

The Chief Constable made clucking, impatient noises.

"Now, now, now. Not so fast. It was Flounder not long ago. Let's be sure before we jump."

"Yes, sir. But Medlicott's the only one who wears spats these days. He's motive, opportunity and ..."

Littlejohn intervened.

"I saw Medlicott just after the murder was committed. He was in his underclothes and would have had to be jolly quick to strip off and get in the condition I found him if he'd been out and killed Browning. And what *is* the motive? It might have been blackmail, but that needs looking into. I'd better have a word with him as soon as I can."

The Chief Constable rubbed his chin.

"Medlicott's certainly a queer fish. I've known him since he was quite a young fellah. Born in these parts, went away, and then came back again and married Anne Bunn. What she could see in him to make her throw over Edgell, I can't think. No accountin' for women's tastes ... His father died in a mental home ..."

He said it casually as though it didn't matter much.

"A mental home, sir? Was he mad?"

"Hardly that, Littlejohn. Let's call him *odd*. Used to knock around town with a bucket and spade collectin' horse-droppin's for his roses. Finally, said he was diggin' for gold among the droppin's ... Wonder if Jubal's tarred a bit with the same brush. Anybody can see there's somethin' *odd* in the family. Those two girls of his are *odd* ... damned *odd* ..."

Littlejohn turned over the case at his solitary lunch. Cromwell was absent at the funeral feed in Salem School, which Littlejohn had seen him entering like a Bunn himself, with Aunt Sarah leaning on his arm.

Jubal Medlicott, with insanity in his family.

Wilfred Flounder, a rabbit who might suddenly have turned resentful and ferocious.

A parson who, through Ned Bunn, had indirectly lost his only son. A parson who read Sartre, Donne and Kierkegaard...

And all the seething, black, funereal mass of Bunns who had invaded Enderby that day. It might be any one of them; a needle in the Bunn haystack.

At least, there was one clue. The spats. Jubal's spats.

It was late afternoon before cars, taxis and umbrellas, all travelling in the direction of the station and the bus stop, announced that the rally of the Bunns was over. Not long after the main contingent had dispersed, the Medlicotts appeared, clad in raincoats, carrying umbrellas, on their way to *Whispers* on foot. They couldn't afford a conveyance and none of the relatives, flustered and annoyed by the contents of the will of Ned *Wood*, had seen fit to offer them a lift. Mrs. Medlicott, small and frail, struggled along with the rest. Suddenly, Jubal detached himself from his party and, after a word or two, made for the shop. The twins turned as if to follow, but he waved them away, bared his teeth in a smile and indicated their mother, who needed company and possibly assistance home. The beating rain gave no time for argument.

Medlicott, paying a flying visit to the shop, which was officially closed for the day, had left the door ajar, and Littlejohn pushed it open and entered. The place was large and old-fashioned with a big window on each side of the door. The blinds had not been drawn. In one window, a number of dummies clad in Mr. Medlicott's handiwork. Nondescript suitings, cut on rather old-fashioned lines, as though Jubal had been unable to keep up with current fashions. *Latest London Cut. Note the Price.* All the dummies, which included three small boys, wore wooden smiles and looked well-pleased with themselves. Their waxen hands stuck out like semaphores and they all held attitudes of listeners to some enthralling news. The other window contained shirts, ties, underwear, caps, pullovers and collars, hanging from brass rods or lying in piles here and there. Stuck on the window-pane was one of Medlicott's invoices, held in place by a gelatine lozenge. *Closed for the day owing to bereavement* in florid script.

The shop covered a lot of ground. The counters which ran down two sides were vast and the public space was cluttered with more dummies, old chairs, an umbrella stand and a showcase with more ties and cheap-looking shirts. The place had originally been equipped for a large trade and had doubtless at one time enjoyed it. Now it was drab, neglected and out-of-date. The silver of the heavy mirrors, sprinkled here and there, was peeling off and the polished fittings were worn and dull.

Mr. Medlicott was bending before a small, old-fashioned open safe in one corner, stuffing pound notes in a wallet. At the sound of Littlejohn's footsteps, he sprang upright, turned, hastily shut the safe and locked it and crushed the wallet in his inside pocket. He looked ruffled and guilty, as though he might have been robbing someone else's property.

"We're closed...Just called for something I forgot."

There was a flash of anger in the dark eyes and then the toothy smile reappeared as Jubal recovered his poise.

"It's you, Inspector...What did you want?"

"A word or two with you, sir. I didn't wish to disturb you at home again at a time like this."

Medlicott gave Littlejohn a searching glance, took off his gold-framed spectacles and began to polish them on an artificial silk handkerchief. He looked a different man without his specs. The eyes seemed to vanish deeply in his head and gleamed short-sightedly from among the trimmed whiskers.

"Come and sit down here."

There was a kind of office in one corner, where the safe stood; glass partitions with a desk behind and two chairs visible.

"Was it about last night, Inspector?"

Medlicott sounded anxious and a bit humble. He put on his glasses and gazed at his shoes through them. He wasn't wearing his spats.

"Partly... And then about your whereabouts, sir, on the night Mr. Edwin Bunn died. We've been informed that you were out of doors at the time of the murder. Is that true?"

Medlicott's mouth fell open, revealing a row of brown bottom-teeth, broken and irregular.

"Who told you that?"

"Is it true?"

Medlicott paused. He was weighing up the chances of sticking to his tale or making a clean breast of it. He moved his hands from the arms of the old chair in which he was sitting and rubbed their palms on his handkerchief. Littlejohn noticed that the place where his hands had been was damp.

"I was out... But I never went near Ned's shop..."

He spluttered it quickly, as though afraid if he didn't get it out, the confession would choke him or die on his lips before he could speak.

"Why did you say you were at home, sir? And why did your family confirm your first statement?"

Medlicott blew his nose loudly, one nostril at a time, trying to think up an excuse. He mopped his beard and forehead.

"What would you have done, Inspector? It looked so bad, me being out at that very time. I asked the girls and my wife to bear me out if anybody asked. I must take the blame. They would do anything for me ..."

He started to sob. Tears sprang from his eyes and disappeared in his beard.

"I don't want to involve them ... They're all so dear to me."

And yet, Browning had said Medlicott was a philanderer!

"Where were you at the time, then?"

Medlicott started and looked surprised, as though he hadn't expected it. The red lips gleaming among the whiskers were dry and he licked them quickly. His face took on an earnest, pleading look.

"I know you won't believe me, but I swear before God that it's true. I got a telephone message to go and visit a friend. When I got there, my friend hadn't telephoned. It was a hoax ..."

"Who took the message? ... Miss Mander? ... Whose phone did you use?"

"No. She was out. Somebody rang up Cuffright and he came up to tell me. He'll confirm that ..."

Medlicott waited like one who expects a blow.

"Whom was the telephone call supposed to come from?"

The little dapper tailor stiffened and his jaw tightened.

"I'm sorry, Inspector, but I'm not in a position to say."

"You mean you *won't*, sir?"

"Exactly."

And he nodded his head vigorously to emphasize it.

"You're aware, of course, of the serious position you're putting yourself in, Mr. Medlicott. If you want to clear yourself of suspicion, you'd better make a clean breast of the whole affair."

Medlicott drew himself up to his full five feet eight. He almost stood on his tiptoes for emphasis.

"I have nothing whatever to do with the murders, Inspector. I refuse to discuss my private affairs with you and I strongly resent any suggestion that my behaviour has been in any way suspicious."

"Your telephone call, I gather, was supposed to come from a lady..."

It seemed a bit merciless to rub it in, but it had its effect. Medlicott looked to lose two inches in height and sagged miserably.

"I still refuse to answer."

"You know, of course, that I can ask Mr. Cuffright who came on the phone for you?"

"Ask him then... Ask him then, and be damned to you. You're a meddling, officious, suspicious..."

Medlicott was beside himself now. He stamped his feet in his rage.

"That will do, sir. Abuse won't help. I'd better see you later. Meanwhile, think it over, and I hope you decide to be sensible."

"Leave me alone. Why can't I have a bit of peace. Everybody seems against me."

Jubal staggered off into the dark places of his shop, among his ready-made suits and overcoats, and Littlejohn left him there.

Outside, Littlejohn could see an ancient taxi with a list to starboard, making slow progress towards the market square, as though towing a huge weight behind. It was Aunt Sarah giving Cromwell a lift home to *The Freemasons'*. The Inspector caught up with them as the vehicle stopped at the pub door. When Aunt Sarah spotted Littlejohn she decided to descend as well.

"I want a word with you, Inspector. I'll come in for a cup of tea and a talk."

The cab groaned and swayed as they hoisted her out and she ordered the emaciated driver to return in half an hour.

"...And I mean half an hour; not twenty-five minutes or three-quarters of an hour."

The hands of the clock over the bar stood at five o'clock. The hooter of the local brewery started to blow, and was followed by the whistle of a sawmill. Workmen began to pass through the square on their ways home.

Mr. Blowitt was again indulging in a temperamental quarrel with his wife. He had a black eye. The little man who dealt in beds and whose name was Sid Twelves, had again visited *The Freemasons'* for dalliance with Mrs. Blowitt and had been insulted by her husband. Mr. Twelves had thereupon gone for Blowitt and punched him in the eye. ... Mr. Blowitt had been throwing glasses about, abusing his wife and preparing and shouting about taking Twelves up for assault. Littlejohn and his party found her with hands clasped and outstretched in supplication.

"Speak to me, Percy..."

Mr. Blowitt ignored her. He was nailing up a card on the bar. *Join our Christmas Goose Club.*

"Wanton!" he hissed at her, after he had removed the last nail from between his teeth, and Mrs. Blowitt smote her forehead with the palm of her hand and made a tragic exit.

Aunt Sarah thumped on the floor with her ebony stick.

"Tea for three in the parlour, Blowitt, and be quick about it."

The order seemed to infuse new energy in the landlord's sagging frame.

"Certainly, Mrs. Wilkins...Certainly."

Aunt Sarah led the way into the small room in which Littlejohn and Cromwell usually ate their meals. Two commercial travellers were occupying the seats before the fire and another stood on the hearthrug. The man on his feet raised his eyebrows at the sight of the huge old woman. He had been leisurely contemplating himself in the mirror over the fireplace and smoothing down his pomaded hair. He wore a large ring with a red stone the size of a hazel-nut, his moustache was waxed to points, and his eyebrows met over his snub nose. Aunt Sarah went for him right away.

"This is the residents' room, my man."

The man with the ring smiled contentedly.

"We *are* residents, madam." He bowed.

"Don't lie to me. I know this place is full up, so you can't be staying. I'll trouble you to leave and take yourselves to the public rooms. We want to be private."

Whatever it was emanated from this large, pug-faced woman who looked like an inflated pew-opener, it was enough to bend any antagonist to her will. The commercial travellers opened their mouths in astonishment and left in a body, the man with the ring backing out as from the presence of royalty.

"Now to business..."

Littlejohn had time to look Aunt Sarah over properly and he admired her as one who knew her own mind. She wore a long black silk dress, elastic-sided shoes, a lot of rings and bangles which bit in the flesh of her swollen fingers and wrists, a link of large jet beads, and ear-rings to match. The Inspector perceived, too, that what he had imagined, from a distance, to be a bonnet, was in reality a felt hat, distorted almost to the shape of a Balaclava helmet by a shoelace tied under Aunt Sarah's chin to keep it in place.

Mr. Blowitt arrived with the tea in person. His missus had locked herself in her own room and was loudly playing the radio: The Flower Song from *Carmen*. As Blowitt opened the door the music wafted in.

Sometimes I curse the hour I met thee. ...

"Stop that row!"

Aunt Sarah pointed in the direction of the Flower Song with her ebony stick.

"I can't. She's locked herself in."

"Switch off the electricity at the meter then."

Mr. Blowitt made a hasty exit before more impossible orders were issued.

"I want to talk to you about these murders. I don't think any of the family did them."

Mrs. Wilkins went straight to the point. She smiled at Cromwell, who had been very quiet since his arrival.

"Your assistant has been very kind to me, Inspector, and I want you to make a note of it ... Most kind."

She took out a snuff-box from somewhere in the volume of her clothes and noisily sniffed a pinch up each nostril.

"Like to try some? No? I was saying about Mr. Cromwell. A man after my own heart. If he'd been single, I'd have been delighted to see him fixed up with my favourite niece, Helen, and leave 'em all I've got. As it is, he's married and has a family."

Littlejohn gave Cromwell a sideways look and raised one eyebrow. The usually imperturbable sergeant thereupon blushed like a lobster suddenly flung in boiling water.

"I won't have her wed to that Hubert Stubbs. If I die in the effort, I'll stop it. As for the rest of the family being murderers ... well ... You've seen them, Cromwell. What do you think of 'em? Can you imagine that miserable lot of psalm-singers firing guns or throttling people? Name any one of them...I can't. Jubal Medlicott comes from a crazy family, but he's milk and water."

She licked her lips and looked from one to the other.

"What do *you* think?"

"It's going to be quite a problem."

"Problem? Where's the problem? There isn't one. You'll have to look outside the family, Inspector. That parson, Hornblower...A man who's lost his faith through trouble...Lost his son through Ned's interference...Or one of the many people in town who owed money to Ned Bunn. People he bullied and harried because they were in his grip. This man, Blowitt...Oh, yes, I know all about Ned's carryings-on in this town. You see, we Bunns are great letter-writers. The family's *linked* by letter-writing. I don't know why we do it. Not out of love for one another, I assure you. It's a sort of inborn instinct...a family duty...Also, I guess, they keep me warm because of my money. They must write to keep in my good books and as they haven't anything cultural or literary to put in their letters, they fill them with gossip about one another...So, I know all about everybody and I tell you that, though many of the family wished Ned out of the way, they'd only go to the extent of praying to the Almighty to do the dirty work by striking him dead. They wouldn't have the guts to kill him themselves."

She went on and on, like a gramophone, asking no advice or opinions, but simply pumping views and information into her hearers.

"They keep suggesting that Flounder might have done it. Poor little rabbit of a man. A vegetarian, he is, without any blood in his veins...They're out to stop him marrying Bertha, but I'll see right done there."

Aunt Sarah waved her stick and just then her taxi appeared outside and the melancholy driver started to "pip-pip" dismally on the horn.

"I'll see that Bertha gets wed this time, if I die in the attempt. The sooner it's done the better, before she gets too old to have children who can inherit her fortune properly, instead of more distant relatives squabbling and snarling for the leavings."

She fished among her outer garments again, took out a large purse, twisted it open, and extracted half-a-crown.

"Pay for the tea, Cromwell," she said. "And if Blowitt tries to charge you more, black his other eye... I'll see you to-morrow, then..."

And with that Aunt Sarah rustled from the room, emerged on the pavement, and was shoved in the taxi by the thin chauffeur, who drove slowly away with a list to port this time.

"You seem to have made a conquest there, Cromwell."

Cromwell blushed heavily again.

"Where's it get us, though, sir? If the Bunns didn't do it, who did?"

Littlejohn slowly filled his pipe.

"The Bunns are a remarkable family," he said. "Having done their best to provide each other with alibis, they now, in case we distrust their statements, send their principal advocate, Aunt Sarah, to convince us that they're temperamentally exempt from committing murder. The Bunns need watching. They're a closed corporation and unless we break them up, we're going to get nowhere."

Chapter Eleven
The Affairs of Ronald Browning

The local police had been at *Whispers* asking a lot of questions from the tenants, but had gathered little to help them. Nobody seemed to have seen or heard anything of the happenings outside the flats which had led to the death of Browning. One thing they did discover, however, was that Mr. Jubal Medlicott wore size sevens in shoes and that this tallied with the imprints found in the garden at the scene of the murder. They hit the right shoemaker first bang off. The little shop next-door-but-one to Medlicott's.

"Yes. Medlicott wears a seven shoe. Same make he buys, every time. My motter's the same. When you find the right shoe, stick to it," said the shopkeeper, a faded, bilious little man with a shock of tow-coloured hair and a worn-out look from constantly fighting and worrying about competitors. He produced the very style favoured by his neighbour and the police found it fitted exactly with the model they had made. Littlejohn persuaded the eager local Inspector to hold his hand a bit until he himself had carried out investigations in his own way.

It had been raining again when Littlejohn and Cromwell got up and although it ceased over breakfast, the wan trees of *Whispers* shed showers of stained water on the Inspector as he made his way under them to the flats.

The blinds of the Brownings' ground-floor rooms were drawn. The children had been sent to a distant aunt's and Mrs. Browning's mother had arrived to keep her daughter company. She was a little, stocky witch of a woman, none too clean, and she had a reputation among her cronies for seeing into the future through the medium of tea-leaves. This Mother Shipton answered the door and barred the way against Littlejohn.

"Are you a reporter?" she said, "Because if you are, you'll 'ave to pay well in advance, and we shan't tell what we know right away. We'll 'ave to think it over after we've got some more offers."

She stood there, slightly redolent of gin and scratching her dishevelled hair voluptuously.

"What is it, mother? ... Do come inside and let me talk to 'im."

Even in her grief and helplessness, Browning's wife was ashamed of her mother, who'd arrived and taken things in hand uninvited. The younger woman was consumptive-looking and thin, with a long face and washed-out grey eyes. Until poverty and her shiftless husband assailed her, she had probably been quite pretty. Her mother had no patience with her and she had never liked Browning, who had never acknowledged any liability to support his wife's parents.

"I said 'e'd come to a bad end. The stars was always agin him," muttered the old hag.

"I'd like a word with Mrs. Browning alone," cut in Littlejohn. "Police ..."

The crafty old woman backed out. Her eyes never left the Inspector's face until she was through the door into the other room. She was afraid of the police, who were always on her track at home for illegal fortune-telling. With her disappearance, the smell of gin and unwashed linen also went.

The flat was untidy and in the half-light of the drawn blinds he could make out a lot of children's toys scattered here and there; a battered doll, a doll's carriage bought perhaps in a spell of opulence, and a home-made truck knocked together from a soap-box. Browning was always leaving things unfinished, half-done. He plugged walls for pictures and cupboards and they fell down ... Over the broken tiles of the mantelpiece was an unpainted motto he had made in fretwork: *Home Sweet Home.*

The large, fine eyes of Mrs. Browning were fixed on Littlejohn.

"Was it about Ronnie?"

"Yes ... I'm so sorry. If there's anything I can do ..."

She looked surprised.

"Not that I'd know of. My dad's helping me ... Dad's always been good to me ... Not ..."

She paused. She was going to say he wasn't like her mother, but it didn't seem right outside the family circle.

"What did your husband do for a living, Mrs. Browning?"

"He was really a french-polisher by trade, but work was hard to come by. You see, it's done now by spraying-machines and Ronnie only used to get work now and then ... The rest was casual and sometimes he'd go on the unemployment pay."

"Whom did he do casual work for?"

She paused.

"Please answer me truthfully, Mrs. Browning. After all, nobody can harm him, now, and it will help us to find who is responsible for his death."

"Well ... He did a bit of work for Mr. Cuffright upstairs. Mr. Cuffright's a commission agent and Ronnie did errands for him."

A bookie's runner!

"... And sometimes he got odd jobs for others, as well."

"Such as ...? I'm particularly interested in what he was doing at the time of his death. He told me he'd had his eye on Mr. Medlicott of late ..."

"Yes. It was a bit of a mystery to me, sir. I don't know what it was all about, but he did seem to be watching what Mr. Medlicott did for somebody; he didn't say who. Ronnie was a bit close about his business affairs, but now and then, when I complained about it bein' hard to make ends meet, he'd say he'd soon have enough money ... I know the day he died, when the men came about the furniture, he pleaded with them to leave it till he could collect some that somebody owed him. He said it was quite a sum ... In fact, he was very bitter and talked of putting the screw on somebody he knew ... I don't know if I ought to be talkin' like this. After all, he was my 'usband."

She had long hands and feet and kept twisting her fingers. The voice came in a regular monotone. The atmosphere of the dim, untidy room was close and airless. The whole business was depressing.

"Your husband confided in you now and then? When he wanted to cheer you up ..."

In other words, Browning was addicted to fits of swanking and boasting to justify himself when anyone complained!

"That's it."

"Did he ever mention Medlicott?"

"Oh, yes. Whenever the rent was due. This time especially. Mr. Medlicott had been pressing. Ronnie said Medlicott wasn't all he tried to make out. He hinted there was some other woman and that Ronnie was keeping an eye on Medlicott about it...Whether it was about a divorce, I don't know... But he used to go out on the stairs and watch Mr. M. comin' and goin' and say things about him to me after."

"Your husband knew when I called to see the Medlicotts just before he was killed. He was waiting for me on the stairs to tell me about Mr. Medlicott's movements. Did he say anything to you about it?"

"Yes. He said if I heard you coming down, to tell 'im. But he was so jumpy about catching you that he ended up outside the door of our flat waiting for you."

There was a muffled cough behind the inner door, where Mother Shipton was posted, listening to all that was going on.

"So you've no idea who was employing your husband to keep an eye on Mr. Medlicott... He never dropped a hint?"

"No, sir. I've wondered... but I might be wrong... but I've wondered if my husband was doin' it on his own account. He hated Mr. Medlicott because he was nasty when we couldn't pay the rent and Ronnie said Mr. M. wasn't the one to be remarkin' on other people's sins when he was what he was, so to speak."

"I see..."

They were interrupted by someone inserting a key in the lock, and a little, stocky, chirpy man entered. He was elderly and had a grey moustache and a bald head with a fringe of white hair round it like a tonsure. He wore cheap black clothes and a bowler hat which was obviously kept in cold-storage for funerals, weddings and the like. He was bow-legged and rolled as he walked.

"Hullo, gel. I've seen to things. The police say we can bury 'im to-morrer... Oh... Didn't know you'd got company."

He hadn't seen Littlejohn in the darkness and now stood silent and a bit abashed.

Mrs. Browning introduced Littlejohn. The newcomer was her father, Mr. Jack Thewless. A decent artisan of the best type. He shook hands with the Inspector; a hard, clean little hand.

"I've just been to the police-station myself. They're a very decent lot…Don't fret, gel, nobody's goin' to do any thin' to you. Your dad'll look after you."

Father and daughter were evidently close friends. Mrs. Browning started to sob bitterly.

"Bloody shame," said her dad under his breath and then Mother Shipton appeared on the scene. You could feel the old man dry up, almost recoil. He never knew what she was going to say next.

"You've been a long time. Where've you been?"

"I'll tell you later, maw. I'm just havin' a word with the Inspector, 'ere. I'll be with you in a minute…"

"So, you want to be rid of me, do you? Well, wot's to be said concerns me jest as much as you, don't it? I'm 'er mother, ain't I? Well…?"

She'd been at the bottle in her absence and brought with her an aroma of gin like an accompanying cloud. She sat firmly down on a chair and folded her arms.

The same old tale of domestic torment and slavery! The little man didn't know where to look or what to say.

"Let's smoke a pipe in the garden."

The old woman looked at Littlejohn as if she couldn't believe her ears.

"Well!"

But she couldn't say anything else. The two men went outside and walked under the trees to the back and round the block again. The whole property was in a weary state.

The back was worse than the front. The rusty pipes of the plumbing system crawled down the rear, and the ground beneath was sour, with the grass worn away and weeds a yard high sprouting all over the shop. The dust-bins hadn't been emptied for a long time and their contents overflowed and leaked out in piles all round them. Rusty tins, tea-leaves, bottles...

Jack Thewless filled his little briar from Littlejohn's pouch and lit it.

"Aye..." he said. A sigh of relief and perhaps satisfaction, for the little man seemed to have within himself some source of strength and cheerfulness which his hag of a wife could not suppress.

"I was only sayin' to Ronnie at th' football match last Saturday, that no self-respectin' chap should be carryin' on a job like he was... I'd rather hump coal or hawk newspapers than earn me livin' spyin' on other folks."

"He told you what he was doing, then?"

"Not exactly. But he said he was runnin' an enquiry agency. Whether it were on his own or for somebody else, he didn't say. But I gathered he got information for people about other folks' private lives. It's like a cat huntin' in dust-bins, if you ask me. Scavengin', that's what it was."

"Did he mention who he was watching?"

"Quite a number, he said. And he added, you'd be surprised at the things folk did. Medlicott, his landlord, for instance. From what Ronnie let drop, in a casual sort of way, his wife's family weren't too happy about his carryin's-on and were havin' Ronnie to watch him and report. Some other woman, I think. I believe in mindin' my own business, so I didn't press it, though Ronnie was eager for me to do so. A funny chap, Ronnie. He'd keep his doin's secret till he couldn't bear it any more and then he'd start swankin'.

Poor chap, I guess he 'ad to justify himself an' make out how well he were doing. Now he's let on somethin' dangerous and he's left a wife and three little children. He should have took my advice. Still, advice is easy to give an' hard to take ..."

He puffed at his pipe, making little noises of satisfaction at the way it was drawing.

He looked up at Littlejohn almost tenderly.

"You'll see that my girl's done right by, won't you, sir? I'm very fond of that lass. Her mother hasn't been to her all she should be, you see. I'll be quite candid about it. You've no doubt seen for yourself; everybody does. We lost a little boy a long time ago an' since then my wife's not been the same woman."

He looked up at the Inspector again and they both nodded in understanding.

They parted at the door of the flat; Mr. Thewless went inside to take his medicine and Littlejohn climbed the stairs to see Mr. Cuffright. He knocked on the door. There was a lot of scuffling and scurrying in the room behind. The bookie was obviously shifting all the incriminating books and slips, for he had been watching the Inspector from the window.

"Who is it?"

"Police."

More scrimmaging and then the door opened.

"Good morning."

Mr. Cuffright was a heavy, common man with a glowing complexion, crops of pimples all along his collar at the back, a close-clipped head of hair, and a large boozy nose. He was puffing a cigar.

"Come right inside."

Mr. Cuffright was ingratiating. He knew Littlejohn was on the Browning case, so there wasn't much likelihood of any inquiry into his business dealings. All the same, you can't be too careful.

A thick green carpet, a lot of yellow furniture, a closed desk; and a girl with hair the colour of aluminium and a frilly open-necked blouse which showed far too much of her femininity, was working at a typewriter. She paused, looked at herself in a mirror, appeared satisfied that she was presentable after Mr. Cuffright's habitual fondling of her, and then turned to Littlejohn and bared her teeth at him like a dentifrice advertisement.

"You get on with your work, Marlene."

Mr. Cuffright was jealous even of the police. He frequently threatened to swing for Marlene if she proved false.

"And now, sir. What can I do for you? Drink? Get the whisky, Marlene, that's a good girl... No; leave it then, Marlene, the Inspector won't... Get on with your work... Now, sir."

The telephone rang. Mr. Cuffright looked frightened. Probably somebody placing a bet.

"Tell them I'm not in, Marlene. I'll ring back."

She undulated to the telephone followed by Mr. Cuffright's hot, pouched eyes, made movements like those of an Eastern dancer, displaying her various charms one after another, and then speaking in an affected, soothing voice to whoever was calling. Finally, her boss could stand it no more, snatched the instrument from her, and jabbed it down on the hook.

The stuffy air was heavy with expensive scent. Littlejohn wondered if he'd better ask Mr. Cuffright to take a turn in the garden with him, as well!

"Now get on with your work, Marlene."

"It's about the telephone call the other night for Mr. Medlicott. I understand on the evening Mr. Edwin Bunn was murdered, someone rang you up with a message for Mr. Medlicott, sir."

Mr. Cuffright was annoyed and said so.

"Yes, and I was mad about it. Piece of infernal cheek, I called it. Why can't Medlicott get a phone of his own. Me and Marlene were just going out for the evenin'."

The typist thereupon turned to nod approval and at the same time placed on the back of her chair a hand bearing an engagement-ring with a diamond the size of a pea. She breathed on the stone, rubbed it on her blouse, and seemed satisfied that she had shown Littlejohn that the association was perfectly regular. She then began to type again inexpertly with the index of each hand.

"We were just goin' out when the phone rings. Somebody for old Jubal. I 'ad to run upstairs for him. It delayed us a bit. I showed him we weren't too pleased."

"Who was it from?"

"I didn't ask. As a rule, they ring up Miss Mander in the front flat on this floor with the Medlicotts' calls. She's softer than I am. Catch me bein' the telephone exchange for anybody! I'm a business man, I am."

He looked at Marlene to see if she had heard and admired his manliness, but she was engrossed in rubbing something out.

"Was it a man or a woman?"

"Oh, a woman ... Probably one of the Bunn lot. They're always round at one or the other of the family houses. Like a lot of jackdaws congregatin' ... Haw, haw, haw ..."

Nobody else laughed and Mr. Cuffright tugged at his collar.

"Any idea who it might have been, sir?"

"Can't say, I'm sure. Ordinary nondescript sort o' voice. Can't say I ever heard it before."

Littlejohn eyed the telephone.

"You're on the automatic, I see."

"Yes. Thinkin' you might trace the call? Not a chance. It was a local call, I can tell you that, because with the others you usually get the operator's voice first, don't you?"

"And that was all, sir?"

"Yes. Old Medlicott came down after me. In a hurry, he was. Nearly fell downstairs in his hurry."

"You didn't hear what was said, sir?"

"We couldn't help it, but there wasn't much. He listened and kept sayin' *yes,* and then *all right.* Then he hurried off."

"What time would that be?"

"About half-nine, wouldn't it, Marlene?"

"Yes, about nane-thawty. We hed aw ahtdaw things on ... Ay lucked et the clock."

She patted her aluminium waves and bared her teeth again.

"Did you hear Medlicott go out?"

"No. We left right away. I gingered him out. We couldn't wait in all night. Damn' cheek I called it."

And with that, Littlejohn left them to their exotic existence and climbed another staircase to see Mrs. Medlicott again.

Chapter Twelve
Confession

There was a tarnished knocker, a squatting Lincoln Imp, on the Medlicotts' door and it made a ridiculous rapping noise when you manipulated it. Underneath it, a strip cut from one of the tailor's business cards: *Jubal Medlicott*, in a little brass frame.

Mrs. Medlicott timidly opened the door. She expected another importunate creditor and looked relieved to find it was Littlejohn.

"Come in, Inspector."

By daylight the room looked even more shabby and poverty-stricken. The jingling wires of the old piano made a faint strumming echo as they crossed the floor. Here, Ann Medlicott kept solitary house all day from the time her family left in the morning until they came home, tittering and twittering every night. On the back of the door hung a shabby light grey homburg hat, a relic of Jubal's finery.

"Sit down."

She seemed to be waiting for something. Her large blue eyes fixed themselves on Littlejohn's face. She must, when she was young, have been the beauty of the family; a throwback with none of the Bunn ugliness. Even now, there were traces of breeding and good looks in the haggard features.

Life had dealt hardly with her. The clever member of the Bunn family had been ground down, debilitated and aged before her time through worrying, slaving and fretting about Jubal Medlicott. Now she looked in the throes of some wasting disease. Her fingers were long, worn and thin and her hands almost as transparent as paper. Her complexion, the colour of parchment, her hair white, her neck stringy and shrivelled. She had a tired, worn-out walk. And all the time, knowing that without her Jubal Medlicott would go to the wall, she struggled, smiled, and pretended she was all right.

Littlejohn took it all in as he looked at the woman sitting opposite and the poverty-stricken tidy room in which she and her brood lived. She wore a shapeless grey frock with a cameo brooch pinned on her breast. Littlejohn found himself vaguely wondering why the brooch hadn't gone where the rest of the family finery had probably vanished, the pawnshop, until, when the light caught it, he was able to make out that it was a fake made of plastic and pinchbeck.

There was a portable sewing-machine on the table and a lot of cotton and pins. A portion of the cotton nightdress Mrs. Medlicott had been machining still protruded from under the newspaper with which she'd tried to conceal it.

A train rushed through the cutting and into the tunnel just outside. The house shook, the piano played a ghostly melody, and a cloud of steam slowly rose before the window and vanished into the blue.

"You remember the other evening when I was here, Mrs. Medlicott? I asked about your husband's movements on the night your brother was killed. You said Mr. Medlicott was indoors, here, all the time."

Anne Medlicott threw him an anxious look.

"Yes."

"That wasn't true, was it?"

She changed colour from parchment to grey and clutched her throat.

"What do you mean?"

"He has already told me the truth. He was out, in answer to what he tells me was a bogus telephone call."

Her colour came slowly back. She looked a bit relieved. In fact, Littlejohn could have sworn Jubal Medlicott had already confessed to her that he'd told Littlejohn that his alibi was a fake.

"Who told you that, Inspector?"

"Your husband."

She nodded her head.

"But he didn't kill my brother. I do assure you he didn't. He couldn't have done."

"Why?"

"Because I did it."

She said it quite calmly, her chin quivering, her lips tight.

"You!"

It sounded so stupid, but Littlejohn couldn't help marvelling at the love of some women. A frivolous, good-for-nothing of a husband, who'd squandered all the money which could have made her comfortable, dragged her down to living a sordid existence in an attic, made her the poor relation of the Bunns, betrayed her with other women ... And now, because Jubal's alibi had been broken, she was prepared to shield him further by confessing to the murder she thought they suspected him of committing.

"Why did *you* do it, Mrs. Medlicott?"

Littlejohn said it quietly and tolerantly, like humouring a child, but she was intensely serious.

"I wanted my brother's money ... the trust funds, I mean. I'm tired of living this poor existence and the money would have made such a difference to all of us. I just couldn't bear it any longer, so I went and killed Ned. He was always mocking my husband; I had no compunction."

"You entered the shop..."

"I have a key. I'll show it to you. Ned gave it to me when I nursed his wife in her last illness. I kept it. As a matter of fact, several of us have keys. You see, the lock hasn't been changed since we were all at home in the old days. We all had keys then and I suppose they weren't all given up. In any case, I did it."

"You shot him dead with a revolver?"

She smiled as though expecting that one.

"Yes. I used to sell them in the shop when I worked there. We had a little range in the cellar and I could shoot as well as my brothers... Better, in fact."

"And Browning... Did you kill him, too, Mrs. Medlicott?"

"Yes. He used to insult my husband. I could bear it no more. He even followed him around, spying on him."

"What kind of insults?"

That got her to the quick. A spasm of pain crossed her tired face, now flushed unhealthily from her efforts to convince Littlejohn.

"Just insults..."

Littlejohn didn't wish to rub salt in a raw wound, but there was nothing else for it.

"Were you thinking of divorcing your husband, Mrs. Medlicott?"

Another spasm of pain. It was obvious she knew all about Jubal and what people said of him.

"Whatever gave you that idea, Inspector? It's preposterous."

"Just that Mr. Browning seemed, as you say, to be spying on your husband. That's the kind of thing matrimonial detectives do. Browning seems to have followed that occupation as a sideline."

Her face was stubborn; the typical Bunn look.

"Well, I didn't set him on my husband to spy, I can assure you. That's unthinkable."

The confession was just too absurd to follow up. Littlejohn wanted news of more important things.

"Who rang up your husband on the night your brother died?"

"One of his friends was supposed to do so. It turned out to be a false call. Mr. Cuffright came up about half-past nine to bring my husband to the telephone. Jubal took the message and went, as asked, to his friend's office. The place was closed. It must have been a prank; Browning might even have done it."

"Who was the friend?"

She caught her breath and looked afraid.

"I don't know... I didn't ask..."

It was obvious she knew, but Littlejohn hadn't the heart to press it.

"Let us get this straight, Mrs. Medlicott. In the first place, I don't think you killed your brother..."

"But, I tell you..."

"Let me speak, please. You think your husband killed him. He was out of the house on a rough and rainy night without any excuse or alibi. You think he killed Ned Bunn for the trust money. Your husband's creditors are pressing. He's almost ruined, isn't he? To shield him, you take the blame. I can't allow you to do that. It isn't fair, Mrs. Medlicott. Besides, I very much doubt if your husband *did* commit the crime. There's quite a long list of eligibles, you know. The large Bunn family and many more besides. I shall ignore your confession for the time being."

The blue eyes flashed. She thought he was trying to trap her.

"At your own risk, Inspector. I don't withdraw a word of it. Because it's true ..."

Littlejohn leaned back in the old-fashioned armchair. It was comfortable, in spite of its age.

"Do you mind if I smoke, Mrs. Medlicott?"

She looked surprised. She'd expected being taken to the lock-up.

"Of course."

He took out his pouch and started to fill his pipe.

"Who was Ned Bunn's father, Mrs. Medlicott? Did you ever know him?"

She suddenly seemed to leave the present as the past reared its head. A woman who, to forget the sordid day-to-day existence, spent as much of life as she could in the old, better times.

"His name was Jukes ... Fred Jukes. He was a friend of my Uncle Walter Wood, the lawyer. Ned was a small boy when my own father married my mother, who had given Ned her own surname, of course. Father insisted on changing it to Bunn when he married my mother."

"What happened to Fred Jukes, Mrs. Medlicott?"

Littlejohn didn't need to ask. Mrs. Medlicott was full speed astern into the past.

"He was killed in 1914 ... the first months of the war. I told you of dark things which happened in this house. That was one of them, Inspector. Fred Jukes went to Australia, leaving my mother to bear his child, later Ned Bunn. Then, when war broke out, he volunteered, came to England, and, dressed in khaki, sought out my mother. There was a dreadful scene here. My father came home and found him. He knew all about the way Jukes had once betrayed my mother ... There was a fight and people had to intervene. Strangely enough, my mother seems to have defended Jukes. She must have loved him still ..."

She said it in a thrilled whisper, her eyes alight with excitement.

"We were all at home, then, and I remember our all crowding round the door of the drawing-room listening to the harsh voices of the men abusing one another and my mother sobbing. I remember my father saying Jukes could take my mother and her brat with him and he never wanted to see them again. And my mother crying out, 'Jerry, Jerry ... Your heart ...' My father had a bad heart ... And my father shouting 'Damn my heart; what does it matter ...?'"

Littlejohn could see it all; the gloomy house, *Whispers;* the brawling of the jealous men over a woman; the children crowding round the door; the woman weeping and bewildered; and then ...

"It all ended rather tamely. Fred Jukes went, and got killed a month later. My father seemed to think my mother loved Jukes all the time and, after that, kept to his own room and sought feminine company elsewhere ..."

And with that the gentle Mrs. Medlicott rose and for no apparent reason confided in Littlejohn.

"You can't tell me anything about men and their ways, Inspector. I'm not the innocent little woman I might appear to be. I have lived through it all. The last years of my father's life, the stupid intrigues of my brothers, the wild ways of my uncles. Let anyone *dare* cast aspersions on my husband. I can bear it. I come from a family of rakes and loose-living women ... Yes, the women, too. They only grew good and pious when their looks gave out ... Let nobody point the finger ..."

Littlejohn knew that in a fumbling almost incoherent way, she was holding up Medlicott's end, defending him.

"... But that wasn't all. My father changed his will. That's why he left Ned's money in trust. Ned had been like his own son and he was fond of him, but he couldn't leave him equal with us in the inheritance. He simply left an income to Ned and the capital came to us when Ned died. My mother always said it was done to set the rest against Ned. Perhaps she was right... It caused his murder, didn't it? It made me kill him to get the money..."

She was still sticking to her confession. Littlejohn ignored it.

"Did your father, or your mother, die first?"

"My father. Twelve months after Jukes went to the war and was killed. In those twelve months, he painted the town red. Had he gone on, there would have been no money left for the family. He was bent, it seemed, on squandering his fortune. He actually brought home one of his women one night... here... I told you this house could tell tales... My mother met them in the hall; there was a terrible row. She ordered the woman out, of course; and she went, quickly, too. Then, she told my father she had never loved him, but that she, too, like the strumpet she'd just turned back on the street, simply wanted his money. After the quarrel my father went to his own bedroom and they found him dead the following morning, in bed, from an overdose of laudanum... They said it was suicide, but there was also a rumour that my mother poisoned him. That was very likely. It served him right. It also prevented him cutting Ned right out of his will. Ned was my mother's darling. She loved him more than all the rest of us put together. You see, he was not a Bunn. He was the child of her one true love."

"How old was Ned at the time?"

"Nineteen... My father's death kept him out of the army. The tribunal gave him exemption. The engineering side of the business was then active and Ned was in it. My mother died at the end of the war. I think she never stopped loving Ned's father, or ever forgave my own father for what he said about him the time he called here."

It went on and on, like a gothic novel; the sombre house, the drama inside it, the tragedies, the loves and hates of the Bunn clan, and the last of them, living on her memories, penniless in one of the garrets and the rest of the house let off in a lot of little hutches to people like Browning and Cuffright and Miss Mander.

Heavy footsteps on the stairs. As if completely to destroy the atmosphere, the milkman had called. A huge fellow with a cap over his large ears and an overcoat a size too small for him. He entirely filled the doorway and started to argue in a loud voice.

"No more milk. You owe me fourteen shillings..."

"But I have to get the money from my husband. He didn't..."

"He never does... Look 'ere, I'm sorry for you, Mrs. Medlicott, but I got a wife and fambly, too..."

Littlejohn looked at the tired hands, the pleading face, the humble attitude of the little woman, and the insolent pleasure of the lout in the cap. He took two ten-shilling notes from his pocket.

"Here... And now, get out..."

The man gingerly put the two bottles he was holding on the mat, keeping his eyes on Littlejohn all the time, as though if he looked away the Inspector would help him down the stairs with his foot. "Remember, you still owe them six shillings worth of milk..."

"Yes, sir. Certainly, sir."

The heavy feet descended two at a time down the resounding staircase, the piano now playing incidental music on all wires.

"You shouldn't, Inspector. We'll pay you back."

Littlejohn didn't know why he did it. There didn't seem anything else he could do. Somehow, it seemed like browbeating a child and he couldn't stand for it.

"Are you taking me with you to the police-station?"

"I beg your pardon, Mrs. Medlicott?"

"The murder, you know. I did it. I killed Ned and ..."

Littlejohn looked down at her from his full six-feet-one.

"Now, you know you didn't, Mrs. Medlicott. So why complicate the case for us? You're only shielding your husband. I don't think *he* did it, either. So what's the use?"

"Have you proof he didn't?"

"Let me answer by another question. Do *you* believe him guilty?"

"No, I don't."

She thrust out her face doggedly.

"Very well, then. Neither do I. *You* didn't do it and I don't think Mr. Medlicott did. Agreed?"

She smiled, looked relieved, and thrust out her worn hand.

"I trust you, Inspector, and I didn't do it, either. I'm sorry I wasted your time and told lies."

"Don't do it again, then," said Littlejohn, and they both laughed.

CHAPTER THIRTEEN
THE ARRIVAL OF BATHSHEBA BUNN

REWARD OF £500 FOR BUNN KILLER

The large headlines in the morning papers were a bit ambiguous, but everybody knew what they meant. On the day after the funeral, Elmer Bunn, a descendant of emigrants from the Melton Mowbray branch of the family to El Paso, Texas, and a millionaire cattle-king into the bargain, had, on receiving the news of the murder by cable, immediately wired to Enderby:

> offer 1500 dollars for apprehension murderer edwin bunn stop will send pinkerton agent if required stop reply at once stop.
>
> elmer bunn.

Now there lived in Melton Mowbray, an incredibly old and wealthy Bunn called Bathsheba, and she was the ultimate matriarch, a spinster even more formidable than Sarah Wilkins. She was eighty-eight and, at the age of sixty-five, had retired to bed. Thence, she directed family affairs, receiving a heavy mail every morning from Bunns who hoped one day to come into her fortune, in full possession of every scrap of family news, entirely aware of all that went on in Melton Mowbray, and from her headquarters on a rubber super-mattress directing by telephone and ukase all the vital operations of the clan. She took Elmer Bunn's offer, without her consent, as an act of *lèse majesté* and said at once that she was getting up. The news was immediately confirmed by the arrival at the agitated Jasper Bunns' of two heavy tin trunks, a large wicker basket, a bath-chair, a rubber mattress, two crated cats and a parrot in a cage. The family all hoped the adventure would put paid to Bathsheba and release another quarter of a million for distribution.

At noon the same day, a large barouche bearing Aunt Bathsheba arrived in Enderby. She was heavily clothed from head to foot, with only the face of what looked like a very ancient bulldog visible. They almost expected her to bark and many people were surprised when she began to articulate in perfect Queen's English. She ordered herself to be immediately wheeled in her bath-chair to the police-station by her house-boy, a comparatively young man of seventy-eight and obviously on his last legs. En route, they halted wherever two or three were gathered together and Aunt Bathsheba announced to them in a loud, rasping voice that a reward of £2,000 would be paid to anyone giving information resulting in the apprehension of Edwin Bunn's murderer. "And don't you be taking any notice of American offers not authorized by the family. Support the old country. God Save the Queen." Everybody agreed that it was their duty to be patriotic, except a local crank who talked about dollar exports, was subsequently certified as a lunatic, and removed from circulation in a plain van ...

A cable was sent to El Paso:

everything in hand stop arrest imminent stop reward
and extra detectives not necessary stop writing stop

bathsheba bunn full stop

"You see what you're up against," said Edgell the lawyer
to Littlejohn.

They had been discussing the past history of the Bunn
family, particularly the tragedy and death of Jerry Bunn.

"I can assure you that Fred Jukes and all his line have
faded out. As for the death of Jeremiah Bunn... well... only
the chemist who sold the laudanum could tell you how much
he sold and to whom he sold it. He died years ago. Hanged
himself when on the verge of bankruptcy. It might be an
even bet that Jerry Bunn's affronted wife gave him an overdose to protect her own and her child's inheritance. Your
guess is as good as mine. I think we'd all be a bit surprised
if we knew the inner history of a lot of the sudden deaths
certified as being due to natural causes."

Mr. Edgell was standing before the small fire in the little
fireplace of his disorderly private office. His grey appearance was more than usually dishevelled and he had egg on
the corner of his mouth. It was as though the Bunn estate
and the legal demands it was making upon him had driven
everything else from his mind.

"And who told you all about the affair of Fred Jukes,
Inspector? I hope you've not been unduly bothering Mrs.
Medlicott... She's the only one who keeps up interest in the
history of the Bunns and she's not in good health. So trouble her as little as you can, if you please."

He passed his thin, dry hand through his mop of grey
hair, scratched his crown, and with a quick movement sat
down at his overcrowded desk and began to rummage
among the masses of papers on the top.

"I've been running over a list of the family and others who might have profited by the death of Ned Bunn...or Wood, as he prefers to call himself. I must confess that few of them would have any reason to go so far. There are the near relatives in this town...All well provided for, with the exception of the Medlicotts, who are in low water, I admit. As for the members outside Enderby...Who can imagine them coming all the way from Melton Mowbray, or even farther afield on a night like that to commit murder...?"

Littlejohn cast a quick glance in Edgell's direction.

"I've known it happen, sir. I've known people travel from one end of the country to the other for such a purpose, in even worse circumstances. A murderer, fired by his task, doesn't bother much about a drop of rain or a gale."

Edgell shrugged his narrow shoulders.

"Have it your own way, Littlejohn. I was going to add, too, that Ned was a bit of a ladies' man. There may be some motive there. A wronged husband, an angry father...But even then...Murder on such a count is very rare. I'm bound to say that, all things considered, I don't like the way things look for Medlicott. If, as you've been telling me, he was out of doors and can't say properly where, at the time Bunn was shot, things seem even blacker. He's at his wits' end for money and he's often been heard to complain about the trust which keeps his wife out of her inheritance till Ned dies..."

Edgell's face grew grave, a couple of bright pink spots appeared over his cheek-bones, and he sat tapping the finger-tips of one hand against those of the other, his elbows resting on the desk.

"I'd be grateful, in the circumstances, if you'd have me there if you come to question him further. I'd like you to advise him to make any statements only in front of his lawyer. After all, I'm a friend of the family and I have the welfare of all of them at heart."

Littlejohn nodded.

"Quite reasonable, sir."

"You see, Inspector, Medlicott's a perfect fool. It would be like him to go and impulsively shoot his brother-in-law and equally like him to make some stupid statement or take some quixotic stand and incriminate himself. I'm not suggesting for a moment he did kill Ned. As likely as not, Medlicott was out chasing some woman or other on the night in question and has a stupid notion he's protecting her or else saving his wife's feelings... You understand?"

"Certainly, sir. I'll bear it in mind."

Heavy footsteps were heard outside, the door was flung open without more ado, and there stood Aunt Sarah on the mat. She was panting hard and heaving from her efforts. She completely filled the doorway and behind her could be seen the face of the girl clerk from the outer office, her jaws still champing on her chewing-gum.

"This young woman tried to stop me coming in before she brought my name to you... I don't wait for anybody, Simon Edgell, and no little chit's stopping me from seeing you when I choose. Good morning to you, young man."

"Good morning, Mrs. Wilkins."

Every male under sixty was a young man to Aunt Sarah. She stood there for a moment, recovering her breath and sucking hard at a glucose drop. She was loud in her complaints that the Fearnses didn't feed her properly and between meals ate packets of digestive biscuits, boxes and cartons of chocolates, and bags of boiled sweets.

"And why don't you have your offices on the ground floor, instead of two flights up? It isn't good enough to old folks. I wonder you've the strength to climb 'em yourself, Simon, a man of your feeble constitution."

"Sit down, Sarah…"

"Don't try to change the subject."

She bumped down hard on the largest chair, clasped her hands over the crutch-head of her ebony stick, and put her chin on her hands. She ground the sweet in her mouth between her teeth, swallowed it, licked her blue lips and then suddenly sat back.

"I suppose you've heard that Bathsheba's in town and offering a ridiculous reward for Ned's murderer. I'd feel like making an auction sale of it and offering *three* thousand, just to best her, only the whole thing's silly. It's got to stop. It's bringing the family into disrepute, as well as casting a slur on the police. As if they weren't able to get the job done properly without being given a bonus! Not that I wouldn't like the Inspector's nice young assistant to win the two thousand, just to spite Bathsheba; but, no… it's got to stop. You've got to stop it, Simon, or else I'll have to take a hand."

Edgell ruffled his hair with his fingers.

"I can't do anything, Sarah. Bathsheba won't take my advice. You know what she's like once she's roused. After twenty years in bed, this murder's put her on her feet again. It's not likely that…"

Aunt Sarah thumped her stick on the floor and they could hear people start shouting and scurrying about in the room below because it had brought down some plaster from the ceiling.

"Very well. I'll see her then."

She pointed a swollen finger at Littlejohn.

"And I'd be obliged if you'd leave us now, Inspector. What I've called to see Edgell about doesn't concern the crime at all. It's family business and it's private. So, if you don't mind ..."

Littlejohn gave way, rose, and took up his hat and coat.

"I was just going in any case. Good day to you both."

He had hardly closed the door before the pair of them had their heads together and their voices rumbled in conference. The girl in the outer office let him out and cast an admiring glance at him. The steps down were dark and the staircase smelled of dust and dry-rot. An arrow pointed to the rooms above. *Madame Cecile, Palmist.* The floor below Edgell's chambers was occupied by a moneylender. *Lighthouse Credit Company. Loans from £5 to £10,000. Walk Right In.* A man carrying a brush and dust-pan was following the last injunction. He was going to sweep up the debris which had fallen from the ceiling.

Littlejohn stood at the door of the chambers, which adjoined a multiple tailors'. *The Natty Tailors. 400 Branches.* Across the way was a small hat shop with a solitary model on a stand in the window. A creation in white of material like blotting-paper, with a veil of net clinging mistily to it. As Littlejohn looked at it, a woman coiled herself from the waist upwards through the black velvet curtains which formed the background for the hat, and thrust a second masterpiece in view. This time it was an object in green felt, shaped like a parson's hat with a pheasant's feather rakishly thrust through the black band. A number of women shopping or passing by in the market square converged from all directions before the new piece of headgear and stood adoring it ecstatically, like worshippers witnessing a miracle.

Littlejohn recognized the woman in the window. It was Miss Mander, the blonde tenant of Medlicott's flats. He crossed and entered the shop, followed by the eyes of curious townspeople, many of whom looked ready to follow him in.

A very small shop, with a little counter, broad shelves for hats, a chair, a large cheval mirror and a lot of little ones here and there. There was a door behind, which led into quarters for the shop-girl. The place was stuffy and smelled of exotic perfume. Scattered about, more hats, frail and inviting, on stands.

Out of her negligée and neatly dressed in a black skirt, white blouse, sleek hose, expensive high-heeled shoes, Miss Violet Mander was, physically, a beauty. Tall, well-developed, with long, white arms and ruby finger-nails. A flawless pink complexion with chubby cheeks, a rounded chin, straight nose and small ears from which hung little pearls on golden chains; china-blue eyes with a perpetual look of vacant, childlike innocence. A narrow, shallow forehead, its defects cunningly hidden by beautiful light golden hair, which swept back in superb waves.

Miss Mander was walking from the room behind when the Inspector entered. She had another little hat on her clenched fist and looked first at Littlejohn and then at the tiny creation of pink felt and tulle as though surprised to find them both where they were.

"Good afternoon, Inspector."

Miss Mander smiled. It was the smile of a little girl in a religious procession who recognizes a relative among the crowds lining the route.

They talked across the counter, Miss Mander unconsciously caressing and stroking the felt of the hat like a cat.

"Do you remember the night I called to telephone at your flat?"

"Yes. When Mr. Browning was killed."

"That's right."

She was surrounded by a faint aura of heady, expensive perfume, probably erotically named and from Paris.

"Did you see anyone about on the stairs after I came down from the Medlicotts' flat? You remember, as I was talking with Browning at the outer door, you came out from your flat for a moment and then went in again."

Littlejohn didn't mention the man who was with her and who hurried in as well, but the large blue eyes betrayed no embarrassment. Rather did Violet Mander seem to be having difficulty throwing back her mind to the occasion.

Suddenly, she began to look surprised, as though her brain had given up some information she little expected. The eyes grew wider than ever, the thin delicate eyebrows rose, her mouth opened slightly and she gulped.

"Well ... ?"

"I ... er ... yes."

"Who was it?"

She looked hesitant and uneasy.

"I couldn't be sure, because the light on the stairs was bad."

"Who did you think it was, then?"

"Mr. Medlicott ... I think he was in a dressing-gown. He hurried down and past the door."

"When, exactly? Before or after you saw me and Mr. Browning talking below?"

She gulped again, an attractive movement of the throat and shoulders, like a good child obediently taking a dose of medicine.

"After. You went away and Mr. Browning went in his flat and shut the door. Then Mr. Medlicott came down, looked out of the front door, and went out, too."

It all seemed clear. Miss Mander had been bobbing in and out of her flat, watching to see if the coast was clear for her visitor to get away, and people had persisted in coming and going and spoiling it all.

"Did you hear Mr. Medlicott come back up the stairs?"

"I can't say for certain. No...You see, I wasn't looking and listening on the landing *all* the time. You couldn't expect me to be, could you?"

Of course you couldn't! Littlejohn could have laughed outright at the comic situation going on inside Miss Mander's flat. The anxious guest, eager to get away; the whispering, the listening at the door, the peeping, the tiptoeing, the annoyed impatience...

"No, of course not, Miss Mander. And what happened next?"

"You called to telephone."

She looked childishly pleased about that, as though delighted by the recollection of their first meeting, with the "mice" rustling in the large wardrobe.

"Thank you, Miss Mander. You've been a great help."

"I'm so glad."

And she looked it!

Across the way as Littlejohn left the shop, he saw Aunt Sarah, her taxi patiently waiting for her, talking with a tall, seedy-looking, thin man of a middle-eastern cast of features, like a carpet-pedlar. He obsequiously shook hands with her, supported her as she squeezed herself in the vehicle, which tipped dangerously to receive her, and then went indoors to an office in an old Georgian house. There were three plates on the door jamb. *Borough of Enderby, Planning Dept. Midshire County, Rodent Officer. J. Habakkuk, Solicitor.* The oily carpet hawker might have been either a shady lawyer or a rat-catcher, but presumably was the former. And what had the formidable Mrs. Wilkins been doing with Mr. Habakkuk, a professional rival of Mr. Simon Edgell?

Littlejohn strolled to the police station and was surprised to find, judging from the decrepit and now familiar taxi and weedy driver, that Aunt Sarah had got there before him. He paused on the threshold of the Inspector's room to listen to the hubbub of conversation going loudly on behind the closed door.

"You know very well, Bathsheba..."

And a much milder voice, almost whining...

"I only wanted to help..."

"You might have killed yourself and then where would we all be...?"

Littlejohn knocked and entered. It was like another comic scene from a theatre.

Bathsheba Bunn, cowering in her bath-chair with the ancient retainer hanging anxiously over her, and Aunt Sarah towering above her, angry and purple, her ebony stick raised aloft to emphasize her arguments. On the fringe, Cromwell on his feet, a smirk of amusement on his face, his hands in his pockets, and his hat on the chair behind him. Inspector Myers, sitting at his desk with a red face and a look of angry frustration.

Aunt Sarah turned to greet Littlejohn, her stick still in the air.

"Come in, young man. You might as well hear this, too, as it concerns you and an aspersion concerning your ability to solve this case and find out Edwin's murderer."

Poor Browning was a mere sideline; nobody seemed to be bothering about who'd throttled *him!*

"This old and obstinate lady has been in bed and at death's door for nearly thirty years."

The bundle of old clothes in the bath-chair became agitated, groaned and trembled, and the ancient bulldog face protruding from it grew pathetic with fear.

"She's thought fit to get up at the risk of her life and to the grief of her large retinue of fond relations to come all the way here abusing the police and offering large rewards for nothing."

"I only wanted to help, Sarah; you can't say I didn't ..."

"I've told her to pack up and get off back to Melton Mowbray and bed before she takes her death of exhaustion and cold."

"I'm going, Sarah. I said I would and I will."

Littlejohn realized that he was witnessing a battle royal for the headship of the Bunn clan, like those momentous tussles for the queenship of the herd by proud cows in the Swiss valleys! And Aunt Sarah had, once and for all, established her superiority.

Mrs. Wilkins made an imperial gesture with her stick, the attendant policeman opened the door, the house-boy heaved and shoved for a minute without success, and finally got the bath-chair in a state of momentum. Aunt Bathsheba was wheeled out to her barouche which, with cats, parrot, tin and wicker receptacles and rubber bed, at once started the return trip to Melton Mowbray, where she still lives, more tenacious of life than ever as she plots the overthrow of her rival, Sarah, and prays three times a day for her speedy death.

Aunt Sarah lowered her stick, switched off her hearing contraption, marched to the door, and was hoisted in triumph in her shabby taxi-cab.

As she left the room, she cast upon Cromwell a delighted, arch smile.

"The reward's off! I like you, young man, and I won't have any friend of mine insulted by meddling old busybodies. Reward, indeed! Two thousand pounds of good Bunn money down the drain! What do we pay rates for?"

Cromwell, perspiring, the colour of a lobster again under the ironic eye of his chief, sat down heavily and flattened out his hat.

CHAPTER FOURTEEN
THE MAN IN WHITE SPATS

The Browning inquest was short enough. Poor Browning might have been an interloper trying to steal the limelight from the Bunn show. Nevertheless, news having travelled fast in this case, the court was crowded. The tribes of Bunn were absent, with the exception of the Medlicotts and Aunt Sarah. Jubal was called as a witness in case of need. He did not testify, for short of the formalities necessary to allow the victim to be buried, no other evidence was taken and the hearing was adjourned. Aunt Sarah was present and arrived like royalty, causing a lot of commotion, keeping a close eye on Medlicott, who, to her disgust, had brought all his family to bear him up, punctuating the proceedings with interjections, grunts, heavy breathing and thuds of her stick on the wooden floor. Mr. Edgell was there, but arrived late, even later than the Medlicotts, who were well behind time, as usual. Mr. Green was on holiday and his deputy, a young, precise and busy lawyer, had other things to do. The whole business was short and sweet and the audience melted away after it, with disappointed remarks and pointed expressions about the soul-less machinery of the law.

After lunch, Littlejohn again toiled up the stairs of *Whispers* to the Medlicotts' flat. He could almost have cut the noisome fetid air of the staircase. Inside the tenements, sounds of housework, crying children, quarrelling, the inexpert sound of Marlene's typing in Cuffright's rooms. A large squad of relatives had arrived to sustain Mrs. Browning. The rumble of their talk in the ground-floor flat rose like a dull chant. They were burying the victim later that afternoon. Men in black suits and bowlers, crowded out from the Brownings' rooms, strolled in the grounds, like gloomy patients in a sanatorium, muttering among themselves, examining the decrepit buildings and sour gardens, making critical comments about them. The vicar arrived just on Littlejohn's heels and the mourners slowly filtered indoors.

Mrs. Medlicott, in the absence of her family, who had gone from the inquest straight to the shop, had just finished a late lunch. The remnants of a small meat pie, tea things, and a few crusts of bread littered the tray which she hastily removed as she let in the Inspector.

"I'm sorry to disturb you again, Mrs. Medlicott, but I didn't manage to catch you at the inquest. One or two more points have arisen and I must ask you about them."

"Sit down."

A slow goods train passed in the cutting under the window. The house shook, the piano clanged, a pall of black smoke from the engine rose and momentarily blotted out the view.

"On the night Browning died and just before I returned to ask about the telephone, your husband went downstairs and out in the grounds clad in his dressing-gown. That is so, isn't it, Mrs. Medlicott?" She hesitated.

"Yes. That is true. None of us said it wasn't, did we?"

"No. But nothing was said *about* it, either. How was your husband dressed when he went out that night?"

She paused again.

"You left us just as it was time to go out to my sister's. My husband took off his jacket, waistcoat, collar and tie. Then, he decided he wanted another word with you. He put on his dressing-gown and went as if to follow and catch you... Instead, he found you at the front door, talking with poor Mr. Browning. He waited till you separated, went down, and came back at once saying you'd got away quickly."

"Yet, when I returned, close on his heels, he was putting on a pair of trousers and the dressing-gown was nowhere to be seen. I assumed he hadn't been out since I left. What did he want to see me for?"

"He didn't say. But he seemed uneasy about something."

She paused and her jaw began to quiver.

"You're not thinking that my husband ran down and murdered Mr. Browning, are you? Jubal wouldn't hurt a fly."

She, his principal victim, stood there gallantly defending her good-for-nothing husband as though he were the last man on earth to commit a sin of any kind.

Below, they were forming-up for the funeral. The hearse had arrived with the body from the morgue and the mourners were packing themselves in the vehicles behind it with the assistance of the undertaker, who, like a sepulchral toast-master, intoned their names in a loud, hollow voice which echoed round the staircase.

"Mrs. Browning, Mr. and Mrs. Tom Browning, Master John Browning and the Reverend Canon Rumbole, *if you please...*"

"Ar... Mr. and Mrs. Golightly, Mr. and Mrs. Cook and Master Cook, Mr. Bernard Shaw..."

Looking down from the window on the foreshortened view of the cortège, Littlejohn watched the last-called bearer of a great name—a small, red-cheeked man and a representative of the French-Polishers' Union—nimbly climb in a cab and crack a joke with those inside. ... He turned to Mrs. Medlicott who had taken up a heavily-darned pair of man's socks and was threading a needle with which to add still more darns to them.

"The other evening when I called, you were mending a pair of spats, Mrs. Medlicott."

She seemed surprised.

"Yes? I do all the mending for the family."

"What was wrong with the spats, may I ask?"

She laid down the socks in bewilderment. This was a funny sort of crime investigator. Surely...

"I was fastening on the strap which had broken."

"Did you finish the job?"

"No ..."

She stopped.

"What funny questions you do ask, Inspector. I wouldn't have thought a pair of spats was important."

"It's very important, indeed, madam. That's why I'm asking you. Why didn't you finish?"

"They were too far gone. The leather of the strap was rotten. It broke more as I stitched it. I'll show it to you."

The pair of bedraggled white spats—Jubal's finery— were in the workbox at Mrs. Medlicott's feet. She took them out and held the damaged one up for Littlejohn's inspection.

"See?"

"Yes. I suppose your husband had a spare pair and put them on?"

"No. That's why I tried to mend these."

At last! Littlejohn felt that glow of excitement which always filled him when, after a lot of preliminary investigations, he finally struck a trail.

"So, you were repairing ... or trying to repair ... that very pair of spats when I called and your husband hasn't worn them since. Not even on the night I called...not even when he ran downstairs after me in his dressing-gown?"

"No. He had the broken one off and the other on."

Her eyes opened wide and a red spot appeared on each cheek. She felt Littlejohn was making a bit of a fool of her or of Jubal. Jubal and his spats were a local joke!

"Please bear with me another minute, madam. Your husband hasn't worn spats—this pair or any others—since he broke those you're holding now?"

"No. I think I've finally persuaded him to abandon spats. They've long been out of fashion, but it was one of his little foibles. Nobody wears them now. He's the only one in town with them and he seems to think they add a bit of distinction."

"He takes sevens in shoes, doesn't he?"

"That's right."

The sock she was darning fell from her hands and she put her fingers to her mouth with a look of horror.

"Have you found his footprints near one or the other of the scenes of the crimes?"

"Not *his,* exactly, but footprints which might be his. Has your husband any enemies, because, I'll tell you quite candidly, Mrs. Medlicott, I think someone's trying to make it appear that he killed both your brother and Browning?"

"But why? Why? Jubal hasn't any enemies. I'm sure of that. A most friendly and well-liked man...Well-liked by everyone."

"Everyone? Including the members of your own family, Mrs. Medlicott? Do *they* all like him? Don't they rather regard him with bare tolerance?"

She was on her feet to the defence of Jubal. Her loyalty in the face of all that he had done to her was amazing, almost maniacal.

"What do you expect of my family? A lot of cranks and misers. Money means everything to them. Happiness doesn't count. At least, *we're* happy, Jubal and I and the girls ..."

"All the same ... forgive me, if I say it ... don't your family regard your husband as having squandered your own little fortune and reduced you to one of the poorer members ...?"

She smiled; she almost looked proud of it.

"Yes, they do. What is money for but to be spent? Certainly not to be hoarded and left from generation to generation, like the rest of my family do."

The gospel according to Jubal, no doubt! Jubal, the penniless spendthrift, the fancy man in white spats, who had reduced his wife to ill-health and penury by his irresponsibility. And yet, here she was, quick to his defence.

"But I can't think of any of my family trying to fix a murder on my husband. Or killing my brother, Ned. Why?"

"Can't you imagine any member of your family, eager to add to the money he or she already possesses, casting envious eyes on the fortune of Ned Bunn, or more properly, Ned Wood, who was not one of the family at all, really. Bear in mind, part of Ned's fortune was immobilized Bunn money, funds the family resented his having and wanted back. Suppose someone murdered Ned and cast around for a man on whom to pin the crime. Isn't it likely your husband would be chosen?"

"And why Jubal, of all people?"

"Candidly, Mrs. Medlicott, he's known to be on the verge of bankruptcy; he's known to be penniless; he's known to live here in circumstances far removed from those he or his family are accustomed to, simply because his money and your money have run out and until more comes by way of inheritance, there's little chance of improvement. In fact, unless something happens very quickly, this place will have to be sold, too, and you'll all be on the street. Who more likely to commit a crime which will bring a small fortune to you?"

She sat with her head down and tears fell on the stocking she was darning. As she looked up, another train passed, shook all the ornaments on the sideboard, vibrated the crazy piano, and cast another veil of steam across the window ... A train of empty vans ... rub-a-dub-dub ... and then a vast yawning noise as they entered the tunnel. A dog had been locked up somewhere in one of the flats and you could hear him howling dismally.

"I admit it all, Inspector. He might have a very good motive. The shop is finished; we can't make it pay and we owe money everywhere. All my money has gone ... we've lived on it for years now. My family said when I married Mr. Medlicott that I'd never do any good with him. He was a good-for-nothing and would soon go through my money. Times have been bad ... Two wars ... Bad trade. We've not been extravagant and he's not been a spendthrift. We've had the girls to educate ... And all the time the shop has been losing money ... we've kept sinking what we had in that. Out of pride, I guess, just so that the family could not say, I told you so ..."

That was probably about it. Medlicott didn't look like a heavy drinker. Otherwise he'd never have swilled down the cooking sherry the way he did. He didn't seem to smoke either and this place didn't call for much in the way of upkeep. Unless Jubal ran another woman in an establishment which he was financing, he'd spent all his wife's money out of pure stupidity and pig-headedness, keeping alive a dead business because the Bunns had said he couldn't make it pay.

"*Now* it will be all right."

She said it quietly and nodded her head up and down a time or two, as though reassuring herself.

"...I shall get my share of Ned's money...enough to keep us going for quite a long time. My husband can retire...We may sell this place and find a little house away from here...perhaps by the sea...We can live on the capital, because within the next few years surely one or another of our very old relatives will die. Aunt Sarah, Aunt Bathsheba, or Uncle Huxley. Uncle Huxley Bunn has been at death's door several times. He is in a mental home. He was a dentist who doubted his wife's fidelity, gave her gas, and extracted all her beautiful teeth."

Littlejohn suddenly realized that Mrs. Jubal Medlicott was not quite in her right mind! Loneliness, poverty, two twittering girls and an irresponsible husband...They'd driven her into a world of the past where she must have been happy and now she didn't quite know whether she was in a world of reality or one of the shades. Added to that, a large percentage of the Bunns weren't a hundred per cent. mentally. It was probably in the family. Perhaps her confession of murder had some basis in fact, after all. But why frame her husband with it?

Could it be that she was more cunning than appeared and far from doting on Jubal, she hated him and wished him out of the way?

"I'm so sorry..."

The glazed, faraway look faded from her eyes and she inserted the wooden mushroom she was holding into the foot of the sock and began darning again.

"I'm so sorry. My mind dwells so much in the past. I'm alone most of the day and I live with my memories. Perhaps now, with Ned's money, we'll all be together and I won't be so much by myself."

Littlejohn rose to go. There didn't seem anything more to be said.

"I'm sorry if I've upset you a bit, Mrs. Medlicott, but it was necessary. I want as much background as I can get and you seem to be able to give it. I'll try not to bother you again."

"Please don't apologize, Inspector. Your visits are most pleasant and you are very kind. I like to talk to someone about the past, too. They were happy days."

There she was again! It was like throwing a pebble into water. A bit of commotion and upset and then calm as ever. Already she had put away her sewing and was looking chirpily at the clock, waiting for Jubal and the two girls, as though anticipating a whale of a time when they turned in.

A train passed behind, a heavy lorry rumbled in front, the house shook to its very foundations and the piano played. Outside, they were coming back from the funeral. They all seemed a bit gay, as though glad it wasn't any of them they'd left behind at the cemetery. The imprisoned dog howled and scratched for freedom and a blast of fried onions which someone was cooking below rose up the staircase and met Littlejohn as he turned to go.

At the door of *The Freemasons'* Cromwell met the Inspector. He'd been writing up his notes and looked a bit wild-eyed.

"Heard the latest, sir?"

The "latest" met them at the door. A cadaverous, tall man, with red hair, bad teeth, and a Fernandel smile.

"I've had to take charge here. The brewery sent me. No doin' any good with Blowitt. He's locked himself in his room and does nothin' but play the pianner."

No need to tell them that. The furious sounds of one of Liszt's Hungarian Rhapsodies could be heard all over the market square.

"His wife's done a bunk. Run off with a chap who had a bedmakin' works 'ere in Enderby. Left 'im a note to say as he'd 'ad his fling all these years; now it was 'er turn."

The corpse-like man bared his bad teeth and patted them both on the shoulder.

"But don't you worry, gents. Everything'll be O.K., see? That's wot the brewery sent me 'ere for. I'll look after yer."

He clapped his hands together like the custodian of a seraglio, and two new good-looking waitresses materialized and brought in afternoon tea.

Chapter Fifteen
Miss Mander Explains

It was nearing six o'clock when Littlejohn started off for *Whispers* again. The streets were full of workmen and girls returning home and the shops were closing. Night was settling over the dull town, which hadn't a single thing to claim the attention except that, at present, it was in the headlines because two murders had been committed there. Very soon, when all the fuss was over, the place would sink into obscurity again.

Littlejohn thrust his hands deep in the pockets of his raincoat, which he was wearing because it was chilly and there was a thin wind blowing. His pipe was between his teeth. He had run out of his own favourite mixture, had bought some other locally, and it was burning his tongue. On the wind, the smell of malt from the brewery down the street.

There was a light in the hat shop opposite *The Freemasons'*. As Littlejohn stood at the door of the hotel, he saw Violet Mander reach into the window, take out the two model hats, and pull down the blind.

He had postponed a further visit to the Brownings' flat. He was reluctant to worry a bereaved household and, besides, he wanted to give the objectionable Mrs. Thewless time to get to her own home. He was disappointed, however, for the old lady opened the door in answer to his knock.

"Oh, it's you again. You'll have to look sharp. My daughter's just packin' a bag and comin' home with me. You can't expect her to stay 'ere after all that's gone on ..."

She looked annoyed about something and was untidy and half-washed. Her daughter emerged from the bedroom carrying a cheap fibre case, which she put down when she saw Littlejohn. She smiled politely at him.

"You're only just in time, Inspector. Mother insists on taking me home with her and we were just..."

The old woman cut in in a hectoring voice.

"I should just think so. With a murderer hangin' round. You might be the next. You're not stoppin' 'ere on yer own."

They were both in black, which heightened the pallor of the younger woman. Littlejohn rather liked her. A gentle, well-mannered sort of girl, who evidently took after her father. In the full light of the room, she looked very young to have so many children and so much trouble. Mrs. Thewless drew the curtains violently. She was angry at the delay.

"I'm sorry to call at an inconvenient time. I'd no idea you were ..."

Mrs. Browning pointed to a chair.

"Do sit down, please..." And then to her mother, "Would you mind clearing the tea-things, mum, and just rinsing them? We can't leave them like that..."

There were the remnants of a light meal on the table; cups, some scraps of bread and butter, and a jam dish. Mrs. Thewless, more annoyed than ever, scooped them all on a wooden tray and took them in the kitchen. Water started running and they could hear the rattle of dishes being roughly thrown in the washing-up bowl.

"You've come about my husband, sir?"

Her lips began to quiver and she ran to her handbag on the table, took out a handkerchief, and sobbed in it.

"It can wait till later, Mrs. Browning."

She insisted, though.

"I may not be back for a bit. Can you tell me what you want before mother...?"

From the rattle of cups and plates going on, Mrs. Thewless wouldn't be long!

"I just wanted to ask if your husband was interested in anyone else besides Mr. Medlicott? You said he was working as a kind of investigator...Was he looking into the affairs of anyone else?"

She answered at once, without any thought.

"Yes...Miss Mander in the flat above."

And then she blushed.

"Please don't mistake me, Inspector. My husband was only interested in her from a business point of view. You understand...Somebody must have asked him to give them information about her. He was a good husband and father. There was no question of..."

She struggled again with her self-control and regained it. Then she dried her eyes and blew her nose in her little handkerchief.

"Of course...I quite understand, Mrs. Browning."

The outer door was opened and closed. Twittering voices in the hall, and then feet ascending the stairs. Littlejohn paused and listened. It was the Medlicott girls, but he couldn't hear their father's heavier footsteps. He raised a finger at Mrs. Browning, went to the door of the flat, and gently opened it. Polly and Dolly were ascending the dim flight, slowly, because they were talking and gesticulating so much. They turned to each other, waved their hands, pushed one another playfully, giggled and chuckled. They never seemed to take anything seriously.

Littlejohn was back again.

"Did your husband say who employed him on any of his jobs, Mrs. Browning? Or did he ever hint why he was watching these people?"

She had been lost in thought and started at the question. "I beg your pardon?"

He repeated it.

"No. He always kept his own counsel about such things."

She spoke nicely and chose her words well. Littlejohn wondered what she had done before Browning married her.

The old woman was back.

"Come on, now, we've a bus to get."

"Just be putting your hat and coat on, mum. We'll have finished by then."

"I know when I'm not wanted, my girl. But don't come to me if you get yourself in a mess through talkin' too fast to the police."

She had evidently been drinking something in the kitchen, for she hiccupped loudly on her indignant way out.

"I do remember one thing, Inspector. My husband came home one night a bit the worse for drink and said he'd got a job for Mr. Blowitt of *The Freemasons' Arms*. That's how he'd got the drink. Mr. Blowitt must have given it to him as he talked. He never said what it was about, though."

The front door opened, closed, and then opened again. First, light footsteps on the stairs followed by heavier ones, hurrying. Littlejohn gently opened the door of the flat.

Voices whispering. The Inspector looked up the staircase. It was Jubal Medlicott talking softly to Violet Mander, who was struggling with her key in the lock of her own door.

"Don't keep following me. People will see us and talk."

"But Violet..."

Medlicott was pleading, beseeching in a low voice.

"I tell you, no. It's not fair of you to keep pestering me..." Her voice sank out of hearing.

"But... I swear I'll kill myself if you let me down."

"Don't be silly. Can't you see... The police... Leave me alone..."

She slammed the door in his face. She was only an angel when it suited her.

Medlicott seemed to age visibly under the dim landing-light. His shoulders sagged, his head bent and he slowly climbed the remaining stairs, one at a time, like somebody stricken with an illness.

There was a bus-stop in front of *Whispers* and Littlejohn carried Mrs. Browning's case to the gate. She gave him her mother's address in case of need and he wished her well and good-bye.

The old woman remained sulky and hardly spoke.

Then he returned to the flats.

At first there was no answer to his knock and he stood there in the dark passage full of stale air and the cooking smells of evening meals being prepared in the rooms. Bacon, kippers, onions again, and then the whiff of something burning—perhaps milk or a rice pudding—which overwhelmed everything else.

"Who is it?"

The shuffling of slippers across the floor. The voice had a hard, metallic tone. Violet Mander thought it was Medlicott back again.

"Inspector Littlejohn."

"Oh, it's you... Wait a minute please."

The door opened. She had slipped off her costume and appeared in a wrapper and red feathered mules. She gave him a friendly smile and made way for him to enter. This time, she didn't bother to draw the wrapper together and disclosed her firm white throat and bosom, with a thin brassière across it. She spoke with familiarity as though they were pals.

"Come in. I'm just making some coffee." There was a percolator already starting to bubble in the hearth and she hurried in the kitchenette and returned with another cup and saucer.

"You'll have a cup...?"

She seemed naturally tidy and the room was neat and clean. A picture of the Eiffel Tower over the fireplace and a lot of framed photographs on the walls. *Love to Vi from Pablo. To my darling; Monty. All my love, Alf.* Mostly pictures of theatrical fancy-men with superlative expressions of devotion autographed on them.

"You looking at my pictures? I was on the stage for a time. In a repertory company. I was never any good at it."

She handed him the coffee and the movement sent a draught of heavy, exotic, expensive scent in Littlejohn's direction. Then she offered him a cigarette from a silver box. Her china-blue eyes held Littlejohn's as she gave him a light from a lighter and she smiled archly, baring her fine, even teeth. She must have been in her early twenties and had the charm and sophistication of a much older woman. Littlejohn stood by the fireplace, his cup balanced on the mantelpiece. Violet Mander bent with studied art to adjust her slipper and the wrapper opened again.

There was a cord stretched under the mantelpiece and on it, clipped by small spring clothes-pegs, half a dozen nylon stockings. The Inspector gently removed one of the clips, quietly took hold of Miss Mander's wrapper just below the chin, and applied the clip to hold it together.

"Now, suppose we get to business, Miss Mander. This is a professional call, you know."

He smiled at her, but inside he felt rattled that she should try the old technique to avoid a lot of awkward questions.

She pouted and shrugged her shoulders, sat down with a resigned air, and sipped her coffee.

"I saw you with Mr. Medlicott on the stairs, Miss Mander."

"I know you did. I saw you, too."

So that was it! She had something to hide and was trying a diversion.

"Suppose you tell me just how far things have gone between you and your landlord."

"He's rather a dear and a bit of a fool. If he's kissed me now and then, that's as far as it's gone."

The eyes were wide with innocence.

"Was that when he called for the rent?"

She simply pouted and tried to look hurt. There didn't seem to be any anger in her make-up, only pained looks, as when you strike a child for things she hasn't done.

"That's cruel of you, Inspector."

"No, no, no. Let's be truthful. It's better that we should know everything here than have to drag it from you at the adjourned inquests of the murdered men."

Her eyes opened wide again, this time with fear and surprise.

"You don't mean Mr. Medlicott killed...?"

"No. But we have to get to the bottom of the whole business, either quietly or in court. You did have an affair with him, didn't you? Otherwise, why was he pleading and threatening suicide on the stairs a few minutes ago?"

She nodded her head.

"He was very kind to me when I came to Enderby at first. The company I was acting with went bankrupt, I was out of a job, and when I got the place as saleswoman in Mimi's hat shop, I hadn't a bean to call my own. I came here to try to get a flat. Mr. Medlicott befriended me at a time when I badly needed help. He was very kind and pathetically lonely."

"And you don't pay any rent here?"

"I've offered it... I'm trying to get a new flat, but they're hard to get in Enderby. I can't go on like this, now. I'll have to leave town and get a new job if things don't alter. Mr. Medlicott won't leave me alone. It's awkward..."

China-blue eyes, golden hair, innocent ways, in every sense attractive and desirable, yet with a heart of ice and a mind centred on the main chance!

Littlejohn put down his coffee cup.

"Some more?"

"No, thanks."

"You aren't annoyed with me?"

"Why should I be? It's no business of mine, except where it affects my work on these cases. But I do advise you to get out of Enderby when all this is over. Where did you meet Medlicott in the past? Here?"

She was on her feet with the first show of indignation.

"Certainly not! Under his own roof? I'm not that bad."

Littlejohn smiled wryly.

"I don't want to discuss the ethics of it, Miss Mander. Where did you meet, please?"

"At the shop. There's a room behind. I lived there for a few days until I came here. It's too noisy and stuffy at the shop; I couldn't sleep."

The whole house shook convulsively as a large train hurled itself at the tunnel behind. Littlejohn thought of the stuffy stairs, too.

"I agree it's nice to have a home of one's own. Is there a telephone at the shop?"

She looked perplexed.

"Yes. Did you want the number? Enderby 4324."

"Thanks. But I just wanted to ask if on the night Mr. Edwin Bunn was murdered, you telephoned Mr. Medlicott from the shop at half-past nine to ask him to meet you there?"

She was visibly shaken.

"How did you know that?" she whispered.

"Is it true?"

"Yes; but it was called off. He didn't come."

"Why?"

"I cancelled it."

"How? If he'd gone out in answer to your first telephone call, how could you get a message to him?"

She looked bothered. It was a bit too complicated for her simple wits. Her face brightened.

"Mr. Browning called to say it was all right. I needn't bother. I could go home and he'd wait and tell Mr. Medlicott it was a false alarm."

Littlejohn sighed.

"Let's get this quite clear, please. Who asked you to make the call in the first instance, and why?"

"Mr. Browning. He rang me up here and said he must see me right away at the shop. He'd heard Mrs. Medlicott was going to sue for a divorce and that I was involved. I was to ring up Mr. Medlicott and talk it over at the shop."

"And then?"

"A short time after I'd rung, Browning called at the shop again, where I was waiting for Jubal, and said it was all right. The information he'd got was all wrong and I could go home. He said he would be about and would tell Jubal everything was O.K., and that I'd gone."

"And that was all? You went straight home and didn't see Medlicott again that night?"

"That's right."

She looked at the travelling clock on the mantelpiece.

"Will that be all? I have to go out soon."

"How long have you been in Enderby, Miss Mander?"

"Almost two years."

"And all that time you've been in Mimi's shop?"

"Yes."

She screwed up her eyes and studied Littlejohn's face, wondering what he was getting at.

"Who is Mimi, by the way?"

"The shop is owned by a Mrs. Ladbroke of Enderby. She started it herself and it did well. Then, when she married Mr. Ladbroke, she took on an assistant and only came to the shop for an odd hour or two during the day."

"And how did you get the job? Through an advertisement?"

"No. I was recommended."

"By whom?"

She looked at the clock again.

"Could we talk whilst I change into my evening clothes? I'm due out in twenty minutes. I can leave the door of my bedroom open."

"Very well."

She took down the stockings from under the mantel-piece, opened the cupboard in which the "mice" had per-formed on the first night Littlejohn called, took from it a black evening gown on a hanger, and with a parting smile, entered a little room to the right, presumably her bedroom, and left the door open. Littlejohn could hear the bed behind the door creak as she sat on it and then she seemed to take off her slippers and fling them down. A pair of stockings flew from where she was sitting and landed on a bedroom chair within sight through the doorway.

"Who recommended you to Mimi?"

There was a pause. There seemed to be running water and a basin in the bedroom, for there came the sound of a tap and then the splashing of a sponge or something.

"What did you say, Inspector?"

"Who got you the job at Mimi's?"

"Mr. Edwin Bunn."

So! Now that they had reached dangerous ground, she preferred to give her answers out of sight, like a penitent in a confessional-box. There was silence in the bedroom as she waited for Littlejohn's reaction and next question.

"Put your dressing-gown on again, decently, and come here, Miss Mander."

"But I..."

"Never mind your boy-friend. This is more important. Please do as I ask you."

She reappeared, combing her hair as she walked. She was gathering up her negligée and had changed into black underwear. She had washed off all her make-up and even then, her skin was clear and flawless. Her cheeks were quite pale and this gave her added attraction if she'd only known it. She seemed to have everything: fine figure, good looks, a teasing smile, voluptuous, animated... Everything except brains and heart. A lovely, empty, greedy...

Littlejohn paused in his thought, at a loss for a word. He had a faithful bitch waiting anxiously for his return and the term to him was one of high respect.

"Sit down and answer my questions."

"How did you come to be associated with Edwin Bunn?"

She looked as innocent as ever, but there was a trace of cunning in her look. She didn't wish to be mixed-up in the local scandal of Ned Bunn's murder.

"It was quite simple, Inspector. I was with a repertory company at Melton Mowbray. They'd been touring but only lasted a short time at their last place. In the end, the organizers couldn't pay us our salaries. News got out and that brought the creditors along. Mr. Bunn was one of the largest creditors. He'd supplied the theatre and the production with fittings. He arrived with his solicitor and he met the players, too. He was rather kind to us all. He helped several of us to get work... It seemed that Mimi's wanted a shopgirl. Before I took up acting I was in a London stores."

"And after you settled down here, what then? Did Mr. Bunn inflict himself upon you? Did he make himself a nuisance to you?"

"Not at first. Then he called a time or two at the shop to see if I was settled down. He tried to take small liberties, like pressing my hand. Then he asked me if I'd like to go out to dinner with him... I didn't want to start anything there, so I said I couldn't. He went off in a rage and I didn't see him again for months. Then, a month or so ago, he called again. He asked me to dine and said he was serious. He said he had in mind asking me to marry him."

The china-blue eyes opened wide and she shrugged her shoulders, as though still in a quandary about Ned Bunn's sudden infatuation.

"Of course, you declined."

"I did it nicely. I said I was honoured. But he took it badly. He talked about Medlicott and said he'd see that *his* little game was stopped. He said I'd better look out and that if an honourable proposal didn't suit me, he'd see there was no more dishonourable behaviour in the town."

"And since then, what has happened?"

"Nothing, Inspector. Just nothing. He died a fortnight afterwards. I'm sure I didn't wish him dead."

The telephone rang and she ran to it.

"Yes ... yes, I've just been held up. Of course it's business. What else ...? Very well ... Wait a minute ..."

She answered in clipped syllables, embarrassed by Littlejohn's presence.

"I'm going, Miss Mander ..."

She spoke back in the telephone.

"Of course there isn't a man here ... I'm busy changing my frock ... Very well. Wait for me ... I'll be at the gate in five minutes ... No ... If you try coming up, I'll never speak to you again ..."

She hung up with an exasperated twitch of her hand.

Littlejohn smiled. So her followers didn't come to the flat for her; she met them at the gate. A kind of Box and Cox business! He wondered how many men were actually mixed up in Miss Mander's life. Young or old, it didn't seem to matter.

"Young men rather bore me ..."

She seemed to want to confide in somebody and here she was, telling it all to Littlejohn, old enough to be her father.

"They're so frantic and impatient. I like calm, experienced men. I guess it's because till I was nineteen and daddy died, we were always together and I grew to appreciate older men that way."

Littlejohn wondered from which play she'd found those lines! He took up his hat.

"I'll let you get on with your dressing, then. I'll want to see you again, later, but I'll call at the shop."

"Very well. I'll always be glad to see you, Inspector. You've been so kind."

Before he reached the door she had flung off her wrapper and ran, half naked in strips of filmy black underwear, into the bedroom to put on her frock.

On the stairs, the strong smell of fried onions fought with the scent of bath-salts coming from the bathroom, and behind the door of the odd flat about which Littlejohn knew nothing, there were sounds of quarrelling and of tears.

At the main gate of *Whispers* stood a fast little sports-car, presumably waiting for Violet Mander. The occupant was so anxious to avoid Littlejohn's seeing him that he hid his head and thus attracted the Inspector's attention. It was, without doubt, Hubert Stubbs!

Yewbert had felt affronted and suspicious after the funeral at which the incongruous roses had arrived among the Ned Bunn wreaths and had, manly and off-hand, called on Helen next day for an explanation and reassurance. Instead, he had been met by Aunt Sarah, smiling and affable.

"She won't be long. While you're waiting, young man, would you mind calling at Mimi's hat shop for a new hat I left there?"

Yewbert, amazed at the request, but a bit gratified by the old lady's change of front, hurriedly made off in his car. He stayed a long time at the modiste's and, after delivering the hat to Aunt Sarah, mentioned an appointment and quickly made himself scarce.

"It cost me five pounds, but it was worth it to get rid of him and his pimples," confided Aunt Sarah to Helen much later.

"And, after all, it was, in a way, a sound investment, though I never wore the 'ideous thing," she added, by way of justification for dissipating good Bunn cash.

CHAPTER SIXTEEN
THE TOWN FOOL

The situation was one the two detectives were getting used to at *The Freemasons'*. Blowitt's changes of mood were like the weather; one moment he was in the depths of despair, playing the piano like somebody demented, the next he was brimming with smiles and good humour. When Littlejohn returned from *Whispers* to the hotel he found Cromwell waiting for him and the landlord eager to serve a good hot dinner.

"What's come over Blowitt since I left?"

"He got a telegram from somewhere, sir, and it was as good as a tonic to him. He announced that drinks were on the house, although there were only two of us present, the acting-manager and me."

The two new blondes served the meal, with Blowitt hanging attentively around, and then when coffee arrived Littlejohn got to business.

"Just a minute, Mr. Blowitt."

The landlord turned and beamed on them both. He was expecting congratulations on the food and drink.

"Yes, gents?"

"I believe you employed Browning on some private business a short time before he was killed. What was it all about?"

Mr. Blowitt looked mysterious and seemed to have all kinds of secrets to divulge.

" 'Ave one each on the house," he said, sat down, and rang the bell for the barmaid.

"Three pints o' mild ..."

"Your 'ealths, gents. I thought sooner or later you'd be askin' questions and I'll do all I can to 'elp."

He went to the door, opened it, looked out to right and left to make sure nobody was listening behind it, returned, and took from his pocket a crushed telegram.

"Read it."

Blowitt leaned back, lit a small cigarette, thrust his thumbs in the armholes of his waistcoat, and looked as happy as he could be.

Hinckley. 11.0 a.m.
Effie Moore employed as barmaid at Unicorn here.
Wire instructions.

Clancy.

"Well?"

Blowitt slowly closed one eye.

"Effie was the best barmaid I ever 'ad at this place and left on account of the shockin' behaviour of the late Ned Bunn. She vanished. Now she's found and I've jest wired Sid Clancy to offer her six quid a week an' all found, to come and manage this place. The wife's run away with that little perisher, Twelves. I've got to ..."

Littlejohn gave him back the piece of paper.

"Who's Clancy?"

"Enquiry agent. My business with Browning was for him to try an' find out where Effie had gone. Browning was busy on other business and couldn't do it all himself, see? So he

177

set Sid on the job and he's done it first class. Now with Effie back..."

"Never mind Effie for the moment. I'm concerned with Browning."

Blowitt cast a reproachful look on the Inspector. His luck had turned and he wanted everybody to be jolly now.

"Wot about another on the 'ouse?"

"No, thanks."

Cromwell waved a finger to and fro to signify the same.

"You had a talk with Browning a little time before he died..."

"A week to be exac'..."

"And as you talked, you stood him drinks on the house."

"Yes. Can't I stand a client a drink if I want? You ain't bein' very matey, are you, sir, after the way I've tried to look after you since you came?"

Cromwell made clicking noises with his tongue against his teeth.

Littlejohn lit his pipe.

"During your talk with Browning, the drinks loosened his tongue a bit, I've no doubt. Did he say anything? Did he give any excuse for not devoting all his time to your job?"

Blowitt puffed out his cheeks importantly and looked wise.

"Yes. Come to think of it, 'e did. He said he'd 'ave to get a suitable colleague, that was Sid Clancy, to take on my job, as 'e himself was busy on a legal one. Matrimonial case, 'e said. A lot o' money in it, from what I could gather. Browning seemed a bit above himself about it. Said he'd landed lucky an' if he played 'is 'and right, he'd do well for himself."

"Was Ned Bunn mentioned during the conversation?"

Mr. Blowitt winked again to show how clever he was.

"Yes, 'e was. I sez to Browning that I bet old Bunn was up to 'is tricks agen. Brownin' treated it with contempt, as you might say. 'Wot? 'im? Naw. Gettin' anything out o' Ned Bunn's like squeezin' blood out of a stone. My client's easier meat than Ned.'"

"That was all?"

"Should there be any more?"

"No, thanks. And now, if you don't mind, my colleague and I have work to do and want to talk it over."

Mr. Blowitt winked again and tiptoed from the room to show he appreciated the gravity of the situation.

"I can't make head or tail of it all."

Cromwell stroked his large chin with one hand and with the fingers of the other flirted pellets of bread from the table at a large framed photograph of a group of freemasons.

"I've a job for you, old man. I want you to call and see Mimi."

Cromwell looked alarmed. Violet, Helen, and now Mimi ... It was like a beauty contest!

"... but Mr. Ladbroke said on principle he'd never agree to any wife of his going out to work, so, as the shop was such a profitable business, I put in a manageress."

Cromwell was only with difficulty able to tear himself away from Mrs. Ladbroke, who lived in a large semi-detached villa in a district known as "up town" to designate it as superior to "down town" which held the slums and works.

Mrs. Ladbroke was a well-preserved woman in her early fifties; the sort in whom you couldn't tell where nature ended and art began. She was heavily made up, had doubtful auburn hair, and she was exquisitely groomed and turned-out. Two black poodles with bright button eyes followed her wherever she went. She talked solidly for half-an-hour about her first and second husbands, her business life, her first and subsequent encounters with Mr. Ladbroke, her "second", and how evil rumours had spread around about their relationship before they married. Finally, she got down to Violet Mander, whom she described as a jewel from the point of view of selling hats, but as "a bit on the loose" in her private life.

"...Not that I'm not broad-minded, you know. Times have changed since you and I were young, Mr....What did you say your name was? Ah, yes...Cromwell..."

The sergeant took his cue before it slipped from his grasp.

"I suppose she was left an orphan, or something, at an early age, Mrs. Ladbroke. However, she seemed to find a good patron in the late Edwin Bunn. She'll miss him now he's gone, I've no doubt."

Mrs. Ladbroke looked a bit stunned.

"Bunn...Bunn...I never heard that he had anything to do with Violet. Who told you that?"

"I think she told my colleague herself."

"I can't understand it."

"But surely it was Bunn got her her job with you, wasn't it?"

"With me?"

She tapped her wishbone with a heavily-ringed finger.

"With me? Edwin Bunn had nothing whatever to do with it. It was my lawyer, Mr. Edgell, who recommended her to me. In fact, I'd asked his advice about selling the place when I married for the second time and he suggested that I might get a girl to run it for me. A few weeks later, he said he'd come across the very one; a young actress out of a job. So, I took her on and I've never regretted it."

"And you never heard of Edwin Bunn paying her attention?"

Mrs. Ladbroke's eyes narrowed.

"She's a very pretty girl and I wouldn't be surprised to hear of *anyone* being attracted by her."

Cromwell had taken a dislike to the woman. The hennaed hair, the painted clawlike nails, the way she dressed slightly too young for her age, the stuffy exotic room, the two dogs, caressed like children and self-conscious about it... They all gave the same impression, a feeling Cromwell couldn't actually define. He knew, however, that Mrs. Ladbroke didn't much care how Violet Mander attracted custom to the shop, provided the takings increased. In a burst of dramatic illumination he saw Maison Mimi as Madame Tellier's Establishment! A hat-shop of ill repute!!

"You must know as well as I do that Bunn paid attention to your shopgirl. I'll bet there's not much goes on there that you don't know about."

"I *beg* your pardon, officer. Are you insinuating...?"

"Nothing, madam..."

Cromwell dismissed it with a wave of the hand.

"Nothing. But I am anxious to explore every avenue about the death of Edwin Bunn. And one avenue is, it might have been a crime of passion!"

"Oh..."

Talk of passion was right up Mrs. Ladbroke's street. She read erotic novelettes most of the day, frequented all-in wrestling matches, flirted dangerously with any man who would rise to the occasion, and said her husband didn't understand her.

"But I never thought of that in connection with Mr. Bunn. How blind I've been! He had a reputation for peccadilloes with the fair sex. Surely the crime wasn't committed by an outraged husband or a jealous lover?"

She had it all off pat; Violet, the fair adventuress, the blonde Carmen, stirring the passions of men until they killed one another for her!

The two dogs, which had been playfully vying for caresses from Cromwell, grew excited, tore at his trousers-bottoms, jostled one another, snarled, and then started to fight, snapping, growling, charging and yelling all over the room.

"Jip and Pip...Behave yourselves. Mummy's little darlings mustn't fight."

She seized one and put it in Cromwell's arms and held the other herself. Amid yapping, slobbering and struggling to get at each other, the dogs punctuated the rest of the interview.

"That explains Mr. Bunn's offer to buy the shop...I never thought."

Cromwell thought quite a lot. He thought Mrs. Ladbroke was a poor liar.

"Did Mr. Edgell show any fondness for Miss Mander? After all, you say he found her the job with you. Was he attracted by her when Mr. Bunn took him to the theatre to collect the debts the stock company owed him?"

"Debts? Stock company? I don't quite follow. As for Mr. Edgell...Oh dear, no. A most respectable lawyer. A bachelor, I grant you, and still waters often run deep, but to commit a crime of passion or even prove susceptible to the charms of Violet...It's too laughable...Mr. Edgell...Just imagine..."

Almost suffocating the dog in her arms, she laughed shrilly...a laugh so false and forced, that Cromwell knew at once that he had laid his finger on a likely spot. She was protesting and bluffing so forcibly, that she might as well have told the truth, the nasty truth that she had acted, or was still acting, as a go-between for Edgell and Violet Mander.

"I hope I'm not going to get involved in any scandal through that girl. It would ruin me if the affair was aired in court. You'll do your best..."

She smiled at Cromwell and fluttered her eyelids. The dogs came to his rescue by starting to howl dismally together and the one in the sergeant's arms wriggled itself free and ran to the door in haste.

"It's their mealtime, the little loves. I often say they must have little alarm-clocks in their heads."

Cromwell seized the chance to get away.

"An unpleasant sort of woman," he told Littlejohn after reporting the interview. "I'd much rather deal with Aunt Sarah any day. You know where you are with Aunt Sarah."

Mr. Blowitt was full of beans. Effie was returning to-morrow and he couldn't contain himself with satisfaction.

"Drinks are on the house to-night, gents. It's time I stood you two a round or two. You've brought great credit and a lot of publicity to my 'umble pub. Your 'ealth, gents."

They didn't stay to be convivial.

"I'd like the room to myself for a while, Mr. Blowitt. Could you arrange it?"

"Sure, sir. Anythin' you like."

Littlejohn knew it was no use ringing up Violet Mander at that hour, so he tried Cuffright. He was lucky. A fruity, unsteady voice answered.

"Cuffright 'ere..."

"Could I speak to Mr. Medlicott, please?"

"Look 'ere, this isn't a telephone exchange..."

"This is Inspector Littlejohn."

"Huuuuullo, Inshpector... Be a great pleasure..."

In a few minutes Littlejohn had spoken to Medlicott and asked him to call at *The Freemasons'* at once.

"I hope it's nothing serious," panted Jubal when he arrived. He'd run nearly all the way and then halted at the door. He wasn't used to frequenting pubs.

"Sit down, please, Mr. Medlicott. I want a straight talk with you; straight questions and straight answers."

The dapper little tailor evidently expected the worst. His eyes were anxious and feverish and he kept licking his bright lips, which made a startling contrast to his auburn and grey beard.

Littlejohn, his hands deep in his pockets, his pipe burning, his face stern, seemed to be talking to himself.

"This isn't a court of enquiry. This investigation's gone on long enough and it's time we did some plain speaking. What are your relations with Miss Mander, your tenant, sir?"

"We're good friends. She was a bit alone and helpless when she arrived in Enderby and I tried to make her comfortable in the flat."

"Is it true you don't take any rent for the rooms and that Violet Mander has been your mistress?"

Medlicott took a deep breath and looked too bewildered even to know where he was.

"I...? I, Inspector? Miss Mander's... Miss Mander's...?"

He couldn't even remember the appropriate word. He flailed the air with his arms for a minute. Then he got to his feet and lost his temper.

"Is this all your investigation has brought to light, Inspector? A lot of damned lies and an attempt to blacken my good name. I protest! Who I can protest to, I don't know. But I protest. I appeal to your better nature, Inspector. I implore you to believe me. I have never, *never*, since I married her, been unfaithful to my wife! Never..."

He looked suddenly dishevelled. In his anguish he had buttoned the wrong button in the wrong buttonhole of his jacket, his tie was askew, and his natty light suit looked crumpled and ready-made.

"You *must* believe me... It would kill my wife to think... She's ill as it is."

Tears flowed and were lost in his whiskers again.

Cromwell, the silent spectator, caught Littlejohn's eye, smiled and shrugged.

"Who is it, then, Mr. Medlicott, who has been around the town spreading the tale of your unfaithfulness to Mrs. Medlicott, blackening your good name, as you call it, mixing you up with Violet Mander, and even trying to pin on you the murder of your brother-in-law and of Browning?"

Littlejohn looked him in the face and was surprised to see his expression change from self-pity to one of purposefulness. Medlicott took out a handkerchief, polished his glasses, mopped his damp beard, and straightened his coat and his tie. He was once again the old Jubal, but without the smile.

"I don't know, Inspector, but I want to help you to find out. I tell you here and now that I killed neither of the two men, I was never anything more than friendly with Miss Mander, and I have never been unfaithful to my wife. I ask you to believe me. Now, please ask as many questions as you like and I will answer them truthfully."

"Where were you on the night Edwin Bunn died?"

"I received a message from Violet Mander that she must see me at her shop on an important matter. I went and instead of Miss Mander, I found Browning waiting at the door of the closed shop to say that it was all a mistake and Miss Mander had left."

"What was the matter she wanted to discuss?"

"She said her name had been linked with mine, a private detective was on our trail, and she suspected my wife had engaged him. She must see me."

"You didn't tell me that when I asked you. Were you afraid of the scandal?"

"Exactly, sir. That's why I went when she sent for me. I couldn't bear my wife even to hear a breath of it. She's not well."

"Did you know Browning was a private enquiry agent?"

"He said so when I met him at the door of the shop. He also said Miss Mander had misunderstood something he'd said and he was anxious to apologize to me and put it right."

"What time was that?"

Medlicott thought for a minute.

"Ten o'clock. I got the ten-past bus home to the gate of our house."

"Now, about Miss Mander. *Did* she pay her rent?"

"Not personally. She had a small income looked after by her lawyer, who paid in the rent quarterly."

"Who was her lawyer?"

"Edgell. It seems Ned Bunn met her somewhere at a theatre where she'd been acting and the company went bankrupt. Ned seems to have taken a fancy to her and got his own lawyer to look after her affairs."

"Throw your mind back to earlier this evening, sir. I saw you enter the flats with Miss Mander. You were begging her for something. You sounded like a lover pleading for forgiveness..."

Medlicott was terrified.

"Are things as bad as that? Must everything I do be turned against me? I tell you I'm not her lover. I..."

"What was the conversation about, then? You looked very upset."

Jubal Medlicott suddenly looked old, tired and ashamed again.

"I was begging for money...I...I...I can't pay my way. We owe money all over the place and until Ned's estate is disbursed, I'm cleaned out. Miss Mander pays her rent quarterly in arrears. I asked her for the two months' money owing; it's not quarter-end till next month. I'm ashamed, but I've no pride left. I'm broke. I asked Edgell for a few pounds on account from the estate. He said he'd find it next week. Meanwhile, the milk is cut off, we can't get meat and bread, the light and gas are due to be cut off any time and..."

He shrugged his shoulders.

"It only needs my wife to hear the rumours of my infidelity and I'm done for. We console one another by saying we've always got one another. Now..."

He looked calm, like a man ready to put his head in a gas-oven to get a bit of peace.

"You see, don't you, Mr. Medlicott, that you've got a terrible enemy in this town? He's set out to steadily ruin your good name, your honour, and your family life. He's got Miss Mander in his power, and she has lied about her relations with you. He's murdered your brother-in-law and seen to it that you have no alibi because you were wandering about in the rain at the time of the crime. He's shut the mouth of Browning, who might have done you some good if he'd told the truth, and he's taken infinite pains to lay a trail of clues right to your door in connection with Browning's death."

Medlicott didn't seem surprised; only resigned.

"Yes, sir. I've talked it over with my wife. She's told me all about your visits and your questions and I have told her the truth. She believes me and she also said that you didn't believe I'd killed either of the dead men. I'm grateful for that, sir, most grateful."

"On the night Browning was murdered, you followed me out of your flats, in your dressing-gown. About that time, Browning was strangled in the garden. What have you to say about that, Mr. Medlicott?"

It was pathetic. Whichever way Jubal turned, he seemed to meet trouble. Now, he moved his head from side to side like somebody in pain and licked his red lips nervously.

"I can only say that it was my usual bad luck. After you left, I suddenly remembered it was very dark down the drive and you might get lost in the grounds. I only came down to show you the way. Even an ordinary act of what you might call common courtesy is now turned against me and I find myself just as much without an alibi as I was when Ned met his death."

"Things certainly look black for you from the circumstantial point of view, sir, and we've only your word and your wife's trust in you against an almost overwhelming mass of incriminating evidence. In fact, we've almost enough against you to arrest you."

Medlicott passed his hand rapidly across his forehead two or three times, as though trying to clear his wits, and then shrugged his shoulders with a feeble weary gesture.

"I've done my best to tell you the truth. There's nothing more I can do. I've always been a bit of a fool; never knew the value of money and always tried to be bright and cheerful by way of showing the shop was prosperous, although all the time it was going the wrong way. Now I seem to have landed myself in trouble that I can't laugh off or treat as funny. I guess I'll have to stand my trial and trust to justice to see me through. But why would it all fall on *me*? Why? Is nobody else suspected?"

Littlejohn lit his pipe again and offered a cigarette to Jubal Medlicott. The little tailor took it slowly and then the gesture must have struck him as a kindly one and in his overwrought condition he was touched. Tears flowed down his beard.

"I don't seem to have anybody to turn to."

"You don't need anybody, Mr. Medlicott. The case against you is too good, too watertight. The solution's been handed to us on a plate. All we have to do is arrest and hang you. That's *too* easy for us. It's made us suspicious."

Cromwell nodded sagely to show he was included in the plural.

"You were an obvious suspect, Mr. Medlicott. You were desperate for money and Ned Bunn had it and it would come to you and your wife if he died. You went out and nobody knew where you were when Ned Bunn was killed. If you'd said you were at Mimi's shop, you'd have needed Browning to confirm it and Browning was dead at the time he could have done you any good. There's motive and everything else there. You also knew Bunn's shop inside-out, knew where the firearms were kept, could easily obtain a key, could find your way about the place in the dark. You knew Ned Bunn's habits...You see what a culprit you might be?"

Medlicott nodded without a word.

"Your own wife thought you might have done it...perhaps for her sake, because she isn't well and you could use the money for her benefit. To divert our suspicions, she told me *she* killed Ned Bunn."

Medlicott just sat sobbing with no resistance or spirit left.

"And then, to crown all, footprints round the body of Browning were your size and across the instep of each shoe, there was a groove made by the strap of a spat, such as you wear. That seemed conclusive."

"Yes. I admit it did."

Medlicott was in a daze, taking it all on the chin, no fight in him.

Littlejohn crossed and stood before him.

"Do you hear what I'm telling you? There were *two* sets of footprints with the mark of a spat across each! Were *you* wearing two spats when you followed me down the stairs into the garden?"

"I? No, I wasn't, was I? *I'd only one on.* I broke the strap of the other and my wife was mending it. I couldn't have had two on, could I?"

"Of course you couldn't! That's where the murderer made his first big slip. He wanted it to look like you and in his finicky precision, he overplayed his hand. Now, Mr. Medlicott, who not only wanted Ned Bunn out of the way, but Browning dead, and you accused of both crimes? Who hates you enough for that?"

"Nobody. That's just it. Nobody. I haven't an enemy in the world. People laugh at me, I know. They think I'm eccentric, mad and irresponsible, but they don't wish me ill. I'm just a local joke, the sort of town fool."

Littlejohn was still standing over Jubal. He felt like taking him by the collar and shaking him.

"Have you ever done anybody a dirty trick in your life, sir? Something they've never forgotten or recovered from?"

"No. I've always tried to play the game."

"Good heavens, man! Who was it turned up and married another man's fiancée just before his wedding and at a time when he'd got a houseful of furniture? And the frustrated lover has never married as a result."

"Simon Edgell! Never! He wouldn't do me a dirty trick. He's a friend of the family, calls on us from time to time, sends us Christmas presents, and always remembers Dolly and Polly on their birthdays. You've got the wrong man. You might just as well say I murdered Bunn and Browning!"

"I think you'd better go home, Mr. Medlicott. You seem to *want* to get yourself hanged. Don't say a word of this interview to a soul. We've confided quite a lot in you and if you mentioned what I've said to Mr. Edgell, he might, as a lawyer, make things difficult for us. We're not exempt from slander, you know."

"I won't say a word, sir. Thanks for trusting me and believing what I told you. I can only say again, I haven't murdered anybody. There were times when I'd have liked to kill both Bunn and Browning but I never got a chance."

"Now just stop it, sir," interjected Cromwell impatiently. "Here we are, trying to clear you of suspicion, and you keep convicting yourself with every other word you speak. You'll be asking me to take down a full confession in a minute."

Mr. Blowitt, beaming still, brought in three glasses of whisky and a syphon.

"Thought you might like a little drink to liven up the talk, gents. All on the 'ouse, with my best wishes."

"Sorry, Mr. Blowitt. I'm teetotal."

"Take it as medicine, Mr. Medlicott, sir. You look as if you need it. Never seen you look so all-in."

Jubal downed the whisky, coughed, pulled himself together and looked better.

"I think I'll have another, landlord. For the road, I believe the saying is. And these gentlemen will join me, won't you?"

He was at it again! Penniless, but throwing about what bit he had left! They all had a drink with him, saw him to the door, and, as Medlicott vanished into the dark, they heard him begin to whistle.

CHAPTER SEVENTEEN
THE MAN WHO READ CONRAD

"**I**s Mr. Edgell in?"

The man who answered the door looked surprised and then, with a gesture bordering on insolence, he took out a large watch from his waistcoat pocket and looked at it with raised eyebrows. He was an ex-policeman and general factotum for Mr. Edgell and his wife lived in and acted as housekeeper. Littlejohn handed the man his card.

"Oh, come inside, sir. I didn't know it was you. We don't encourage callers, but you're different. Please wait here."

The house was a large one set on a hill just outside the town. A long wooded avenue and then a broad façade of windows with a wide semi-circular drive in front. It had been built by a pretentious millowner after a trip to the French châteaux, and embodied many classical features in miniature. Edgell had bought it cheaply when the owner's son went bankrupt after running through his father's fortune.

The hall was panelled up to the ceiling and light by electric fittings in the form of candles, imitation wax and all. A wide, carpeted staircase ran up to a landing and there was a little minstrels' gallery at one end. Littlejohn couldn't help comparing the place with *Whispers* and thinking how Edgell seemed to have gone up as the girl he wanted to marry had gone down.

"Mr. Edgell will see you, sir."

Another beautifully panelled room with bare oak beams in the ceiling. This was evidently the library, for there were books from top to bottom of one side, and on two others, closed cupboards half-way and above them glazed bookcases packed with richly-bound volumes in calf, and gold-lettered. A log fire blazed in a large Adam fireplace and there were winged armchairs on each side of it. A table set out with whisky and a wine decanter; a box of cigars, a pipe and a jar of tobacco. Edgell seemed to do himself well in his isolation. There was nobody in the room, but a door at the far end stood open and Littlejohn could hear someone padding about beyond it.

As he waited, Littlejohn, his hands behind his back, examined the books in the open case. They were evidently favourites, for they were well-worn. Galsworthy, Meredith, Conrad, Trollope, and Dickens. One of the Conrad collection was missing.

"Admiring my books, Inspector?"

Edgell had entered quietly and was eyeing Littlejohn from the inner doorway. He wore a black velvet smoking-jacket.

"Sorry to keep you. I was in my dressing-gown when you called and I thought I'd better change."

He looked better than when Littlejohn saw him at the office. He had obviously dined well and there was a healthy pink flush on his usually grey cheeks. His white hair shone under the light of the seven-branched chandelier which he switched on from where he stood.

"Yes, sir. We seem to have similar tastes. I could spend a happy night with any of these."

Littlejohn indicated the row of Conrad's novels with his hand.

"I'm just reading *Typhoon* again. You know it?"

"Yes, sir."

"A remarkable book; a great adventure. And the woman for whom the story of the fantastic affair was written, simply cast away the account without so much as reading it."

Littlejohn pricked up his ears. Edgell sounded to be getting at something, hinting at some episode in his own life.

"...I admire Conrad most for his sense of discipline. One must have inner strength to meet the cruelties of life and...But there, you're not here for a literary lecture. What can I do for you at this late hour? Sit down."

They sat, one on each side of the glowing logs. Edgell offered Littlejohn drinks and cigars, but the Inspector declined the former and asked if he might smoke his pipe. The ex-policeman entered and made up the fire. Edgell waited for him to go.

"How far have you got with these crimes, Inspector? You've been here nearly a week. I was just wondering..."

Littlejohn scented reproach at the delay, tinged perhaps with curiosity about developments. He ignored the question.

"There are one or two matters which puzzle me and I think you might help, sir."

Edgell didn't seem embarrassed. Littlejohn could feel a tension growing in the atmosphere, but it was probably that of a skilled lawyer ready for work. There was a smile on Edgell's usually grim face.

"I'll be very willing to help. In fact, I must confess to feeling a bit guilty about you, Inspector. I've seen very little of you and I feel I could have assisted you. I know a lot about the Bunn family, you know."

In the drowsy heat from the fire, Littlejohn was studying the man sitting opposite. Small, grey, highly intelligent, fastidious, with a fine skin, high forehead, thin nose, firm chin and a petulant mouth. A man who liked his own way and who fumed, chafed and probably got nasty when he didn't get it. He seemed, in his home, to have dropped the fumbling fussy manner he adopted at the office.

"I don't see that family background is going to help us much, sir. Intestine quarrels are always going on behind the family curtain everywhere, but they don't get to killing one another about them."

Edgell stiffened.

"You're a bit independent, aren't you? I'm an older man than you and if you've gathered your experience from one angle of crime, you'll give me credit for gaining mine from another, *and* a more intimate one."

There he was! His weak spot was his pride and arrogance. Edgell couldn't stand anybody crossing him.

"I'm sorry, sir. I didn't mean any discourtesy. I'm ready for all the background you can give me about the family."

Edgell was sulking a bit. He wasn't going to play.

"Why did you call, Inspector?"

"Your name has cropped up in certain directions, sir, and I think you might help us clear up some obscure points. For example, Miss Violet Mander..."

The corners of Edgell's mouth twitched and he gave Littlejohn a momentary look of evasion, something flickering and a bit shifty.

"Well?" His voice wavered now.

"Who is she?"

"How should I know?"

"I heard that you first met her when you were with Edwin Bunn at a theatre in Melton Mowbray looking after Bunn's interests in the bankruptcy of a repertory company. Miss Mander was in the show and Bunn took a fancy to her. He tried to find her a job in Enderby."

Edgell cleared his throat, poured out more whisky for himself, and sipped it.

"Did he?"

"Yes. Or, that's one side of the story. The other was that *you* got Miss Mander the job at Maison Mimi ..."

"That's right. At Bunn's request. A man often puts things like that in his lawyer's hands when he wants to keep in the background himself."

"He also put in your hands the paying of Miss Mander's rent in Medlicott's flats?"

Another flicker of indecision. Edgell seemed a bit afraid. He wasn't quite sure how much Littlejohn knew.

"Bunn was fond of pretty women. It was his weakness. No discipline; couldn't control his appetites ..."

Discipline again! Edgell was arrogant about it; a man who seemed to despise human weakness.

"So, he asked you to pay the rent for Miss Mander. Did she allow that? I gathered he seriously wanted to marry the girl. She turned him down. Didn't she also turn down the rent from Bunn as well?"

"No. I paid it direct to Medlicott and she must have overlooked it."

"Overlooked it! Surely she knew who paid the rent, sir, and if she'd sent Bunn about his business, she'd have no more money from him."

Edgell shuffled in his chair. His long fine, brittle-looking hands gripped the arms and he pouted again.

"What has all this to do with the murders? Bunn's love affairs are over and done with. You surely don't think these were crimes of passion. They were crimes of *greed*... done for money."

Littlejohn removed his pipe and looked straight at Edgell, whose patience seemed at an end.

"Money? I can quite see Medlicott killing his brother-in-law to get his wife's share and make ends meet, but why kill Browning?"

"Hasn't Medlicott already told you, Browning saw him in town on the night of the crime, prowling about near Bunn's shop?"

"Yes. But how did you know, sir?"

"I'm Medlicott's lawyer. It's my business to know things."

"I see. Medlicott told you?"

A faint hesitation, a flicker of the cold grey eyes.

"No. Browning told me the day he died. I had him in to see me about a debt he owed to the furniture company for hire purchased goods. He called to ask for advice. At the same time he seemed talkative about the murder of Ned Bunn and mentioned having seen Medlicott in town on the night of the murder. You recollect, I asked you to have me present if you suspected and questioned Medlicott. You didn't, did you? You questioned him without my being there. I shall make a point of that if Medlicott is charged."

"If we contemplate an arrest in that direction, I'll let you know, sir. Medlicott had every reason for wishing his brother-in-law dead, I admit. He's on the short-list of suspects."

"Who else is on it, if I might ask?"

"Blowitt, Hetherow, Flounder, Miss Mander... Even Mrs. Medlicott."

Edgell bridled.

"I warn you, Inspector. Don't try to make a fool of me. You're simply reeling off a list of names as they come to mind. Blowitt, indeed! What reason might Blowitt have for killing Ned Bunn?"

"Another crime of passion. A matter of a barmaid, I gather..."

"Ridiculous! This is a serious affair, Inspector. You seem to be treating it with levity. I was a bit surprised when they called in Scotland Yard. Local colour's what's required to solve a job like this one. Not a lot of crack-brained theories."

"You think I haven't gathered any local colour during my stay in Enderby, sir? Very well, we shall see. Meanwhile, to get down to practical matters. Where were you on the night and at the time Mr. Bunn met his death?"

Edgell was on his feet in a flash. His polite, engaging hospitality of the start had evaporated.

"What is all this? Do you think I killed my old friend? Because if you do, out with it and no more beating about the bush."

Littlejohn puffed leisurely at his pipe. He found it a bit difficult to appear calm, but that was what was wanted.

"No, sir. Not at all. Just a routine enquiry; one I ask every-one I encounter in this case. Part of our practical work."

"Are you being sarcastic?"

"No."

"I'll tell you where I was. I was out of town. I was at Melton with Mrs. Wilkins. She asked me to call about her new will. I left there at ten o'clock and got here at home at ten-thirty. Will that suit you?"

"Driving your own car, sir?"

"Yes. I nearly always do. I was nowhere near Enderby when Bunn was killed. As for Browning, if you're hunting alibis there, too, I was here, indoors, sitting where I am now, before the fire. Nobody entered, because the staff have orders not to disturb me after dinner until I'm ready to retire. I read a lot, as you will see and ..."

"That's quite all right, sir. I'm not asking you for a cast-iron alibi. Why should I? *You* didn't murder Bunn and Browning."

"One would think I had done, the way you go on, Inspector. Is that all? What I thought was a friendly call seems to have degenerated into an unpleasant argument and I'd rather put an end to it."

"I'm sorry, sir. I simply called to ask for help in filling-in gaps in the enquiry."

"I'll see you to the door."

Edgell did more than that. Although wearing slippers and a smoking jacket, he accompanied Littlejohn down the drive to the gate. He seemed anxious now to smooth matters over.

"You'll admit, Inspector, it's a bit irritating to be disturbed just before bed by a reminder and a lot of questions about Ned Bunn. It's worried me a lot. We'd been friends a long time, you know. No ill feelings, I hope."

"Not at all, sir. Thank you."

He shook the dry, brittle hand Edgell held out to him and hurried off in the dark. At Medlicott's flats, Cromwell met him in the garden.

"She's not in, yet. It's nearly eleven, but I guess the night's yet young to her. I put my head indoors once or twice. The telephone in her flat's been ringing like blazes, on and off, for the last quarter-hour."

"I thought it would! You'd better stay with me. We'll wait until she gets back."

If Violet Mander was a late bird, Yewbert hadn't been brought up that way and his father still held him under his thumb. At eleven-fifteen the fast little car drew up at the gate. Yewbert held open the door for Violet and together they walked up the drive to the front door. There was an eloquent silence as Yewbert embraced his companion in the dark, and a sound of scuffling as she broke free and unlocked the door.

"Wednesday night, then, Vi?"

"I'll let you know if you ring me up. Good night."

"S'long, Vi..."

Yewbert almost tripped to the gate in his new-found amorous energy. Littlejohn and Cromwell were at Violet's side before she'd turned the key in her own lock.

"Sorry, Miss Mander, but I'll have to trouble you again."

She turned. She still looked fresh and smiling, although Yewbert's fumblings had smeared her lipstick round her mouth and there was even the shape of his lips or moustache in red on the nape of her neck!

"Come inside. I don't know what the other people in the flats will think about callers at this hour. However..."

She was wearing a modest fur coat which she flung on a chair, revealing her black evening gown, from which her head and bare shoulders and arms seemed to emerge like a flower. She kicked off her brocade shoes, dusty as if from dancing somewhere, and flexed and unflexed her feet before putting on house slippers. Perhaps the eager Yewbert had been tramping upon them to the sound of jungle music.

"What did you want, Inspector?"

She stood by the gas-fire without asking them to sit down, perfectly natural, asking a perfectly natural question.

"Why did you tell me Medlicott was your lover, when all the time he wasn't? And it wasn't true, either, that he let you off the rent. Now, Miss Mander, this is very serious. I want a perfectly truthful statement here and now, in the presence of my colleague, and if, later, it proves incorrect, there'll be trouble."

For the first time, she looked afraid and a bit lonely and defenceless. She feverishly tapped the cigarette she had lit and her eyelids started to twitch.

"I... I don't know. I..."

"You had been *asked* to tell the tale you told me. You never were Medlicott's mistress, he never pestered you with his attentions, he never let you live here rent-free. Am I right?"

"Yes."

They could hardly hear the answer.

"Who is at the back of all this? Wait! Don't tell me Edwin Bunn, if it wasn't Bunn at all."

"Mr. Bunn did pay me attentions. He did ask me if I'd like to marry him. And, if he hadn't died, he would have bought Maison Mimi from Mrs. Ladbroke, because he told me he was going to own it and then we'd see who was boss. Those were his very words."

"Who got you the job there?"

She hesitated.

"It was Mr. Edgell. He came with Mr. Bunn to the theatre at Melton and was very nice to all the players, specially to me. He offered to find me work and a few days later wrote to offer me the job with Mrs. Ladbroke."

"So, it wasn't Bunn?"

"Not at the time."

"But Edgell told you to say, if anyone asked about it, that Bunn was acting through him?"

"Yes."

"He also paid the rent and said Bunn had done it?"

"Yes."

"Why?"

"Do I have to answer that?"

"Yes."

"He asked me to marry him."

Another! Littlejohn let his arms fall limply by his sides. Would it never end?

Violet Mander showed spirit for the first time.

"It wasn't what you think. I doubt if he loves me in the way the others say they do! He has never said so. He's never tried to kiss or maul me like the rest. Hubert Stubbs ... faugh ..."

She rubbed the back of her hand over her mouth in a flash of temper, smearing the lipstick across it.

"He said, if I'd been younger he'd have adopted me as his daughter. I reminded him of someone he once knew. He was lonely, with no relatives, a large house, a lot of money with nobody to leave it to. He couldn't do a thing about it unless I married him. He told me to take my time and I haven't given him an answer yet."

"He asked you to help entice Medlicott out of doors the night Bunn was killed, didn't he?"

"Yes. He said Browning had been talking about my relations with Medlicott and I'd better ring up Mr. Medlicott to come and talk it over at the shop. Browning came after I'd rung up and told me it was all a mistake. I could go home and he'd apologize to Mr. Medlicott."

"Why did you lie to me about your relations with Jubal Medlicott?"

"Mr. Edgell said if ever anybody asked about who paid for the rent and such things, I must on no account mention his name. On the spur of the moment, I made up the tale about Mr. Medlicott. You see, he sort of suggested it by pleading on the stairs for the rent. You suspected something, and that gave me a chance with the story."

"On the night Browning died, you had someone in the room when I was talking to Browning downstairs. Was that Edgell?"

"Yes."

"What was he doing here?"

"I don't know... Honestly, I don't. But he came in and said he wanted to stay till the police had left. He tried twice to get away by the back door. The second time, he managed."

Littlejohn pointed to the large cupboard.

"He wasn't in there when I called? Who was?"

She smiled for the first time.

"I told you the truth, Inspector. It was mice. There are some about and that night there was a mouse in the cupboard. I was terrified. I almost asked you to open the door and catch it."

Littlejohn could have laughed outright. Hitherto, the mouse had been Edgell's alibi in Browning's murder. If he'd been in the wardrobe all the time, he couldn't have been throttling Browning! Now...

"How was Mr. Edgell dressed when he called on you, Miss Mander?"

"As usual... In his grey suit and coat."

"Did anything in his get-up strike you as unusual or incongruous? His shoes, for example."

She hesitated.

"Yes, now I come to think of it, there *was* something funny. He had on a pair of spats. I'd never seen anybody but Mr. Medlicott in spats before."

The telephone rang urgently. Miss Mander crossed the room and took the instrument from under the silken skirt of the blue doll.

"Leave it!"

She stopped in the act of taking up the receiver.

"Let it ring..."

They stood transfixed whilst the bell rang and ended in apparent exhaustion.

"But why?"

"It's not safe, Miss Mander. And now, I don't want you to stay here overnight. There's a desperate murderer about and I can't run any risks. Have you any friends you can stay with?"

"Not at this hour, Inspector. Besides, what would I say about turning up so late with a tale like that?"

"My colleague here will take you over to Melton right away. Pack a bag for the night and he'll see you safely to a hotel."

Still amazed, Violet Mander threw a few things in a case and Cromwell set out with her in the police-car for Melton Mowbray.

Littlejohn switched off the lights of the flat and turned out the gas-fire. As he left, the telephone started to ring again.

CHAPTER EIGHTEEN
"THROSTLES NEST"

Cromwell hadn't much difficulty getting a room for Violet Mander at *The Greenwood Tree* in Melton Mowbray, although the night-porter, after a look at his companion, gave Cromwell an artful leer which made him go hot under the collar. If the sergeant hadn't wanted to ask the fellow a favour, he would have ticked him off for his cheek.

"There isn't a telephone in the room, is there?" Cromwell said, after his ward had been comfortably established and they had wished each other good-night.

"No. Wantin' one?"

The porter was old and decrepit and had a tired, disillusioned look, as though he'd served every night of his life in hotels of ill-repute and you couldn't tell him anything he didn't know.

"That's just the thing I don't want. The lady's highly-strung and she's being pestered by a fellow she doesn't like. On no account must she be disturbed."

The porter nodded sagely and spat on the two half-crowns Cromwell slipped in his hand.

"And another thing; if she comes down and asks for the phone, don't let her use it. Say it's engaged ... Any excuse. I'll be here first thing in the morning and I'll see you right if you help me."

The porter thereupon closed one eye.

"Looks as if you was wantin' her kep' away from the said pesterin' feller. Maybe, yore in the runnin', too, eh? Can't say I blames yer. She a redlar smasher, an' no mistake. Trust me, mister..."

Next morning Cromwell and Littlejohn were at *The Greenwood Tree* early and Miss Mander found them waiting for her at breakfast. She looked cool and fresh after the night's adventure. She never seemed to look anything else. Two sleepy commercial travellers eyed her and her companions with amazement, for she was still wearing her evening gown.

"I've telephoned Mrs. Ladbroke that you won't be at the shop to-day. Your aunt's sick..."

Cromwell smiled and poured her out a cup of coffee. She looked puzzled.

"But why?"

"We're taking you back with us, but we want you to attend a gathering we're arranging in connection with the death of Edwin Bunn. Some of the things you've told us have an important bearing on the case."

Littlejohn told her quietly and nodded reassuringly.

"Very well. Since it's all settled..."

Neither of the two detectives knew Melton Mowbray, but the police were very helpful and quickly told them where Aunt Sarah lived. *Throstles Nest*, just outside the town. The local superintendent sent a constable to show Cromwell the way. The bobby was so overawed by the presence of Scotland Yard that he barely spoke a word there and back, but cleared his throat loudly as though getting ready to sing a solo and tugged at his collar nervously until he almost choked himself.

"Nice day, sir."

"Busy at the Yard nowadays?"

"Nothin' ever excitin' happens here, but I must say I like the place."

"That's the house over there."

Cromwell might have expected it. A typical Bunn residence. Square, ugly, built behind walls. To prevent the public from spying on what was going on inside, the interstices of the wrought-iron gates had been boarded up, like an asylum or mysterious foreign embassy.

Cromwell let himself in. Beyond, the house was set in a large well-kept lawn, relieved by flower beds. It was a tidy, solid structure with sash windows at which were draped long, expensive, plush curtains of a bygone generation. The front door was closed and, although there was no strength in the autumn sun, there was hung before the door a large striped blind to protect the paint. A massive, prosperous-looking place, with a wrought-iron balcony on the first floor. Gravel paths and a coach-house and stables converted into a garage. You could imagine old furniture indoors and perhaps a trim maid or two and a manservant. Instead, from somewhere at the back there emerged a bent old man in a shabby jacket and corduroy trousers held up by a belt with a tarnished brass buckle. He made belligerently straight for Cromwell.

"Hi! You be trespassin'. This be private property."

"I'm not trespassing. I want to speak to someone in charge."

"If you be sellin' anythin', the missus be away."

"For how long?"

Cromwell pretended to be a stranger to the affairs of *Throstles Nest*, but, from his knowledge of Aunt Sarah, he could have told them a lot about it. Stuffy, full of old-fashioned, heavy, ugly furniture, antimacassars, skin rugs, family photographs in frames. And perhaps copies of the *Financial Times*, for Aunt Sarah's regular estimate of her wealth in investments and to enable her to sum up what to buy and what to sell.

"For how long?"

"She didn't say. She never tells me anythin'. Better ask the missus."

"Is your wife in?"

"Yes; but if you be sellin' anything she's an 'oly terror. Better teck my advice..."

The party was interrupted by the sudden appearance of Hinksman's better half. She was breathing heavily as though she'd been hastily summoned and had run all the way.

"These men be askin' for Mrs. Wilkins, missus."

"And might I h'ask your business?"

A woman who evidently fancied herself and tried to talk accordingly, and flinging aspirates about in the effort. Grey-haired, with an abundant bosom and rear, she'd probably married Hinksman, the gardener, as a last resort, thought herself a cut above him, and despised him because she now had the idea that she might have done better.

"I gather the lady of the house isn't at home. I wonder if you could help me?"

The embodiment of a type now becoming very rare— the old family servant, brought up from girlhood in the same house, faithful, but a bit bitter with the resentment of years of knuckling under and putting up with the same foibles day after day throughout a lifetime.

"...If your husband hadn't told me, I'd have thought you were the mistress here..."

That did it! Mrs. Hinksman gave her husband an acid look for betraying her and then smiled kindly on Cromwell.

"In what way can I 'elp you?"

The attendant constable appeared, stood first on one foot and then on the other, rather piteously puzzling what was going on and where it was all going to lead.

"I'm from the police, as you'll have guessed, madam, and I was rather anxious to see Mrs. Wilkins just to check the statement of a gentleman who was here on Monday, October 26th. A Mr. Edgell, of Enderby. I understand he was Mrs. Wilkins' lawyer. He's told us he was here in the evening and we always have to check up on statements to make sure. I'm certain you'll do just as well as Mrs. Wilkins."

"Better, if you ask me. She's gettin' old, you know, and a bit of a trouble, if you understand what I mean. In fact, too much trouble for the likes of us, even if I have been with her for forty years."

The lips grew thin and the face peevish. The woman had a grievance and was eager to give vent to it in the right quarter.

" 'It me, she did, with her owld stick on account o' treadin' on they geraniums. As if Oi could 'elp it, me with me rheumatics an' not so limber as Oi used ter be ..."

The old man gave tongue. He seemed bitter about everything, including his wife's scornful treatment of him. The sort of man who, having grown to hate his better half, now disgraced her by knocking around in large dirty boots and corduroy trousers loosely held up by a leather belt and looking ready to slip down to his ankles any time.

"You leave me to talk to the gentleman. He isn't h'interested in your grievances."

The old man looked already out of his depth and stood trembling with fury at the affront and ready to go off in a temper.

"You don't find things too comfortable here, madam?"

The gardener burst out before they could stop him.

"Comfortable? Dang 'er, no. We be givin' notice as soon as 'er comes back. Folk next door a' bin after us for long enough and now we be goin' to 'em. That'll be one in the eye for the ole cat. 'Er with no 'elp about the place, a-seein' of us workin' loike mad for the folk next door..."

The old woman cut him short.

"That will do, Reuben. Our own h'affairs are private and personal and the gentleman isn't h'interested. You were sayin', sir?"

She smiled at Cromwell to show that the matter rested between him and her.

"What time did Mr. Edgell leave here on the night I mentioned?"

The woman didn't hesitate.

"Just before half-past nine..."

"You're quite sure? Sure it wasn't nearer ten?"

She looked put-out at being doubted.

"Of course not. I can tell the time, can't I? I know the time the lawyer left particularly..."

"Why? You'll pardon my asking. I don't want to seem to doubt you, but you know what policemen are..."

He said it with a winning grin and the accompanying bobby sniggered as though enjoying some private constabulary joke.

Mrs. Hinksman smiled a cruel smile.

"My husband can perhaps explain better..."

She placed her arms akimbo and indicated that the ball was passed to the old chap.

"Oi be allowed off the chain every noight for an hour whiles Oi go and gets me pint at the local. Half-past eight to half-past noine. Then Oi gotta be 'ome. Dead on half-past noine, else there's ructions from the missus."

Mrs. Hinksman nodded vigorously.

"Early to bed and early to rise is the motto here. My husband gets in at half-past nine prompt to be ready for mornin' and then we go to bed just after ten, because as she's got older, Mrs. Wilkins gets up earlier. Shoutin' for her breakfast, she is, just after seven."

It wasn't hard to guess that the couple were completely fed-up with their mistress and took every opportunity of airing their complaints.

"And Mr. Edgell?"

"He left just before my husband got home. The kitchen was in darkness and I think he must have thought we were both out, because he opened the gates himself and drove quietly away. As a rule he h'asks my husband to do it for him."

"So he sneaked quietly off..."

"Well, I wouldn't quite say that. He just thought we were havin' our night out, havin' already seen my 'usband on his way to the public house."

She mentioned the pub with venom. It was obviously a bone of contention. She looked the thrifty sort and every pint probably cut her to the quick.

"Thank you very much, Mrs. ..."

"Mrs. Hinksman."

"...Mrs. Hinksman. Did Mr. Edgell come often?"

"At one time he came two or three times a week, but now not half so often. A great friend of Mrs. Wilkins, but now the young lady's gone elsewhere and doesn't come any more, Mr. Edgell isn't seen so much about."

The old man cackled hideously at some private joke and bared his almost toothless gums and showed his tongue and uvula. His wife gave him a disgusted look.

"The young lady? Who was she?"

"I shouldn't really be gossipin' here. *She'd* be h'annoyed if she knew."

The thought of annoying Mrs. Wilkins stimulated her.

"A young lady called Miss Deane ... Valerie Deane ... Used to come here for hospitality. Mrs. Wilkins was quite fond of her, she having once fancied the stage herself and, but for the family, they say, would like as not have been actress, though with her looks I doubt her success at it."

"An actress?"

"Yes. There was a stock company came here about two years since. Played at the theatre for quite a while. The mistress went to the theatre every week; sometimes twice. And with the same people bein' here and in all the plays week after week, the local people sort of had them to their 'omes and gave them hospitality. Miss Deane came here sometimes twice or three times a week for tea before the play, you see. And one time Mr. Edgell was 'ere. After that, he started to come reg'lar when the young woman was here to tea. Disgustin', I called it, an old man like Mr. Edgell being gallant to a girl of Miss Deane's age."

"How did it end?"

The old woman looked bitter.

"Not as you might imagine, by the lawyer makin' a fool of himself and December marryin' April. Oh, no. The theatre company went bankrupt and the players was all out of work. Mr. Edgell found Miss Deane a job in Enderby, I've heard. Wanted 'er on his doorstep, I should say. But it ain't none of my business old men makin' fools of themselves."

She gave her husband a cutting look and he passed his huge paw across his dry lips to signify in which directions his own foolishness lay.

"Valerie Deane, eh? What did she look like, Mrs. Hinksman?"

The old man's mouth opened as he prepared to give a description and then he glanced at his wife and decided on prudence.

"A young 'ussy. Pretty as a picture on a chocolate-box lid, but an artful one. She soon had ole Edgell twisted round her little finger, believe you me."

"Dark or fair?"

Mrs. Hinksman eyed Cromwell as though she suspected him of getting off the business in hand.

"Fair and blue-eyed, brazen in the showing of too much of herself. Not the sort I'd like a boy of mine to be takin' up with. Why?"

"I wonder if I know her..."

Mrs. Hinksman drew herself in with a deep breath.

"Not the kind a decent young man like yourself would be wantin' to get tied up with. In any case, you wouldn't have much chance. A policeman! She don't want policemen. Millionaires is what the likes of her are h'after... or silly old men like Mr. Edgell, with more money to throw about on a pretty face than wits to bless theirselves with..."

Outside the gates of *Throstles Nest* a car-horn blew.

"We'll just call round and pick Cromwell up on our way back to Enderby," Littlejohn had said to Violet Mander and now they had drawn up before the house and were making their arrival known.

Cromwell hurried to the gate to meet his chief, took him aside, and told him what he had learned from the Hinksmans.

"You know this place, Miss Mander?" the Inspector asked when the sergeant had finished his tale.

"Yes. Mrs. Wilkins who lives here was very good to me when I was playing with the repertory company in Melton. She extended her hospitality sometimes several afternoons a week. It was very sweet of her, because when you're in a town like this you get lonely, and it's nice to have a place like home to call at."

Her china-blue eyes opened wide like those of a child.

"You met Mr. Edgell here, didn't you?"

"Many times. He was Miss Wilkins' lawyer."

"He was very fond of you?"

Again the look of clear innocence.

"He was a perfect gentleman to me. So nice and kind."

"And then he asked you to marry him?"

"That was later, after I'd been working at Mimi's quite a long time."

She looked a bit out of her depth, too, in the face of enquiries. Littlejohn could picture her easily enough on the stage they had in the solitary theatre in places like Melton Mowbray. Not the subtle or tragic heroine of melodrama, but the girl who stood around, looked pretty and hadn't much in the way of acting to do, in farces or pleasant comedies. Dressed in clothes lent by the fashionable small-town dress-shops and acknowledged on the programme: *Miss Valerie Deane's clothes by Maison Jules.* Lovely ensembles, chic turnouts, attractive hats, or even a bathing costume now and then. And the bright sparks of the town would send her flowers and try to make appointments.

"Did Mr. Edgell ever ask you to marry him before you left the theatre?"

"Not exactly."

"But he suggested ...?"

"He was always a gentleman."

The long lashes over the blue eyes flickered. Perhaps she hadn't been such a bad actress after all!

"Did you ever have a young man of your own, Miss Mander? A good-looking girl like you ..."

She actually looked coyly at Littlejohn, as though he, too, were going to join the company of Ned Bunn and Edgell!

"Yes...Yes, I went out with one or two, but never settled. As I said, I was with daddy so much when he was alive, that I grew to like older men better. They seem more mature and gentlemanly."

"What did your father do?"

"He was a railway official. He died years ago."

Gus Mander had been a bit of a character, a rolling-stone, who drifted from one job to another and was rarely at home. Actor in third-rate shows, potman in a London pub, a bookie who welshed, a traveller for educational courses of £1 down and ten monthly instalments of £1, and finally a shunter on the railway, where he had been killed by run-away waggons. A railway official sounded best of the motley list; it gave people the impression of Mr. Mander seated high above a busy terminus, directing Royal Scots and Golden Arrows amid a lot of maps and flashing lights.

"I missed daddy and after he'd gone, I seemed always to be seeking him again in fatherly men."

Another touching line or two from some play she'd been in at one time or another!

The local constable and the Hinksman pair had come to the gate to see what was holding things up.

"Why, Miss Deane! Where 'ave you come from?"

The old woman looked feline at the sight of the young and pretty actress and her husband bared his spare teeth and touched his forelock out of respect for beauty.

"Good morning, Mrs. Hinksman...Hullo, Hinksman. I was just passing through. I hope you're both well and happy."

It went straight to Hinksman's heart and he looked at her proudly. His wife, however, was untouched.

"We're all right, thank you."

You couldn't quarrel with Violet Mander. She seemed to want to please everybody. A good soul, obviously, either by nature or training. It was a way of obtaining an easy passage through life. Hospitality, free flats, clothes, any number of admirers young and old to keep her entertained... And she preferred the older ones, who had money and who reminded her of daddy, the railway shunter... She had knocked about the world and knew what she wanted and when she found exactly what she was after, either in a Yewbert or an Edgell, she would be quick to put it on a permanent footing. Till then, she had her beauty, her innocent ways, her fascinating china-blue eyes and the sumptuous figure which, just at present, was almost causing Mrs. Hinksman physical pain.

Littlejohn thought a minute.

"Mrs. Hinksman, I'd be grateful if you'd get your things and come along to Enderby with us."

The old lady looked surprised.

"Me? With you, in the car?"

She eyed Violet Mander's evening outfit spitefully. They could see her wondering what sort of a gathering they were going to; two policeman in lounge suits—one smart tweeds and the other sombre navy-blue with a bit of shine on it—and a girl in a black evening gown which got every ounce of her charm and beauty from her, even at ten o'clock in the morning.

"Yes. I just want you to confirm officially what you've told us about Mr. Edgell's visit here on October 26th."

For the first time, Violet Mander looked alarmed.

"Mr. Edgell...? Why are you checking on him?"

As though Edgell didn't need any checking at all... a paragon.

"Pure routine, but necessary in the case of everybody connected locally with the Bunn family."

"Oh, I see..."

The eyes looked straight into Littlejohn's, full of hope and trust, as though sudden illumination had dawned on their owner.

"I'll come, but don't think I can stay away long. There's a lot to be done here and the milkman and the bread and such like..."

Mrs. Hinksman took the old man aside and gave him a lot of muttered and careful instructions which he accepted with nods and gruff affirmations. Then she went indoors, stayed there for five minutes, and emerged clad in a long black coat, a black felt hat without any trimmings and just a shade too large for her, and a white silk scarf which might have belonged to Aunt Sarah, so different was it from the rest of the get-up. She carried an umbrella and a pantechnicon of a black leather bag, with large clasps of imitation amber. She climbed heavily in the rear of the police-car and sat down primly beside Violet Mander, who looked at her as though Mrs. Hinksman's company was the one thing in the world she needed to fill her cup of happiness to the brim.

They looked rather a motley crew, tweeds, sombre serge, a costly evening gown, and a portly thin-lipped woman in black like the poor relation at a funeral. Hinksman and the local constable waved them off and continued waving rhythmically until the car vanished down a turn in the road.

CHAPTER NINETEEN
CONFERENCE AT
"THE FREEMASONS"

The car pulled up at *The Freemasons' Arms* and Littlejohn and his party got out. Mr. Blowitt was waiting at the door, apparently unable to contain himself for the arrival of his new manageress. In honour of the occasion he had put on a light grey suit, wore brown shoes the colour of tangerines, and there was a rose in his buttonhole. He looked like a disciple of Jubal Medlicott, a toff.

"We'd like the private room for an hour or two."

Blowitt turned his radiant face on Littlejohn.

"Of course. You've only to say the word, an' it's as good as done. Like any food or drinks servin'?"

"No, thanks."

Mrs. Hinksman was dubious about entering licensed premises. In spite of her husband's alcoholic tendencies, she was herself a member of the Particular Baptist sect, a staunch supporter of the Band of Hope, and strictly T.T. in all circumstances. Her nose was high as she crossed the threshold and she recoiled at the blast of beer which greeted her there. Violet Mander, wearing her fur coat over her evening dress, excited the men hanging about the market place to noisy admiration and the women to visible envy and disgust.

Blowitt put a match to the ready-laid fire in the snug— the room from which Ned Bunn had walked to his death— and bade them all be seated. Then he went back to the front door to keep his vigil for Effie.

Littlejohn led Cromwell back to the car.

"Just run along and bring back Aunt Sarah, old chap. She'll doubtless be delighted to see you and relish a ride with you. Don't tell her who's here. Just say I'll be obliged if she'll call at *The Freemasons'* and that there have been important developments."

"What if she turns a bit awkward? She's the sort who if she knows you particularly want her to come, might say she can't or won't."

"Use your charm of manner. I'm relying on you."

Cromwell looked sorry for himself. Even the car seemed to resent the mission and he had to make half-a-dozen efforts on the starter before she'd move.

The two women in the private room were sitting stiffly opposite one another when Littlejohn returned. Both wondered what was in store and the older woman kept eyeing the younger up and down, rudely appraising her clothes and strongly disapproving of her low-cut gown, bare flesh, sleek legs...In fact, everything about her. To make matters worse, Violet had been improving her make-up with lipstick and puff. There was a heavy scent of powder and a lighter one of *Passion de Paris* on the air. Mrs. Hinksman, between the smells of various kinds of alcohol and erotic perfumes, felt herself in a hotbed of sin and vice and her lips were a thin line as she wrestled inwardly against them.

Outside, a long-distance motor-coach drew up and a tall, buxom Juno got out. Her hair was peroxide-gold, she wore a shabby black costume and, as she drew near, she looked tired and bedraggled. She carried a large fibre suitcase and the weight of it made her go over on her high heels and totter from side to side as she crossed the street. Blowitt hurried to meet her, danced round her like a faithful dog, took the case from her hand and, grasping her arm, towed her rapidly across to the pub. She was a couple of inches taller than he was. They could hear him taking her into his private quarters, talking breathlessly.

"Come an' have something to buck you up, Effie. You look tired, Effie ... I'm glad you've come back, Effie ..."

It made it all the more difficult for Mrs. Hinksman.

"Will you want me to stay here long, sir?"

"Not long. Sergeant Cromwell's just gone to get Mrs. Wilkins."

Both women were on their feet together.

"What's she comin' for? I really can't meet her here. I ought to be at home and that's where she expects me to be when she's out. It's not fair of you to ..."

"Don't worry, Mrs. Hinksman. This is very necessary and it's better here than at the police-station."

"Well, what am I supposed to do when she gets here? She'll give me the sack for this."

"I thought you were giving notice in any case."

"Yes, but I wanted to *give* it, not *be given* it."

She sat down sulkily, fished in her bag, took out a mint imperial, and started to suck it as though somehow it gave her inner strength.

Violet Mander waited until she'd finished and then she began to question Littlejohn, as well.

"Why do I have to meet Mrs. Wilkins? Where do I come in? I'm sure if Mrs. Ladbroke sees me, I'll lose my job, too. Do you really need me?"

She looked so pathetic that if Littlejohn hadn't known her thoroughly by this, his heart might have been softened. "Calm yourselves, both of you. You are needed in this interview, though I must tell you I can't make you stay if you don't wish to. But it's better to go through it here in private than elsewhere ... the police-station or even the Assize Court."

That silenced them both for a bit whilst they tried to straighten their thoughts and think out what Littlejohn had said. Mrs. Hinksman crunched her peppermint between her teeth.

The Inspector stared out into the market place, puffing his pipe. He offered his cigarette-case to Violet, who took one, and he lit it for her. Mrs. Hinksman started to cough in protest and her peppermint seemed to do her no good. Littlejohn was at a bit of a loss with her. He didn't know what to offer her, how to entertain her, or what to say to her in the way of light conversation. He need not have worried. She had her own thoughts and they were very superior ones as she compared herself with the world around, especially with her husband, her employer, and the abandoned Jezebel in whose company she was being forced to spend the time. Mrs. Hinksman was very self-contained. She had been saved, and well she knew it.

"Here they are."

The car drew up with Cromwell looking unhappy in front and Aunt Sarah indignantly occupying the whole of the back and making the springs bounce and squeak. There was a scrimmage as Cromwell helped her out. He had to slide the front seat as far as it would go in the direction of the windscreen, and even then there was hardly space enough for Aunt Sarah's exit. It was like a scene in a pantomime. A small knot of loafers started to give ribald advice and pass sarcastic comments.

Then the noise approaching the snug indicated that Cromwell had had a bit of trouble carrying out his orders. Aunt Sarah was kicking up a row, snorting, stamping, wheezing heavily, as though intent on dying on her companion's hands. In her anger, her voice grew loud and vulgar.

"If he wants me, why can't he come where I am? Sr' Agnes's place is better than this low pub and ten times more comfortable. And what am I supposed to do now I *am* here?"

Her huge bulk filled the doorway, and then she saw Mrs. Hinksman and Miss Mander.

"So!"

It was a roar.

"And what, might I ask, is the meaning of this? Why aren't you in Melton Mowbray looking after the house instead of gallivantin' all over the shop? What are you doing here? Have you been telling the police things about me?"

Littlejohn cut her short.

"*I've* brought her here and Miss Mander as well. The responsibility is entirely mine and you'll see the reason for it all before we've finished. Won't you sit down?"

"I will not."

Aunt Sarah looked round for a large enough chair, however, and flopped in it.

Cromwell remained in the doorway looking miserable. It was easy to see he'd had a rough passage getting Aunt Sarah where she was.

"That young man threatened me. Said something about getting a warrant if I didn't oblige."

She rounded on poor Cromwell. He was no longer her favourite policeman.

"Well, young man. What about it? Where's the warrant? Let's be looking at it. Otherwise, I'll ring up my lawyer right away and put the whole matter in his hands. You can't make a fool of me, you know."

Cromwell looked plaintively at his boss.

"Mr. Edgell will be here very shortly. You can take it up with him then, Mrs. Wilkins. Meanwhile, I'm sorry we've had to bring you here like this, but your help is absolutely necessary now. It may mean a miscarriage of justice unless you co-operate."

Aunt Sarah was by no means convinced. She shuffled in her chair, her lips were blue, and she still panted from her exertions.

"Get me a glass of brandy, young man. I'm not feeling well."

Cromwell, eager to do something to placate her, however menial, flew eagerly out of the room, returned quickly, handed Mrs. Wilkins half a tumbler of neat spirit, and smiled knowingly. He'd helped himself to it in the absence of Mr. Blowitt, who was still making Effie comfortable and paying pathetic homage to her.

Aunt Sarah's temper immediately subsided as she smacked her lips over the drink. She might never have been in a rage at all. She paused until the liquor had got properly inside her, and then smiled back at Cromwell.

"Now what do you want?" She hiccupped noisily.

It wasn't hard to guess that the shrewd old woman had known matters were reaching a climax when Cromwell called for her and she had tried to bluff her way out of it. Now, faced with Violet and Mrs. Hinksman, she had a good idea what was before her and was ready for a battle of wits.

"To put it briefly, Mr. Edgell has told me that he was at your home in Melton Mowbray at the time Edwin Bunn met his death. He says he left at ten o'clock. Is that so, madam?"

"Yes."

Mrs. Hinksman reared in her chair. She wasn't *going* to be made into a liar, Mrs. Wilkins or no Mrs. Wilkins. She hadn't come all the way from Melton for that. She'd had enough of being used as a domestic doormat.

"You're wrong there, Mrs. Wilkins. He left at half-past nine, an' well you know it."

She nodded her head for emphasis, looked hard at the brandy glass, which her mistress was still holding, and made a noise like "faugh" as well.

It looked as if Aunt Sarah was going to have a stroke. She fought for air.

"You keep your mouth shut, Belinda Hinksman, and don't let me have any more of your impertinence. When I say a thing, I mean it. It was ten when Simon Edgell left *Throstles Nest.*"

"Oh no, it wasn't. I don't tell lies, if other people do. It was half-past nine."

Aunt Sarah looked all round the room, making little pecking motions of the head as though she couldn't believe her own ears and seeking from the very air inspiration as to how to deal with this rebellious menial.

"Shut your mouth!"

It looked like going on all day! A real slanging-match.

"Please go and get Mr. Medlicott, Cromwell, and, at the same time, ask Inspector Myers to step across. Ask him, please, to bring with him a warrant for the arrest of Jubal Medlicott for the murder of Edwin Bunn."

Aunt Sarah slowly lumbered to her feet, waving her ebony stick about her, looking ready to intercept Cromwell violently.

"What's all this?"

The sergeant slipped out with obvious relief.

"Your statement, Mrs. Wilkins, completes the process of elimination I've been working on. That leaves Medlicott as the guilty party."

"Wait a minute, Inspector. What has that traitor been saying?"

She pointed at Mrs. Hinksman with her stick. Belinda rose with tight lips and fully on the warpath.

"No need to try to frighten me. I told 'im the truth and my husband said the same. It's two against one, even if you *are* Sarah Wilkins of *Throstles Nest;* and me and me 'usband gives you notice."

"No, you don't. You're sacked! Pack up your belongings, you wicked and unfaithful servant, and if you're not out by week-end, I'll have you thrown out, bag and baggage."

It was now Littlejohn's turn to say *wait a minute.*

"You persist in your statement about the time Mr. Edgell left you, Mrs. Wilkins?"

"Yes, I do."

"Very well. You will be subpoenaed for the trial of Medlicott to say it in court and Mr. Harry Habakkuk will also be called to give evidence and to produce the sealed packet you recently left with him."

Aunt Sarah looked ready to have a fit.

"What do *you* know about sealed packets? I never ..."

Littlejohn didn't, but it was a reasonable assumption on the face of things. Why else, if Edgell were family lawyer, should Aunt Sarah be employing another solicitor and a young and obsequious one, eager to obey her to the letter?

All her wrath had evaporated and she looked a bothered and lonely old woman at her wits' end.

"I've reason for believing that you left with Mr. Habakkuk a statement sealed in a packet, to be opened in certain circumstances, and that it contains vital evidence connected with the death of Edwin Bunn."

"Has Habakkuk been talking, then?"

She said it craftily, trying to seek out the chinks in Littlejohn's armour.

"No."

"It's Edgell!"

"I decline to discuss the matter. It's there and we shall take steps to avail ourselves of it."

"You can't. It's against the law."

"This is murder and nothing is going to stop us finding out all about it. Now, are you going to tell me the truth? I *know* you're trying to protect an old friend and I admire you for it, but matters have gone too far, Mrs. Wilkins."

She obviously didn't know what to do. Anne Bunn had, since she was a child, been her favourite relative. The arrest of Medlicott would be the last straw. It would kill Anne. Besides, Jubal was one of the clan, even if only by marriage, and even if he *was* a fool ...

"How can such a statement save Jubal Medlicott? It doesn't sound reasonable."

Again the cunning look, the cornered animal seeking a way out.

"That's our business. Will you make a proper statement?"

"Very well. But not because that hussy, Belinda Hinksman, has played the Judas on one who's always treated her like her own flesh and blood. It's because of Anne ... Poor Anne ... Such a sweet little thing, too, when she was young ..."

There was a sob in her voice. Littlejohn remembered that she, too, had once been something of an actress.

Aunt Sarah looked across at Violet Mander.

"Hullo, Violet. How do you come to be mixed up in this silly affair? Are they bullying you, too?"

Violet gave her the innocent look which seemed to be part of her stock-in-trade.

"Oh, no, Mrs. Wilkins. They've been most kind and considerate. Although I don't quite know where I come in."

"Poor Anne. What a state she's got in. As pretty as a picture in her prime; and now, a withered old woman before her time."

The brandy was taking effect on Aunt Sarah and making her maudlin.

"I keep looking at you, Violet..."

She raised her stick, pointed at Violet Mander, and addressed the room in general.

"Vi, there, is the image of Anne when my poor niece was her age. Same blue eyes, same cast of features, same look, as though she were surprised at what she saw in life. The image of her! Though I must say she daren't show as much of herself as Vi does; her father would have put her across his knee and slapped her if she'd tried."

Aunt Sarah lowered the stick and shrugged.

"Now look at her. Old and ill and with a silly husband and a couple of stupid daughters on her hands. All her money and her good looks gone. A sort of caricature of Violet..."

Then she flew into a rage, gnashing her teeth, thumping her stick on the floor.

"Let it be a warning to you, Violet. Looks don't last. It nearly makes you stop believing there's a God..."

Belinda Hinksman was up in arms at once. She wasn't going to stand for that. Her face was red, her hair seemed to grow wild and dishevelled of its own accord, and she clenched her fists till the knuckles grew white.

"How dare you? But then you never believed in Saving Grace, did you? You're a lost woman, Mrs. Wilkins, a lost woman. Me and my husband gives you notice."

"Don't try to get out of getting the sack by preaching at me, Belinda Baggs, or Hinksman, or whatever name you call yourself now you've married your clod of a husband."

Littlejohn let it go on. Between them they had brought to light a startling fact. When Anne Bunn was young, she resembled Violet Mander! Not like a Bunn at all! The beauty of the family; and now here was her younger replica; or, at least, after all the years, the older generation thought so.

The car was back again at the front door of the pub. Cromwell was bringing in Jubal Medlicott. It was like the comings and goings at a wedding!

Jubal looked at his wits' end. He'd been pushed around, questioned, suspected, insulted so much since the murders that he didn't know whether he was on his head or his heels. His wife had done her best to turn him out as spick and span as usual, but there was a difference. The light seemed to have died out in him. There was no bounce or polish left; he was tarnished and moth-eaten. The absence of his spats emphasized his old shoes, cracked and worn across the insteps and down at heel. His suit had been pressed, but he'd no flower in his coat. His usually bright spectacles wanted polishing and instead of the once prancing little steps, he half shuffled in the room and looked around shamefacedly.

"Hello, Jubal."

"Hello, Aunt Sarah."

That was all. He didn't seem to notice the rest.

"Sit down, please, Mr. Medlicott. I promised I'd call in Mr. Edgell if we sent for you to question you again."

Medlicott was in the act of sitting on a chair by the fireside. He hung suspended in mid-air, his legs bent, his rear protruding like a duck's.

"But I've told you all I know. You've got me bewildered till I don't know what I'm saying. I can't sleep at night and it's affecting my wife's health. It's not right the way you're treating me."

He bumped down in the chair and exchanged thin smiles with Violet Mander. Both of them looked as ready to weep as to smile.

Littlejohn turned to Cromwell again.

"Did you let Inspector Myers know?"

"He's out, sir, but they're trying to get hold of him. They'll send him across."

"Perhaps you'll step over to Mr. Edgell's office, then, and tell him to come along."

Cromwell looked happy to get away again.

Aunt Sarah rose with difficulty and crossed the room to where Jubal sat slumped by the fire, stood in front of him, and tapped his shoulder with her swollen finger.

"He's got you here to arrest you, Jubal. You always were a fool, you know, just a harmless fool, and how you got yourself mixed-up in this sorry business I can't for the life of me think. But you can depend on me. I know a thing or two, and nobody's going to touch you."

Medlicott wasn't interested, however. He gave Aunt Sarah a glazed look, threw up his hands, opened his mouth, and pitched full length on the floor, unconscious.

Chapter Twenty
The Defeat of Aunt Sarah

It seemed to take them an age to bring Jubal Medlicott round. The commotion brought Mr. Blowitt from his retreat whence he was followed by Effie, who turned out to be a tower of strength in the confusion. She seemed to know everyone except Littlejohn, took them all for granted, put Jubal on a wooden couch, gave him brandy, and revived him with it. He was full of apologies and shame for his fit of weakness.

In the mix-up Blowitt came and went, excited, wringing his hands, delighted by Effie's efficiency, almost beside himself with conflicting emotions. He carried stimulants to Mrs. Wilkins as well and tried Belinda Hinksman, too, and was rebuffed. At length he returned, looking nervous and pale, gazed through the window and registered acute anxiety. Cromwell and Inspector Myers were crossing the market square together. They walked solemnly like two figures representing the relentlessness of fate, neither speaking, their faces set and grim. Mr. Blowitt seemed in a hurry.

"If you'll come to the bar, Miss Mander, I'll find you a little pick-me-up, too. You look all-in. Come along."

Violet Mander followed like a lamb, meek and showing no surprise. Littlejohn was hoisting Medlicott back in his chair where he sat slumped and white.

Aunt Sarah was fortified by more brandy but when Cromwell and Myers entered, fear and tragedy were written all over her face. She made a great effort to pull herself together, but her features twitched and her looks grew wild. She kept glancing apprehensively at the door even after the officers had entered.

"Where's Edgell?"

Littlejohn stood bolt upright, his face anxious and set.

"He said he'd come right away, so I went to see if the Inspector was about. He'd just got in... Edgell should be here by now..."

There was a second's silence. The sun was shining outside and the noises of vehicles and shouting in the market square contrasted sharply with the hush in the room. Belinda Hinksman sat straight as a ramrod in her chair, like one who resented the company and the place she was in, but was making the best of it. Aunt Sarah, in sharp contrast, looked broken, her lips quivered and she began to sob.

Myers was stiff and disapproving. He thought all this should have gone on at the police-station.

"You sent for me, Inspector?"

Littlejohn didn't heed him. Instead, he rushed from the room, followed by Cromwell, leaving the rest surprised and aghast.

When the officers arrived at Edgell's chambers the girl in the outer office met them leisurely, her jaws rotating round her chewing-gum.

"He left just after the gentleman called..."

She indicated Cromwell.

"Where does he park his car?"

"In the street behind *The Freemasons*'."

They tore out, ran up an alley, and found themselves right behind the hotel in a narrow cobbled thoroughfare with cars parked in a string down one side. There was only room for other traffic to pass in single file. One end was blocked by a dust-cart into which dustmen were casually tipping the contents of bins which festooned the back doors of the property fronting on the market place. Half-way down the street stood a brewery lorry which had been discharging barrels at *The Freemasons'*. The driver of the lorry was slowly backing out, trying to make way for a car wedged between his vehicle and the dust-cart. The occupants were Edgell and Violet Mander. Edgell's head was thrust out of his car and he was angrily shouting orders to the brewery drayman.

Then he saw Littlejohn...

The gathering in the snug was suddenly roused by noises and shouting. Banging doors, running feet, furniture being overturned, and a crash of glasses falling on the floor.

Myers appeared in the lobby with Mr. Blowitt, with the faces of the women in a huddle trying to look out and see what was going on.

"What's all this...?"

Steps mounting the stairs, others in pursuit, shouts, and then the heavy slamming of a door. Myers followed and then Blowitt.

Inspector Myers was angry, almost violent. He felt he was being edged out of the case and now he was going to show them who was who.

"What's the meaning of...?"

Littlejohn and Cromwell were applying their shoulders to the door of the room they had occupied since they'd arrived in Enderby. It resisted their efforts. *The Freemasons'* wasn't a very old place, but the brewers had, in reconstructing it, tried to make it look like one, and put in heavy oak doors on the ground and first floors to give it an antique finish.

"Edgell's got Miss Mander in here and the door's locked. Give us a hand. Have you another key, Blowitt?"

"Won't be much good, sir. There's bars on as well."

"Get an axe, then."

"But..."

Blowitt's eyes nearly left their sockets at the thought of such an outrage.

"Get one..."

The oak door was set in a deep frame and the policemen couldn't get at it to give it their joint weight.

Inside, there were voices. Edgell's cracking like a whip, then pleading; Violet Mander's raised to a pitch of hysteria.

"No...I tell you. No. I don't want...Please...I'll do anything but not..."

Then a revolver shot.

The officers threw their weight against the door again. Below, Blowitt was ascending with the axe, a stupid little thing he used for chopping firewood.

"I can't find the big one. It must have been pinched. Will...?"

Another shot. Then silence.

The lock and the bolt gave way together and the door crashed open.

The large, rather shabby room which Littlejohn and Cromwell had grown to know so well, and where not a single article of furniture stood steadily on all its legs at once. The two large beds with brass knobs and on one of the knobs, the cloth cap Cromwell sometimes wore after dark.

Edgell and Violet Mander were stretched across the bed which had belonged to Ned Bunn. The lawyer's arm was round Violet's waist. He was dead. They thought Violet Mander was dead, too, but as Littlejohn bent over her, her china-blue eyes opened, she tried to speak, smiled faintly, and then died.

People were trying to get upstairs to see what was going on and Mr. Blowitt was barring the way waving his silly little axe.

"Get down. There's nothing you can do. Get down or I'll..."

Littlejohn appeared at the bedroom door and beckoned the landlord.

"Did you tell Miss Mander that Edgell was waiting for her at the back door?"

Blowitt licked his lips and looked sorry for himself.

"Yes, sir. He said he only wanted a word with her and to tell her on the Q.T...Is she...? Are they...?"

"Both dead..."

"This is a nice mess, and no mistake. I'll be glad to hear what it's all about."

Myers was as pale as death and nasty about it all. He thought he could have made a better job of the investigation himself and he didn't hesitate to say so afterwards all over the place. "If you ask me, Scotland Yard have messed the whole thing up. Made a complete failure of it."

In the snug, the women were sitting in a terrified group. Effie was the only one who looked herself. Aunt Sarah sagged in her chair like a bundle of old clothes and Mrs. Hinksman was praying and sobbing noisily at the same time.

Blowitt entered, his forehead bathed in sweat, his face like putty. He had been bracing himself at the bar and when he breathed a gust of alcohol swept the room.

"The police surgeon's here. I've taken him up. It's opening-time; do you think it'll be all right...?"

Myers looked ready to murder Blowitt.

"No, it won't. Let 'em go thirsty for once."

"But some of them want lunches."

"They can do without!"

Through the window came the noises of a large crowd of spectators, peering, craning their necks, trying to get in to see the sights. Four policemen elbowed their way in, sternly pushed away the mob, and waved them off. There were complaints at their officiousness and people started to line-up on the kerb opposite to get a good view of what was going on.

Aunt Sarah had recovered a bit and Effie gave her another drink of brandy and water.

"I knew he was mad about her. But what did he want to do that for? He'd had his life. Hers was only just beginning. To go and ..."

Effie hovered round, trying to calm her.

"You knew Edgell killed Edwin Bunn, didn't you, Mrs. Wilkins?"

Littlejohn was the first to speak about the murder.

"She can make a statement at the police-station. We ought to be getting along."

Myers was showing his teeth again.

"I'm conducting this case, Inspector. You'll have your turn later. Now, Mrs. Wilkins ..."

Aunt Sarah looked pitifully at him.

"Yes. I didn't know at first. But after I arrived here, I started to make enquiries around and when I found Ned had been up to his tricks with Violet Mander, I knew Edgell wouldn't stand for that. You see, it was really on account of Ned that Edgell lost Anne years ago. They never got on. Ned always said it was through Edgell that he wasn't treated like the rest of the family. Edgell, he said, never forgot he was a bastard. So whenever he could do him a dirty trick, he did.

Anne used to work in the shop and Ned encouraged Jubal Medlicott to keep calling, till Anne got carried away with his fancy ways and married him. Edgell was mad about her, but she never cared much for him ... So ..."

Until his name was mentioned, they'd all forgotten about Jubal. Where he had been and what doing during the hullabaloo nobody seemed to know. Now, he materialized in the chimney-corner, his head between his hands, rolling from side to side. He had been helping himself to the brandy bottle and was drunk.

The ambulance arrived amid a clanging of bells. The heavy tramp of men with stretchers sounded on the stairs.

"I'm going up to see to things. I shall expect a full statement at the station later."

Myers went huffily. He hadn't forgiven Littlejohn and was, as far as he was concerned, running the last lap of the case on his own. The air seemed to clear as Myers left the room. The party became more intimate. Aunt Sarah, broken and in tears, Jubal drunk in his corner, Belinda Hinksman petrified by a situation she thought could only exist in highly indecent fiction which she never read; and Effie, cool, experienced, disillusioned and kindly, as women of her type usually are. Cromwell was still upstairs with the surgeon and the local men.

Littlejohn sat on a chair beside Aunt Sarah.

"Did you challenge Edgell about the murders?"

"Yes, I did. You see, he made the mistake of mentioning that he left Melton at half-past nine on the night of Ned's murder. He introduced it in conversation, casually, and I corrected him. Then he got so insistent that I was suspicious. Besides, he called for nothing at my place that night. He must just have been giving himself an alibi."

"Was that the day you found me in Edgell's office and asked me to leave you together?"

"Yes. I had my suspicions, because I knew Ned and Edgell weren't too friendly. But I'd also heard from various members of the family that Jubal was suspected. He couldn't or wouldn't give an alibi for himself on the night of the crime. I was sure Medlicott wouldn't kill anybody. A harmless man, even if he is a fool..."

"Wassat? Me?"

Jubal had wakened from his stupor and called out from his corner.

Aunt Sarah's old temper flashed out and then died away.

"Go to sleep, you. This doesn't concern you at all."

"Sorry, I'm sure..."

And Medlicott obeyed orders and went off again.

"I wasn't going to have Jubal in trouble; for Anne's sake, I wasn't. I wasn't going to let you hang him. So, I told Edgell I'd keep quiet just as long as nobody else suffered. Also..."

Her voice came in a crafty whisper.

"Also, I made it a condition that he wrote me a letter saying he accidentally killed Ned...a kind of confession. I wasn't going to have him kill *me* as well. I lodged it at the bank through Habakkuk, the lawyer. It's there still and I'll give it to you. Habukkuk doesn't know what's in it. I made a new will with him and said that, if I died violently, my executors, the bank, were to open the letter and deal with it as they saw fit. If I died in my bed, the letter was to go to Edgell. You see, if Edgell died first, it wouldn't have mattered. The letter was then put in my strong-box at the bank and I alone have the key."

"I'm surprised you agreed to that, Mrs. Wilkins. It's quite a penal offence, you know. Why did you do it?"

The old woman sighed.

"I was wrong, I admit. But our family did Edgell a terrible injury. He ought to have had Anne, you know. Ned was responsible for his losing her and for his lonely life after, because he was really a one-woman man who never loved anybody else. I was sorry for him. Besides, there was Violet."

Littlejohn lit his pipe.

"You mean, he met her and she looked so much like the woman he'd loved so long ago, that he fell in love with her?"

"Madly. All the lost love since Anne jilted him seemed to be for Violet. He met her at my place. I was once connected with the stage a bit and used to entertain the actors who came to the local theatre. Violet was there with a stock company for a month or two before they went bankrupt. She came a lot. I got very fond of her; almost as if she was my own..."

Tears flowed again. The whole of Aunt Sarah's massive frame shook and she bawled loudly because it was too much strain to weep quietly. Mrs. Hinksman crossed to her, put her arms round her, and tried to comfort her.

"There, there, don't go on so, Mrs. Wilkins. I won't give notice. I'll stay with you. It's only Hinksman wants to leave and 'e don't matter. You've got your old Belinder..."

Aunt Sarah forgot her grief.

"Don't you make out, Belinda Hinksman, that you're withdrawing your notice. It's me that's withdrawing the sack. You can stay on if you want. I'll be glad to have you back."

"But I gave me notice..."

Littlejohn intervened.

"Now, now, you two. No more squabbling. This isn't the time or place..."

The venomous looks they both gave him silenced him. He suddenly realized that this was their way of life and they got a lot of entertainment, even happiness from it. They were always sacking and giving notice, but they never parted.

"Well, now that's settled, Mrs. Wilkins, suppose you tell me the rest. What about your conscience and poor Browning? You couldn't square that, could you? You couldn't forgive Edgell coming behind a helpless man and just choking him with his muffler, could you?"

Aunt Sarah gave him an amazed look.

"Browning. I know nothing about Browning. I read he was dead in the paper, but who killed him, I didn't know. How could I be expected to know who murdered him? I wasn't there, was I?"

Littlejohn shook his head at her.

"You crafty old woman! You were very fond of Edgell, weren't you? You were prepared to let him off his crimes provided nobody else suffered. But let me tell you, Browning was part of a plot to get Medlicott down to town on the night Ned Bunn was killed, part of a scheme to destroy any alibi he might have had. Browning did jobs of work for Edgell. Most likely he owed Edgell money and was in his clutches. Then, he turned awkward and tried blackmail. I'm sure that even before that, Edgell was determined to kill him if necessary. He tried to put the blame for that on Medlicott, too, by leaving prominent footmarks, with spats, the size Jubal wore. He must have carried his hatred through life, but till Bunn started his tricks on Violet, it wasn't powerful enough to make him kill anybody. When Bunn looked like tormenting Violet and perhaps ruining Edgell's happiness, as he'd done before—and, by the way, he'd done the same to Blowitt—Edgell saw red, killed Bunn and tried to incriminate Medlicott."

"I tell you, I'm not interested in Browning. Why should I be? He wasn't one of the Bunns..."

She wouldn't budge, but Littlejohn knew her well enough by this and was sure she had held that secret as well.

"I was fond of Simon Edgell. He was like one of the family. A discreet man, who'd always been around helping us all..."

"Yes, Mrs. Wilkins, and full of family secrets, some of them not too savoury. The death of Jerry Bunn, for example. Was it natural or was it...?"

"Stop! No use washin' old clothes, Inspector. Let the dead rest in peace."

"Edgell wouldn't have done if you'd dared not support him in trying to cover his crimes. It was blackmail kept your mouth shut, Mrs. Wilkins. He knew enough to make the name of Bunn a disgraceful byword if he'd cared to talk. So you gave him an alibi...You also had to chase away Miss Bathsheba Bunn, whose offers of large rewards might have brought a lot of unsavoury information to light."

"I've said I was wrong. What more do you want?"

Suddenly a hush fell over them all. Stumbling, lumbering footsteps on the stairs, slowly, one at a time, bump, bump, bump. They were bringing down the bodies. The outer door opened. Another pause and the ambulance, gong-gonging furiously, whined away. Mr. Blowitt entered. He'd had another bracer or two and was half-seas over.

"They've gone, Effie."

He seemed only concerned with her.

She gave Mrs. Wilkins a pat on the arm.

"You'll be all right now?"

"Yes, thank you, Effie."

Mr. Blowitt breathed a fog of alcohol over Littlejohn.

"Can we open now? We've put a rope across the stairs so's nobody can go up and mess about."

"Very well, if the local police agree. Ask Mr. Myers."

Aunt Sarah had pulled herself together now that it was all over. She blew her nose on a large handkerchief.

"Simon Edgell was crazy about Anne. I know it was like crucifying him to watch her going downhill because Medlicott was so rotten at business. Edgell offered to help her, but she wouldn't hear of it. She said it would be wrong after the way she'd treated him."

She pointed her stick at Jubal, asleep in his corner, snoring, with his mouth open and blowing out his whiskers with every gust of breath.

"You wouldn't think to look at him that he was the start of it all, would you? Life's funny. Fate uses the most ridiculous people to play leading parts in the terrible dramas of life. Violet was remarkably like Anne when she was young and what she lacked in similarity, Edgell must have painted in in imagination. He gave her the mad, pathetic love of an ageing man. You can't blame him, Inspector. She had such good looks and style and she played up to him so. He created the job for her with Mimi, just to get her near him, and then Ned started his tricks. Do you blame Edgell getting mad and making up his mind to settle with Ned once for all?"

"It was planned with mature cunning, a real lawyer's crime. Alibi, the right time and place, and, if he didn't succeed that time, he could wait. As it was, he had a dark night and rain confusing the issue. I suppose he crept out the back way."

"He didn't say. He never gave me any details."

"You've been very wrong, you know, Mrs. Wilkins. You knew of the crimes and who did them, and yet you kept quiet. It was your duty to tell me or the local police."

She sighed again and rose unsteadily, for the brandy had got in her legs.

"I'll take my medicine. Who'd have thought I'd die in prison. How long will they give me?"

"I don't know. You'll have to make a statement at the local police-station. Myers will see to that."

He looked at the slumbering Medlicott and at Belinda Hinksman, who didn't understand a word of what was going on. She only knew that in her wildest nightmares she'd never experienced anything so unbelievable as her present situation, and once back at *Throstles Nest,* she wasn't stirring out into the wide, wicked world again.

"I shall have to put in my report, of course. Edgell's lack of alibi; his motives; his hatred of Ned Bunn; and, finally, the confession, a letter left behind ... Was it addressed to you?"

"No. Just a plain sheet of paper starting, *I wish it to be known,* and signed by him. It just said he killed Edwin Bunn by accident, intending to scare him."

"Better get it and give it to me, and I'll include it with my report."

"You mean ...?"

"Do as I ask, Aunt Sarah."

"Aunt Sarah. That sounds very friendly of you ... All right. If you want me to adopt you, I will."

And every Christmas until her death, Littlejohn received a card and a pound of tobacco from Aunt Sarah, and when she died, Cromwell inherited a hundred pounds.

The Case of the Famished

Parson

George Bellairs

CHAPTER ONE
THE TOWER ROOM

Wednesday, September 4th. The Cape Mervin Hotel was as quiet as the grave. Everybody was "in" and the night-porter was reading in his cubby-hole under the stairs.

A little hunchbacked fellow was Fennick, with long arms, spindleshanks accentuated by tight, narrow-fitting trousers—somebody's cast-offs—and big feet. Some disease had robbed him of all his hair. He didn't need to shave and when he showed himself in public, he wore a wig. The latter was now lying on a chair, as though Fennick had scalped himself for relief.

The plainwood table was littered with papers and periodicals left behind by guests and rescued by the porter from the salvage dump. He spent a lot of his time reading and never remembered what he had read.

Two or three dailies, some illustrated weeklies of the cheaper variety, and a copy of Old Moore's Almanac. A sporting paper and a partly completed football pool form. ...

Fennick was reading "What the Stars have in Store." He was breathing hard and one side of his face was contorted with concentration. He gathered that the omens were favourable. Venus and Jupiter in good aspect. Success in love affairs and a promising career .... He felt better for it.

Outside the tide was out. The boats in the river were aground. The light in the tower at the end of the breakwater changed from white to red and back at minute intervals. The wind blew up the gravel drive leading from the quayside to the hotel and tossed bits of paper and dead leaves about. Down below on the road to the breakwater you could see the coke glowing in a brazier and the silhouette of a watchman's cabin nearby.

The clock on the Jubilee Tower on the promenade across the river struck midnight. At this signal the grandfather clocks in the public rooms and hall began to chime all at once in appalling discord, like a peal of bells being 'fired.' The owner of the hotel was keen on antiques and bric-a-brac and meticulously oiled and regulated all his clocks himself.

Then, in mockery of the ponderous timepieces, a clock somewhere else cuckooed a dozen times. The under-manager, who had a sense of humour, kept it in his office, set to operate just after the heavy ones. Most people laughed at it. So far, the proprietor hadn't seen the point.

Fennick stirred himself, blinked his hairless eyelids, laid aside the oracle, stroked his naked head as though soothing it after absorbing so much of the future, and rose to lock the main door. Then he entered the bar.

The barmaid and cocktail-shaker had been gone almost an hour. Used glasses stood around waiting to be washed first thing in the morning. The night-porter took a tankard from a hook and emptied all the dregs from the glasses into it. Beer, stout, gin, whisky, vermouth. ... A good pint of it. ... One hand behind his back, he drank without stopping, his prominent Adam's-apple and dewlaps agitating, until it was all gone. Then he wiped his mouth on the back of his hand, sighed with satisfaction, selected and lighted the largest cigarette-end from one of the many ash-trays scattered about and went off to his next job.

It was the rule that Fennick collected all shoes, chalked their room-numbers on their soles and carried them to the basement for cleaning. But he had ways of his own. He took a large newspaper and his box of cleaning materials and silently dealt with the footwear, one by one, as it stood outside the doors of the bedrooms, spreading the paper to protect the carpet.

Fennick started for the first floor. Rooms 1, 2, 3, 4 and 5, with the best views over the river and bay. His gait was jaunty, for he had had a few beers before finally fuddling himself with the dregs from the bar. He hummed a tune to himself.

Don't send my boy to prizzen,
It's the first crime wot he's done. ....

He tottered up the main staircase with his cleaning-box and stopped at the first door.

Number I was a single room. Once it had been double, but the need for more bathrooms had split it in two. Outside, on the mat, a pair of substantial handmade black shoes. Fennick glided his two brushes and polishing-cloth over them with hasty approval. They belonged to Judge Tennant, of the High Court. He came every year at this time for a fishing holiday. He tipped meticulously. Neither too much not too little. Yet you didn't mind. You felt justice had been done when you got it.

Fennick had been sitting on his haunches. Now and then he cocked an ear to make sure that nobody was stirring. He moved like a crab to Number 2 gently dragging his tackle along with him.

This was the best room, with a private bath. Let to a millionaire, they said. It was a double, and in the register the occupants had gone down as Mr. and Mrs. Cuhady. All the staff, from the head waiter down to the handyman who raked the gravel round the hotel and washed down the cars, knew it was a lie. The head waiter was an expert on that sort of thing. With thirty years' experience in a dining-room you can soon size-up a situation.

That was how they knew about the honeymoon couple in Number 3, too. Outside their door was a pair of new men's brogues and some new brown suede ladies' shoes. "The Bride's travelling costume consisted of...with brown suede shoes...." Fennick knew all about it from reading his papers in the small hours.

There were five pairs of women's shoes outside Number 2. Brown leather, blue suede, black and red tops, light patent leather, and a pair with silk uppers. All expensive ones.

Five pairs in a day! Fennick snarled and showed a nasty gap where he had lost four teeth. Just like her! He cleaned the brown, the black-and-red and the patent uppers with the same brushes for spite. The blue suede he ignored altogether. And he spat contemptuously on the silk ones and wiped them with a dirty cloth.

Mr. Cuhady seemed to have forgotten his shoes altogether. That was a great relief! He was very particular about them. Lovely hand-made ones and the colour of old mahogany. And you had to do them properly, or he played merry hell. Mr. Cuhady had blood-pressure and "Mrs." Cuhady didn't seem to be doing it any good. The magnate was snoring his head off. There was no other sound in Number 2. Fennick bet himself that his partner was noiselessly rifling Cuhady's pocket-book....

He crawled along and dealt with the honeymoon shoes. They weren't too good. Probably they'd saved-up hard to have their first nights together at a posh hotel and would remember it all their lives. "Remember the Cape Mervin ... ?" Fennick, sentimental under his mixed load of drinks, spat on all four soles for good luck.... He crept on.

Two pairs of brogues this time. Male and female. Good ones, too, and well cared for. Fennick handled them both with reverence. A right good job. For he had read a lot in his papers about one of the occupants of Room 4. An illustrated weekly had even interviewed him at Scotland Yard and printed his picture.

On the other side of the door were two beds, separated by a table on which stood a reading-lamp, a travelling-clock and two empty milk glasses. In one bed a good-looking, middle-aged woman was sitting-up, with a dressing-gown round her shoulders, reading a book about George Sand.

In the other a man was sleeping on his back. On his nose a pair of horn-rimmed spectacles; on the eiderdown a thriller had fallen from his limp hand. He wore striped silk pyjamas and his mouth was slightly open.

The woman rose, removed the man's glasses and book, drew the bedclothes over his arms, kissed him lightly on his thinning hair, and then climbed back into bed and resumed her reading. Inspector Littlejohn slept on ....

Fennick had reached the last room of the block. Number 5 was the tower room. The front of the Cape Mervin Hotel was like a castle. A wing, a tower, the main block, a second tower, and then another wing. Number 5 was in the left-hand tower. And it was occupied at the time by the Bishop of Greyle and his wife.

As a rule there were two pairs here, too. Heavy, brown serviceable shoes for Mrs. Bishop; boots, dusty, with solid, heavy soles and curled-up toes, for His Lordship. Tonight there was only one pair. Mrs. Greyle's. Nobody properly knew the bishop's surname. He signed everything "J. C. Greyle" and they didn't like to ask his real name. Somebody thought it was Macintosh.

Fennick was so immersed in his speculations that he didn't see the door open. Suddenly looking up he found Mrs. Greyle standing there in a blue dressing-gown staring down at him.

The night-porter hastily placed his hand flat on the top of his head to cover his nakedness, for he'd forgotten his wig. He felt to have a substantial thatch of hair now, however, and every hair of his head seemed to rise.

"Have you seen my husband?" said Mrs. Greyle, or Macintosh, or whatever it was. "He went out at eleven and hasn't returned."

Fennick writhed from his haunches to his knees and then to his feet, like a prizefighter who has been down.

"No, mum...I don't usually do the boots this way, but I'm so late, see?"

"Wherever can he be...? So unusual...."

She had a net over her grey hair. Her face was white and drawn. It must have been a very pretty face years ago.... Her hands trembled as she clutched her gown to her.

"Anything I can do, mum?"

"I can't see that there is. I don't know where he's gone. The telephone in our room rang at a quarter to eleven and he just said he had to go out and wouldn't be long. He didn't explain...."

"Oh, he'll be turnin' up. P'raps visitin' the sick, mum."

Fennick was eager to be off. The manager's quarters were just above and if he got roused and found out Fennick's little cleaning dodge, it would be, as the porter inwardly told himself, Napooh!

It was no different the following morning, when the hotel woke up. The bishop was still missing.

At nine o'clock things began to happen.

First, the millionaire sent for the manager and raised the roof.

His shoes were dirty. Last night he'd put them out as usual to be cleaned. This morning he had found them, not only uncleaned, but twice as dirty as he'd left them. In fact, muddy right up to the laces. He demanded an immediate personal interview with the proprietor. Somebody was going to get fired for it….

"Mrs." Cuhady, who liked to see other people being bullied and pushed around, watched with growing pride and satisfaction the magnate's mounting blood-pressure…

At nine-fifteen they took the bishop's corpse to the town morgue in the ambulance. He had been found at the bottom of Bolter's Hole, with the tide lapping round his emaciated body and his head bashed in.

The first that most of the guests knew of something unusual was the appearance of the proprietor in the dining-room just after nine. This was extraordinary, for Mr. Allain was a lazy man with a reputation for staying in bed until after ten.

Mr. Allain, a tall fat man and usually imperturbable, appeared unshaven and looking distracted. After a few words with the head waiter, who pointed out a man eating an omelette at a table near the window, he waddled across the room.

They only got bacon once a week at the Cape Mervin and Littlejohn was tackling an omelette without enthusiasm. His wife was reading a letter from her sister at Melton Mowbray who had just had another child.

Mr. Allain whispered to Littlejohn. All eyes in the room turned in their direction. Littlejohn emptied his mouth and could be seen mildly arguing. In response, Mr. Allain, who was half French, clasped his hands in entreaty. So, Littlejohn, after a word to his wife, left the room with the proprietor....

"Something must have happened," said the guests one to another.

WANT ANOTHER PERFECT MYSTERY?

GET YOUR NEXT CLASSIC CRIME STORY FOR FREE ...

Sign up to our Crime Classics newsletter where you can discover new Golden Age crime, receive exclusive content and never-before published short stories, all for FREE.

From the beloved greats of the golden age to the forgotten gems, best-kept-secrets, and brand new discoveries, we're devoted to classic crime.

If you sign up today, you'll get:

1. A Free Novel from our Classic Crime collection.
2. Exclusive insights into classic novels and their authors and the chance to get copies in advance of publication, and
3. The chance to win exclusive prizes in regular competitions.

Interested? It takes less than a minute to sign up. You can get your novel and your first newsletter by signing up on our website www.crimeclassics.co.uk

Made in the USA
Lexington, KY
29 May 2018